The Forgotten Story

The room was noisy but peaceful. It was square and low raftered and full of smoke, its ancient bow windows looking out on to the winking lights of the river and harbour.

Into this comfortable scene a lighted match was dropped. Tom Harris was speaking to Patricia, and Ned, lolling opposite her, made a remark. That was the match. Tom abruptly leaned across the table and smacked Ned across the face with his open hand.

In a second Ned was up, had grasped Tom by the throat and was pulling him across the table, trying to force his head down . . .

WINSTON GRAHAM

The Forgotten Story

FONTANA/Collins

First published by Ward Lock 1945
First issued in Fontana Paperbacks 1974
Sixth impression January 1983

Made and printed in Great Britain by
William Collins Sons & Co. Ltd, Glasgow

PROLOGUE

On a stretch of yellow sand on a beach of north Cornwall, just below Sawle cliffs, there lies the remains of a shipwreck.

Every tide submerges it; seas have dashed over it, men have come and gone, but something still survives: a few spars deeply overgrown with seaweed and mussels round which venturesome children sometimes play. Indeed, at dead low tide when a heavy ground swell has sucked away the sand it is possible to make out the way the vessel struck, broadside on, and to see the backbone and the iron ribs lying exposed among pools and dripping a little in the sun.

There are still some who remember the wreck and will tell you the date she came in, a handsome ship, on the ninth of December, 1898. But these have been years of flux in the village of Sawle; successive wars and depressions have seen rapid changes, and few are left to tell the tale. Those even who remain and remember find that no one is interested in something that happened in Victorian times. Their own children could not tell you anything: they are far too deeply involved in today to bother about the past. Although the information is still to be had for the asking, they do not ask and will not listen.

So with the instability of unaired memory, the facts themselves are harder to come by with each year that passes. You may learn the vessel's name – that she was registered at Falmouth, that she was carrying a mixed cargo and bound, some say, for Liverpool, that some of her crew were saved, though whether all or how many it is hard to recollect. Some will nod and draw at their pipes and tell you that there were passengers aboard, but of course they do not remember names or details.

For this information you may if you are curious turn up the files of the local paper and find a photograph of the ship and the bare bones of the story, just as the tide will ever and again draw back the sand from the bare bones of the wreck, like a wicked child pulling away a cover and saying with secret gloating: "See what I did!"

But there is no flesh upon the bones, and for this it is

7

better to rely upon what is still to be gathered in Sawle. There the men who remember will tell you that on the evening of December the eighth, 1898, a strong wind blew up round the coast and that before the night was far advanced the wind had reached the force of a heavy gale. In the morning, almost as the late dawn broke amid the scream of the wind, a farmer called Hoskin, out on the cliffs on business to do with his cattle, glanced out over the grey scud of the sea and saw, only just visible on the low horizon among the shifting mists of the morning, a sailing vessel driving before the gale.

One minute she was there, the next she was invisible again, her sails blown to shreds, her decks swept by the hurrying seas. But Hoskin had seen enough and, dog at heels, hurried across two fields, climbed a stone wall into a lane, and ran down the steep hill to where the sometime mining and fishing village slept in the fold of the hills with the wind roaring among its cottages and ruined chimney stacks.

Rousing the rocket crew was a matter of minutes, but by the time they had struggled up with their apparatus in the teeth of the wind upon the lower cliffs which guarded the entrance to Sawle she had already struck.

A boy named Coad saw her come in. One moment she was leaping and plunging like a horse among terriers, the next she had sharply stopped and was heeling over as if about to capsize. From the extremity of the swing she partly righted herself, and the great waves, unable to move her, began instead to smash into her exposed side, sending up fans of sea and spray.

Hardly able to see or speak for the wind, the rocket crew dragged their gear to the nearest point on the cliffs, pushed it to the edge and fired their first rocket, carrying its thin lifeline over the broken sea towards the wreck.

Normally the distance would have been amply spanned, but so strong was the wind that the rocket fell into the sea some distance short. The crew wiped the spray from their faces and tried again. By now in the growing light it was possible to see figures clinging to the deck of the ship.

There was little time to spare if the rescuers were to be useful, and they fired two more rockets before deciding to wait upon some slackening of the wind. But the gale, though often rising to new heights, seldom dropped below a constant pitch of fury, and although they chose the best moment of the morning the line again fell short.

Helpless now, while others from the village came on the scene, they watched the ship settle in the water. All around them the rocks were grey with flying scud, and now and then a back-wash from a returning wave would sweep the slanting deck. Almost everything had been carried away – but the tiny figures still clung there mutely appealing for help.

Then one of these figures was seen to crawl away from the poop and work his way towards the bows.

"Thur's a fool thinks he's going to swim ashore," said the leader of the rocket crew. "Fire another rocket, Joe; try an' stop 'im; he'll not go to save 'imself that way."

Another rocket hissed and sputtered away from the cliffs. One or two of the men made gestures at the ship, but before any more could be done the figure in the bows of the ship had slipped over the side. A wave hit the vessel and everything upon it was hidden from view in an explosion of white and green water; the mist and spray from this was blown across to the watchers and some minutes passed before one of them shouted and pointed with a gnarled finger at the sea some distance from the wreck.

A head could be seen bobbing and disappearing on the bubbling crest of a great wave. They caught sight of the swimmer again two minutes later. He was being swept towards Angader Rock, which barred the entrance to Sawle Cove. But he was not seen again. Men do not live in Cornish seas when a gale is calling the tune. The watchers cursed in broken snatches and strained their eyes towards the wreck.

Then one shouted: "Try Sawle Point. Cann't we get the gear down thur; the wind'll be abeam of us."

With sweat mingling on their foreheads with the spray, they hauled their tackle away from the cliffs, dragged it round the edge of Trelasky Cove and with a clumsy impatient care began to half-haul, half-lower it towards the edge of Sawle Point.

The seas were breaking over this, but as the point lay almost due west of the ship they would no longer be firing into the wind but across it. Slipping and sliding in their haste, hobnailed boots sparking on the rock, they set up their gear and prepared to fire their next rocket.

From here the ship lay pointing north-east with her

stern towards them; the angle of her deck was acute, her masts reaching towards a gleam of yellow sunlight among the racing clouds. Her mizzen mast was at a greater angle than the other two.

They fired the first rocket well out to sea and away from the ship, and there was a moment's silence and then a cracked cheer as the line was seen to have been blown full across the poop. All along the cliffs people waved and opened their mouths in sounds which were lost as soon as uttered.

One of the figures on the ship snatched at the line as it passed him and quickly made it fast.

Now began the task of paying out by means of this thin rocket line first the whip, which was an endless rope much thicker than the line and had to be secured to the main mast, then the hawser, and finally the breeches buoy.

You may still hear all this from the lips of a man who saw it. You will be told that just for a moment when the mizzen mast collapsed it looked as if the breeches buoy would be carried away, with only two of the crew rescued. You will be told what happened when the survivors came ashore, of the efforts of the Sawle people to provide them with dry clothing and food, of how some of them were accommodated at the Tavern Inn and others in the cottages near.

But from that point the account becomes vague. Even though he remembers the sensation which shortly followed the rescue, a sensation which set it apart from all other wrecks of the century, the shipwreck is still the main concern of the narrator. This much he saw; the rest he read about. At the time it was a topic on everyone's lips; but lips and ears are not eyes, which take the lasting impressions.

Turn up the newspapers of a few weeks later and you will find that much was written in them on this later sensation. But reading the faded pages, one is struck once again by a sense of inadequacy, of seeing the bare bones of the events and being not quite able to imagine the flesh which hung upon them. This person lived and that person died, this woman made a public statement to the press, that woman left the country quietly and was hardly heard of again. Like palaeontologists trying to reconstruct an extinct animal we patiently fit the pieces into place and from them

10

build up a probable structure which will pass for the real thing. At heart, though, it is artificial, an inverted creation, reaching from the overt acts back to the unstated reasons and not growing, as life grows, from the need to the wish, from the desire to the intention, from the reason to the act.

In Sawle, therefore, the curious will find something at once to excite their interest and to frustrate it. A description of a shipwreck and the shadowy outlines of something more. The spectre of human hopes, defeated or fulfilled and now forgotten, the shadows of human conflict and affection, generosity and greed, must stalk sometimes on December nights over the remains of the wreck.

To this the newspaper, crackling as we turn its pages, can only add a faded epilogue.

But further inquiry is not as fruitless as it might appear. Still living in another part of the world are people who remember these events because they were an intimate part of them, who perhaps cannot tell you the end, for their own lives are not yet ended, but can, if you get them in the right mood, explain exactly how it all began.

Book One

CHAPTER ONE

On a sunny afternoon in mid-June 1898, a train drew into Falmouth Station, and among the few passengers who alighted was a boy of eleven.

He was tall for his age, reedy of build, with a shock of fair hair, good open blue eyes and a clean skin. He was dressed in a brown corduroy suit, obviously his best, and a wide new Eton collar with a bow tie. In one hand he carried a cloth cap, in the other a wicker travelling bag secured by clasps at the top and bound by a leather strap.

He stood there irresolute, blinking a moment at the stationmaster, who had taken off his silk hat to mop his damp forehead in the sun, then followed the other passengers to the ticket barrier.

Just outside the barrier, eyeing the outcoming passengers with a purposive gaze, was a tall girl of about nineteen. Occasionally she would put up a hand to steady her wide-brimmed hat against the wind. When the boy passed through the barrier she took one more glance up the platform and then stepped forward.

"Are you Anthony?" she asked.

He stopped in some surprise, changed hands with his bag and then set it down and blushed.

"Are you Cousin Patricia?" It was noticeable that their voices had a resemblance, his low but not yet beginning to break, hers contralto and of the same timbre.

"I am," she said. "You look surprised. Did you not expect someone would meet you? Come along. This way. The train was late."

He followed her down towards the town and presently fell into step beside her on the pavement, darting glances about him, towards the crowded harbour and the noisy docks, and the tall chimney of the sawmill, then sidelong at his companion who now was holding her hat all the time.

"So you're Cousin Anthony," she said. "How tall you are! I was looking for a *little* boy." When he blushed again, "Are you shy? Haven't you ever been a journey by yourself before?"

15

"Yes," he said stoutly. "Often." Which wasn't quite true. He had in fact never been to a seaport of this sort before. Born and bred on Exmoor, he had not even seen the sea for four years — almost a lifetime — and that had been no more than a glimpse from the top of a high cliff and upon a grey day. Today the harbour sparkled and shone. Ships of all sizes mingled bewilderingly in its blueness, and away to the east the lovely line of St. Mawes Creek glittered in the sun. But this was not why he blushed.

"I was frightfully sorry to hear of Aunt Charlotte's death," said the girl soberly — or at least with an attempt at soberness, for all her movements were instinct with the joy and vigour of life. She brightened up. "What shall you do? Have you come to stay with us long? Joe will tell me nothing."

"Joe?"

"Dad. Your Uncle Joe. Everyone calls him Joe. He's frightfully close about things."

"Oh," said Anthony. "No. That is, I don't rightly know yet. Father wrote to Uncle Joe. He says it just means me staying here till he can make a home in Canada. Of course, I'd go out straight away, but father says where he is now isn't fit for children."

"What's he doing?"

"Prospecting. He's been out two years, you know. Mother and me were going out as soon as he could make a home. Now, of course . . . it's all different."

"Yes," said Patricia, nodding sympathetically. "Well, you must stay here and make your home with us."

They walked on in silence. The memory of his dire misfortune cast a black shadow over Anthony's mind for some moments. Even yet he could not accustom his mind to the change. He still felt that his mother existed in this world, that she had gone away for a few weeks and would soon be back; already his mind was stored up with things he wanted to say to her, little questions he wished to ask, matters which had cropped up since her going and which seemed to need her personal attention. He felt mature and lonely. Nothing would ever be the same.

"Well," said Patricia, lifting her skirt to step fastidiously across a littering of old cabbage stalks which someone had carelessly tipped, "there's plenty to do here. Boating and

16

fishing and helping in the house. I suppose you know we run a restaurant?"

Anthony nodded.

"There's always plenty going on at Joe's. Mind you, it's mainly an evening business; but there's always plenty to do during the day. If you can lend a hand you'll never need to feel in the way, even if your father won't have you for another couple of years. There's plenty of fun too. Look down there; that's Johnson's; our chief rival."

Anthony peered down a narrow, dirty street leading to a quay. In doorways ill-clad urchins sat and played, but he could not make out anything which looked like a restaurant. The glance served to bring his attention back to his present surroundings, and especially to the girl at his side. Youth has the resilience of a young birch tree: you may bend it till its head touches the earth, but in a minute it will spring erect again, head to the sun and no thought of contact with the soil.

Anthony had been startled at the first sight of his cousin. She was wearing a high-necked white lace blouse with a fine white drill skirt and a wide-brimmed hat turned up at the side and trimmed with broad green velvet ribbon. In one green-gloved hand she carried a parasol. She was very pretty, with curly chestnut hair swept up from the ears, large expressive brown eyes and the complexion of an early peach. She was tall and slender and walked with a grace which was curiously interrupted at intervals by a sudden lifting upon the toes like a barely suppressed skip. She talked vivaciously to him – treating him as an equal – and bent her head graciously from time to time in acknowledgment of a greeting from some passing friend.

He noticed that many of the sailors, even those who did not know her, looked at her from across the street or glanced round as they passed. For sailors were prominent in this strange, exciting little town; dark men and lascars, Dutchmen and French. The whole town was different from any he had been in before: it was foreign and smelt of fish and seaweed and strong tobacco. It smelt of all sorts of things he had not smelt before; as they walked along amid the sun and shadow with the dust playing in whorls between the ramshackle houses his nostrils were assailed now with the odour of untended refuse from a squalid courtyard, now with the sudden strong smell of salt air and the sea. That fresh wind was like a purifier pushing through the slits of streets straight from the Channel and distant lands.

"I wonder if you'll ever have a stepmother?" said Patricia. "I have, you know. Dad married again last year. My mother died two years ago, nearly."

"I'm sorry," said Anthony.

"Yes, it's never the same. Good afternoon, Mrs. Penrose; breezy, isn't it? She's all right in her way – Aunt Madge, I mean – she looks after Dad, but not like Mother did. Dad doesn't love her: he married her because she was a good cook."

For the second time Anthony felt faintly shocked. Patricia's outspokenness was something new to him and as fresh as the wind. A large fat seaman with some tattered gold braid round his cuffs stepped off the pavement to make way for them and beamed at the girl. Anthony stared away from the sea up, up a seeming endless flight of stone steps climbing the hillside, with grey slate cottages running in uneven terraces from them. But Patricia's way was not up the steps. She still went on, along the endless winding main street which skirted the whole western part of the harbour. The wind was less boisterous here and the sun more strong, but she did not raise her parasol. He wondered if it was carried only for ornament, since the handle was so long and the silk cover really so small.

A plump little lady passed them and carefully averted her head.

"Is there anyone else lives with you?" Anthony ventured. "I mean, I haven't any other cousins, have I?"

"No. There's Joe and Aunt Madge and me. Then there's Joe's brother, Uncle Perry. He came home from America last year. He's made money and is looking round for somewhere to retire; but he hasn't found anywhere yet. Then there's Fanny, the scullery maid ... oh, and one or two others who're about, but they don't live in. Are you tired? Shall I give you a hand with that case?"

"Thanks, no," said Anthony, overcome by the thought.

She did not in fact press for the honour. "Well, we're nearly there. Just up this hill and down the other side."

They climbed a short rise where the street became so narrow that the two sides seemed about to meet; the crooked bow windows of an antique shop peered fastidiously down upon two conger eels for sale on the marble slab opposite; then the street dropped again, and Patricia turned off down a short and precipitous side-way which stopped abruptly upon the brink of the harbour.

Here, above the door of the last building on the right, there was an old and weather-beaten signboard, sorely in need of a coat of paint. On this signboard was the simple legend: JOE VEAL'S.

CHAPTER TWO

You entered Smoky Joe's — as the café was universally called by its clientele — through a narrow shop door, and immediately encountered Smoky Joe himself. Indeed it was not physically possible to dine in the café, whether upstairs or down, without first coming into contact with the pro-prietor; for it was his unvarying custom to sit brandishing a carving knife and fork on the opposite side of the counter as you entered the narrow shop; and so belligerent was his look that no one had ever dared to pass closely by him without first learning what there was to eat and then order-ing on the spot the meal he wanted.

Spread on this counter were the viands which made up the choice. At one end there might be a roast turkey or a couple of chickens, with a huge leg of lamb and a piece of sirloin on succeeding dishes. Further down there was a choice of three or four kinds of pudding or tart steaming over an elaborate gas-ring.

The decision made, one could, if one wished, linger to see the portion cut off; one paid up, and the dishes were set aside to be taken into the kitchen where they were piled with vegetables and presently delivered to the customer wherever he had taken his seat.

The system was a good one. Bad debts were never incur-red, complaints seldom; and so succulent was the aspect and smell of the dishes on the counter when one entered that scarcely anyone was ever put off by the gruff and grudging manner of the Tyrant with the carving knife.

In appearance Joe was short and thin with a pale slate-grey complexion and eyes like a small black terrier. His heavy black moustache drooped over a mouth which was at

19

once obstinate and astute. In the shop he always wore a dark alpaca coat the length of a frock coat and a high wrap-round collar with scarcely any tie.

Anthony saw nothing of this on the afternoon of his arrival, for he was ushered down some steps and by a back door into a big low kitchen, where a thin red-faced girl not much older than himself was trying half-heartedly to tidy up the disorder, and a big woman with a distasteful expression was making pastry.

Aunt Madge was a disappointment. This lovely creature who had escorted him all the way from the station, talking cheerfully to him as if they were old friends, had warmed and brightened his heart. He had forgotten his tiredness, his loneliness, the fact that he was thirsty and hot. He had been uplifted in her company. Aunt Madge restored his perspective.

"Late," she said. "Have you been. Round the sea front, I thought. Pat, you should have . . . Fanny needed help. Take him to his bedroom. A cup of tea presently."

Anthony found himself following Patricia up the stairs with an impression that he had not yet really met Aunt Madge at all. In the kitchen there had been a large rather over-dressed woman, a fleshy rather than a fat woman in early middle age, with fair hair going grey, with a pince-nez straddling a short nose, and a discontented mouth built upon a pedestal of chins. But he did not think she would recognize him again. Being introduced to her was like making an appointment with somebody who forgot to turn up.

These old black winding stairs with rickety banisters and creaking boards. They climbed half a flight and two full flights to an attic.

"You'll find yourself a bit at sea at first," said Patricia, on whom her stepmother's welcome had left no impression. "It's with being altered for the restaurant that has made the house confusing."

She opened an old door and showed him into a bedroom with a ceiling which sloped three ways from a central part where it was possible to stand upright. There were all sorts of odd crossbeams. A large iron bedstead decorated with brass knobs was the chief article of furniture. The window was on floor level.

"You can see most of the harbour from here," she said helpfully.

He went to the window and again his spirits began to rise. The view was fine.

"Thanks awfully ... Patricia," he said. "You've been ... Thanks awfully for meeting me at the station."

"That's all right," she said, pulling off her hat and shaking out her curls. She met his frank gaze and smiled. "You'd do the same for me. Tea in ten minutes. Don't wait for someone to shout, will you?"

She ran off down the stairs humming.

Tea was the one meal at which Joe Veal consented to sit down and partake of food in the bosom of his family. He never ate breakfast, and dinner and supper were served to him on a little table behind the counter of the shop where he could supervise the orderings and preferences of customers. But the café was usually empty about tea time; the trip-bell was set to work over the shop door, and Joe and his pipe came down into the kitchen to tea.

Anthony ate buttered scones and drank several cups of hot tea, and absorbed all the newness about him and glanced diffidently but candidly up at the faces of this family into which fate and unfair bereavement had suddenly thrown him. Two months ago he had been at school at Nuncanton in the Vale of Exmoor; he had taken his home and his existence for granted, accepting it as unthinkingly as he drew breath. Now he was here among this family of strangers – related to him perhaps, for Uncle Joe was his mother's brother-in-law – but still strangers, of a quantity and quality unknown.

Anthony instantly took a liking for Perry, Uncle Joe's brother. Uncle Perry was bigger and younger than the other man and had a jovial, rollicking air. He had strong black hair which he wore rather long, and a lock of it was inclined to fall across his forehead when he laughed. He had a plump fresh-complexioned face and roving black eyes. It was a face which might have belonged to a buccaneer.

Joe made very little of the boy by way of greeting. He took his strange square pipe from a corner of his mouth and said, "Well, Anthony," and shook hands with a jerky gesture like someone turning the handle of a door, then put his pipe back in its corner. Anthony thought he looked

21

not unkind but over-busy about his own concerns, which was natural in a man with a restaurant to supervise. Anthony felt that he ought to offer some thanks for the hospitality which was being extended to him, but by the time he could muster a sentence the opportunity had passed.

Uncle Perry's greeting was different. He said, "*Houd vast*, now; so we've taken another hand aboard. Greetings, boy! I could do with a second mate." He laughed as if he had made a joke and thrust back his hair and looked at Aunt Madge and laughed again.

And Aunt Madge, ear-ringed and small-featured and momumental, went on pouring tea.

After the meal Anthony was left to wander about the building and to make himself at home. The building was old and ramshackle and as smoky as Joe himself. From the shop one went down five steps into the lower dining-room or up five steps into the one above. Both were square rooms with windows looking out upon the bay and very low black rafters which made tall men instinctively bend their heads. The one kitchen served both rooms by means of a manually operated dumb waiter. The family lived and fed mainly in this kitchen, but Mr. and Mrs. Veal had a private drawing-room next to their bedroom on the second floor. Besides these there was an office into which Joe retired from time to time and smoked his curious pipe and counted his gold.

As the evening advanced customers began to come in. Fat brokers from the town who knew where there was a good meal, Chinese dock hands, captains of casual tramp steamers, sailors out with their girls, passing travellers, local clerks and apprentices, Belgian fishermen. They varied from week to week as one ship left the port and another put in.

Anthony watched the rooms fill up in some astonishment. Everyone smoked, and very soon the atmosphere was thick and blue. Everyone talked and argued, and presently a man with one leg came in and sat in a corner and began to play an accordian. He did not play it loudly and the sound only just emerged from among the sea of voices, but there was something in the music which added a touch of colour to the room.

The boy from Exmoor could not get over the fact that he had come to live in such a place, which to him seemed to be the height of the exotic, that *his* relatives owned and ran it. When Aunt Christine died two years ago his mother had come to Falmouth for the funeral. He could not understand why his mother had not come back to Nuncanton full of talk about this place.

Two boys of about seventeen dressed in white coats did the waiting: Patricia superintended and sometimes helped out whichever boy was busiest. Through the fog of smoke Anthony perceived that she was tremendously popular in this company. There was pleasure in merely watching her weave a way among the crowded tables. Anthony did not reason that the charm and piquancy which at a glance had subjugated a boy of eleven would be likely to have the same effect on hardened, weather-beaten men of fifty or sixty; had the thought occurred to him he would have felt it disgusting that old men should have any feelings at all. But he enjoyed her popularity without analysis of its causes.

There was great competition for her attention but no advantage taken of it when gained. Neither did it occur to the boy to see any connection between this good behaviour and the presence of the severe little man sitting in the shop with a carving knife.

Later in the evening, when the smoke in the restaurant was making his eyes prick and water, and when the clamour of dish washing in the scullery was no longer a novelty, Anthony moved hesitatingly towards the shop, found a vantage point, and watched fascinated the procedure by which each customer chose and paid for the food he was to eat.

In a lull Joe Veal saw the boy standing awkwardly in a corner, his rather scared, frank blue eyes taking everything in. He beckoned with a dripping carving fork, and Anthony came and stood by him and stared down at the almost empty dishes.

"Why don't you go to bed, boy? Too excited to be tired, I s'pose."

"I'll go soon," said Anthony. "I thought perhaps you might want me. Do you – do you close soon?"

Smoky Joe showed a row of small, yellow, false teeth of which one had been filed away to provide a suitable lodgment for his pipe. It was not so much like a smile as a display of a set of coins.

"Close, boy? Not just yet awhile. In a trade like this you

23

always have to remember you're the servant of the public, see? Can't just close and open when you want. Did Charlotte leave you any money?"

Anthony blinked. "Mother? I don't rightly know, Uncle. Mr. Parks, the solicitor, said something, but I didn't quite catch . . ."

Smoky Joe's pipe had a sudden downward curve an inch from his lip, and the queer, square bowl emitted smoke from opposite the top button of his waistcoat. He took this bent stem from his mouth and wiped his moustache with it.

"Never trust lawyers. Scum of the earth. The law's like a basket, full of holes; and it's the lawyer's job to find the holes and slip through them. Slippery, they are. There was one I knew in Java . . . This Parks, did he give you any money for yourself, eh?"

"Yes," said Anthony, staring hard at the skeleton of a roast duck. "Three pounds he gave me before I left. He said that he had come to some arrangement with –"

"Oh, some arrangement. Yes, some arrangement. That's lawyer talk. We want more plates, Fanny! You're slow with the plates! Lawyers are always coming to some arrangement." Uncle Joe fastened his terrier-like eyes on the boy. "Where is it?"

"What?"

"The three pounds the lawyer gave you. It isn't safe for a boy of your age to carry sov'rins loose in your pocket. Might lose them. I'll keep them for you."

Anthony hesitated. "There's only two now. I had to pay my railway fare."

"Well, two, then," said Joe Veal, holding out a dry and scaly hand. All his skin looked dry and mottled as if the natural oil had long perished from it.

Anthony felt in his jacket pocket and took out a purse. In it were two sovereigns, a shilling and a florin piece.

"I'll have those as well," said Uncle Joe, taking all the coins and slipping them into a deep recess of his greasy waistcoat. He puffed at his pipe and stared meditatively at the boy for a moment. "You're a big fellow for your age. Going to be a big man, I reckon. Is your father big?"

"Yes," said Anthony.

"But, then, it don't signify. Look at me, I'm small. Your aunt was small. But Pat's shot up like a weed. Maybe we

24

could make use of you in the restaurant, eh? How would you like that?"

"I think I should like it," said Anthony. He put his empty purse back in his pocket.

"Wait," said Joe. "Don't ever let 'em say I was mean." He put down his carving knife, reluctantly it seemed, and pressed some keys of the automatic till. There was a "ping" and the drawer shot open. He took out twelve pennies and handed them to Anthony. "There. That's pocket money. That'll do to buy sweets. You can spend that; different from a sov'rin. Make it last a month; then come to me for more." His expression changed and his moustache bristled as two smart young seamen came into the shop, and said, "Evenin', Joe."

"No lamb," was his belligerent reply. "You're too late. There's a bit of beef left," he admitted reluctantly. "It's tough."

Soon afterwards Anthony went to bed. He waved to Pat, who gave him a brief, brilliant, glinting smile which warmed his heart afresh; then he slowly climbed the two creaky flights of stairs and groped a way into the attic.

There was no candle in the room, but darkness had only just fallen, and he could see what was necessary by the loom of light in the west and the glitter of the first stars. From his window he could see the lights of Flushing across the creek and all the winking eyes of the ships, big and small, riding at anchor in the roadstead. The lower window would not open, but through the upper one came the strong smell of seaweed and tidal mud.

For a long time he knelt by the window absorbing the strangeness of the scene. He felt as if he were in a foreign land. But presently tiredness got the better of interest and he slowly undressed and said his prayers and climbed into bed. It was a large double bed, and once in it he was suddenly beset by loneliness and bereavement. Years ago he had slept in a bed like this, but beside him there had been the warmth and softness and all-including guardianship of his mother. Nothing then had been for him to do, to decide, to consider: it had been sufficient for him to *be*, to exist unthinkingly, in the aura of that loving, understanding, comforting protection.

Now he was alone in an alien world.

Much later he woke. He had been dreaming that someone was quarrelling violently, crying wild curses and threatening to come to blows. He had been dreaming too that someone played upon a piano and rough men sang jolly choruses. The sounds still seemed to echo in his ears.

Pitch dark and there was no means of telling the time. A soft summer wind soughed across the estuary.

He turned over and tried to go to sleep. Then a door banged and he sat up.

Silence had fallen again. He lay in bed and wished he was not such a baby, that such a waking in the middle of the night should make his heart beat faster.

Another door banged and there was the clatter of a pail. Then down in the very depths of the house, as if from the inmost recesses of its rickety old soul, someone began to sing:

"They heard the Black Hunter! and dr-read shook each
    mind;
Hearts sank that had never known fear-r;
They heard the Black Hunter's dr-read voice in the
    wind . . ."

It was a man's voice, quavering and drunken. Another door banged. Then came the sound of feet on the stairs.

The attic was the only room on this floor; it was really built into the roof. But the feet were on the flight of stairs lower down.

All the same Anthony wished there had been some means of locking his door.

All the sounds in this house seemed to echo; due perhaps to the way in which it was built about the well of the staircase. Anthony could hear the over-careful feet stumble against one of the steps and the curse which followed.

"Hearts sank that had never known fear-r. (Rot and blast the thing! Who left it lying about?)

"They heard the Black Hunter's dr-read voice in the wind!
They heard his cursed hell-hounds run yelping behind!
An' his steed thundered loud on the ear. . . ."

Presently the drunken voice died away and silence reigned. In the distance the siren of a ship hooted. After a

26

long time Anthony felt his muscles relax, and drowsiness
crept quietly over him like an unreliable friend.

Later still he was awakened by hearing someone being violently sick.

CHAPTER THREE

Daylight brought a more homely aspect to his new domi-
cile. From his window he saw that the tide was out, and
many of the little boats loafed on their elbows in the mud.
Seagulls crossed and recrossed the sky, flying lonely and
remote as a cloud, wings scarcely moving, or suddenly
darting down and fighting in a screaming, undignified
pack for some morsel which one of their number had
found. Two lighted on the flat end of the roof immediately
below the attic window and side-stepped warily along to
the corner piece. In the distance a small tramp steamer
moved lazily out to sea.

Last night he had not put the twelve pennies Uncle Joe
had given him into his purse, and this morning when he
came to put on his trousers they fell out of his pocket with
a clatter and rolled in all directions about the room. One
had rolled beneath the bed and he pulled away the strip of
carpet to get at it. As he retrieved it he was surprised to see
a cork embedded in the floorboards.

Interested, he lifted up the valance and wriggled further
under the bed amid the dust and fluff. Then he took out
his penknife and with very little difficulty was able to pull
the cork out. He put his eye to the hole which resulted and
found himself looking down into the room below.

A small room, with a desk and a filing cabinet and an
armchair. There was a pile of letters on the desk and newspapers and magazines on a chair. Tacked to the door was a
nautical calender.

He was suddenly afraid of being surprised in this prying
position; he felt that someone was just about to enter his
bedroom and find him there; he thrust back the cork and
replaced the carpet and hurriedly resumed dressing.

When he went downstairs it was still early but he found
Aunt Madge up and swatting flies. She seemed to have a

27

particular aversion for them, for there were six flypapers hung about the kitchen. She was dressed in a pink kimono with lace and frills and ruches and long sleeves of which the wide lace cuffs were stained with bacon grease. On her head was a pink lace cap.

She looked at him from above her chins and evidently recognized him.

"Ah," she said. "You slept? Fanny's late. You could get . . . sticks for the fire."

Under directions Anthony went out upon the stone-paved quay, which was directly accessible from the kitchen door, and found a pile of driftwood and an axe. He began to chop up the wood. This was a job to which he could bring some skill, for he had always done it at home, though with good stately logs to work on, not miserable chunks of deal and pine, many of them half rotten with worm. He came on one spar which split into pieces at the first stroke and he found it honeycombed inside like a model of the catacombs. This idea so interested him that he went down on his knees to trace the burrowings more closely; and he was still there when Patricia came out.

"Good morning, Anthony. Did you sleep well? Have you got some sticks? Madge seems to be in one of her moods this morning."

She was wearing a pretty black and white striped apron drawn in at the waist with a big bow at the back, over a simple high-necked blouse and dark skirt.

"Look at this," he said. "Isn't it pretty? What's made it like this?"

"Barnacles. Haven't you ever seen them?"

"No."

"They're big black worms with heads like mussel-shells and long ferny red tongues. The sort of thing you see in a nightmare. But Madge'll start reading you a sermon if she doesn't get her fire soon."

Breakfast was a feminine meal. Neither Perry nor Joe put in an appearance. Little Fanny arrived down red-eyed and weary as the meal was about to begin, and Anthony saw what Aunt Madge's sermon was like when directed at someone else.

She did not show any signs of anger. Seated in immobile serenity with a cup of tea steered unerringly from time to time to the plump little opening from which emerged so much sound, she talked on and on at Fanny in a pained rather hoarse voice with majesty and persistence. Sometimes she put an *H* in front of a word to give extra emphasis. Having said what she had to say, she shook her ear-rings, adjusted her pince-nez, and started anew. Finally Fanny burst into tears and went breakfastless to brush out the upper restaurant.

At this Aunt Madge turned up her eyes as if in surprise at a rebuff, and poured herself another cup of tea. She had a peculiar habit of putting her eyes away under her small lids as if she were withdrawing them for inner consultation.

"Girls," she said to nobody. "Difficult. Can't reason with. Hi try to be patient, to *lead* . . ."

Anthony was kept busy all the morning. Uncle Joe appeared, wizened and sallow, about eleven, Uncle Perry, dark-eyed and plump-faced and laughing, an hour later. Before lunch Anthony went shopping with Patricia. When it was done she hired a landau and took the boy along the sea front, past the new houses shining in the sun. The ride was in the best possible style. Pat prudently dismissed the landau a hundred yards or so from JOE VEAL'S and they reached home in time for the midday meal.

Mrs. Veal clearly suspected that they had been up to no good; she went round and round the subject while she was dishing out the stew, but they gave her no satisfaction. Finally Uncle Perry diverted her by launching into a long account of what had happened to him once in the Barbados, and Patricia caught her cousin's eye and winked.

The Barbados story went on indefinitely. At least, thought Anthony, Aunt Madge can cook. I shan't starve in this house. "Yes," he said to Uncle Perry, with his mouth full. "No," he said, taking another piece of home-made bread to wipe up the gravy. And, "Fancy," he said, leaning back and wondering if the pudding would be as good.

"Fanny," said Aunt Madge, and waved an ostentatious hand. "See if Mr. Veal . . ." She smoothed down the geometrical frills of her yellow silk blouse and adjusted her pince-nez to look at Patricia. "Hubby called this morning."

For the first time Anthony saw the girl's face lose its soft contours; colour moved across her neck and cheeks.

"What did he want?" Her voice was brittle and calm.

"Wanted to see you, of course. I told him you weren't . . .

29

Pity, I think." She glanced at the plate Fanny had brought back. "Mr. Veal hasn't eaten ..."

"Mr. Veal says he don't want any pudding, mum. An' he says two Roast Porks have gone upstairs, an' these are the plates."

"I'll do them," said Pat, rising. It seemed as if she welcomed the opportunity of movement.

Anthony was served with steaming hot lemon pudding with treacle sauce. For the moment he could not touch it.

Patricia returned to the table. "If he thinks I'm going back," she said, still in the same brittle voice, "he's mistaken."

Anthony slowly moved his eyes to her left hand. On the third finger there was a gold ring.

"Think you ought," said Mrs. Veal. "Marriage vows. Taking these things lightly."

Patricia poured herself some water. "It's my own life, and I – don't want to live it with him. Why should I always go on paying for one mistake."

"Hi don't approve." Anthony suddenly found himself under Mrs. Veal's gaze. Her pince-nez had slipped a little and her eyes were looking over the top like unmuzzled guns. "Not eating pudding. Young boys not saucy."

He hastened to eat several mouthfuls. Hours he had been in Pat's company and never noticed that ring. It shouldn't have made any difference, but in fact just at the moment it seemed as if nothing would ever be the same again. He was suffering the shock of broken puppy dreams.

"Three weeks," said Aunt Madge. "No time. After a good trial. . . ."

"What did he say?"

"He said, 'Good morning, Mrs. Veal,' he said, 'I want to see Patricia.' Into the kitchen quite sudden. The pork. Almost burned. 'Marriage vows,' I said. 'Mr. Harris, I don't approve. Made in the sight of God.' "

"You'd no business to take his side against me," Patricia said quietly. "You shouldn't have given him encouragement."

"There, there," said Uncle Perry. "It isn't as if anyone was going to make you go back."

"I don't see why they should try," Pat said mutinously.

"More pudding, Perry," said Aunt Madge. "Manners at

30

the table. . . ." Her chins went up and down as she ate some cheese ."Those flies. In from the river."

"Marriage should be like it is in the Pacific Islands," said Uncle Perry. "If you fancy someone there you just have a tribal dance." He laughed infectiously.

"Perry . . . Please."

Uncle Perry winked at Anthony and pushed his lank black hair away from his brow. It was the second wink Anthony had received that meal, but he no longer felt in a mood to appreciate them. When Patricia pushed the cheese across to him he refused it. He felt terribly uncomfortable and his cheeks were burning. When at last he could get away he went straight out to the woodpile and spent all the afternoon in the hot sun chopping firewood.

Presently Uncle Perry came out and sat on a mooring stone and watched him, and after a while began to talk.

Perry Veal was a good story-teller with an eye for picturesque detail and the slightly suggestive phrase. In spite of himself Anthony at last laid down his axe and sat beside the dark man listening with his ears and blue eyes open wide. More than half the allusions were lost on him, but that made his interest all the more intent. Here before him was a man who knew everything in the world that was worth knowing, and the boy would have given a lot to have understood all the sly nods and oblique references which as often as not made up the point of a story. He felt as some men do when an after-dinner speaker persists in concluding all his bawdy stories in French.

But he learned much, and in the process temporarily forgot the tragedy of this afternoon when the sweet green shoot of his first romantic attachment had been broken off and trampled in the dust. He remembered it again only when Uncle Perry lit his short black "nose-warmer" and began to tell a story of a friend of his who had married a native queen in Patagonia.

"Four feet six broad she was, boy; handsome arms and shoulders; a fine figure of a woman. Well, there's not much a native queen don't know about marriage, you can take it from me." He drew at his pipe with a wet sucking noise, then spat over the side.

"Cousin Pat never told me she was married," Anthony blurted out, committing the impropriety of interrupting his

31

uncle in full spate. "When was she married? What's her husband? Don't they get on?"

"Eh? What's that?" Perry's winking dark eyes grew vague. He took his pipe from his mouth and stared at it, then knocked out the contents upon the palm of his hand. This black half-burned tobacco he rolled again into a ball between his palms and thrust it back into the bowl of his pipe. Then he blew away the ash, took a little fresh tobacco and pushed it down on top of the old. He struck a match and the wet sucking process began afresh. "Pat. Oh, Pat." He laughed. "She's fickle, boy. A little filly who doesn't know what she really wants, see?" He nodded and sucked and his black hair fell across his brow. "At that age, boy, they're nervous. Not properly broken in, as you might say; mettlesome. First touch of the bridle and they're up and away. But she's tasted flesh. She'll go back one day. Once they've tasted flesh, they always go back to it. That's what the tiger does, boy. In Madras; when I was in Madras in '91 –"

"Who is he, her husband?" the boy persisted. "Have you seen him?"

"Seen him? Of course I've seen him. He's a lawyer from Penryn. They were only married in April. Couple of little budgerigars inching up to each other on the same twig. Sweet, they were. Little love birds. Then they were married. She went to live in Penryn. Handsome house, money no object. Eating off silver. Then of a sudden she comes home all of a sweat, nostrils quivering. 'Go back?' she say. 'Not I!'" Uncle Perry's pipe had gone out again. "Little filly. ... Wants breaking in, that's all. She'll go back."

At that moment they heard the subject under discussion calling them to tea. Anthony felt he had that afternoon become an adult. Never before had he been admitted to the confidences of a man. He was tremendously grateful to Uncle Perry for being treated as an equal. The enormous mysteries of life bulked large in the hot June sun. All the same he felt that Perry had gone over the mark in his talk of Patricia. As he sat at tea with the family all his admiration for the charm and prettiness of the girl filled him afresh.

The evening passed much as the previous one had done. Feeling more at home, the boy began to make himself useful, and during the evening rush hour his quick legs were a help. Recovering from the shock of dinner time he set himself whenever possible to help Patricia. The fleeting smiles that she gave him were sufficient reward. She was not so vivacious as the previous evening, and it was evident to the boy that her husband's visit had upset her.

The fact that the unknown man was a lawyer made Anthony think of someone like Mr. Parks, who was thin and grey-bearded and dry and talked through his nose. The idea that this beautiful fresh young girl should have tied herself for life to such a creature, covered with the dust of the law, appalled him. For the first time in his life his inquiring mind turned upon the subject of divorce. He resolved to ask Uncle Perry. Uncle Perry would be sure to know not only all about divorce in this country but also in Asia, Africa and the South Sea Islands.

Anthony decided to stay up later tonight to see all that there was to be seen, but by nine o'clock he could hardly keep his eyes open. He had slept badly last night and had been up very early two mornings together. So after a struggle nature had its way; he wished the kitchen staff good night and climbed the stairs to bed even before the old man with the one leg had begun to play his accordian.

Dead tired, he slept much better. Once or twice he was conscious of shouts and music. Then after what seemed a century of sleep he heard again the drunken voice singing as it climbed the stairs to bed.

No song of a ghostly rider tonight. This time it was about a lady called Aluetta.

CHAPTER FOUR

The next day was a Sunday, and even Smoky Joe's was compelled to remain closed. Shortly after breakfast Joe himself appeared in an old frock coat with a grey woollen muffler wound round his throat and a straw hat in his hand. He beckoned to Anthony.

"Can you row?"

Anthony shook his head. "I rowed on a lake once, that's all."

"Never mind. You'll soon learn. I want you to row me

out to a ship in the roads. It's a nice morning. You'll enjoy it."

Anthony was of the same opinion. He rushed upstairs for his cap and joined his uncle on the quay. Joe was pulling in a small dinghy by its painter, and Aunt Madge with folded arms was watching.

"Currents," she observed didactically. "No experience. Tide is going out. You should send over . . ."

"Fiddlesticks," said Joe, breathing heavily with the effort. "Anybody can row. And *I* haven't forgotten how. Here, boy, down this ladder and jump in."

Swelling with responsibility, Anthony climbed down the iron ladder attached to the quay and got into the boat. After a moment Joe joined him.

"Cold wind on the water," said Mrs. Veal to the doorpost. "No coat . . ."

This remark was ignored until they drew jerkily away from the land; then Joe said:

"Women. They coddle you. Your aunt wants to make a baby of me. See that she doesn't make one of you."

It occurred to Anthony, struggling with the oars, that his aunt had taken no noticeable step in that direction so far. So he just smiled, showing his good regular teeth, and nodded. When they were about a hundred yards out Uncle Joe pointed over the boy's shoulder.

"See that barquentine. No, there, letting go her heads'ls. That's where you're to row me."

Anthony caught a crab in his effort to do two things at the same time, and operations were suspended while Joe give him one or two lessons. Anthony thought how thin and old and dry his uncle looked in the morning light. After each sentence his moustache clamped down like a trap door from which nothing more must be allowed to escape. His small eyes were like gimlets in the sun, glinting as they turned to stare about the bay.

The ship indicated was well out in the roadstead, almost halfway across to St. Mawes. She had only recently arrived, and between her and them there were all manner of craft. Anthony was in a fever of concern lest he should run into or be run down by one of these vessels.

"You stick to your rowing, boy; I'll tell you what to do," said Joe, pulling his hat lower over his eyes. "Don't pull your guts out; take it slow and steady. He-eave – o-o-o. He-eave – o-o-o. That's it."

Joe was in a better mood than he had previously seen him, more human and approachable out here than when crouched like a terrier over the till. None of the Veals, except Patricia once, had offered the boy any word of sympathy on the loss of his mother, and barely consciously the boy resented it. Joe at least, who knew her, might have said something. Instead of that he had asked about the money, nothing more. Not even a word on Anthony's prospects of joining his father. The prospects might be discussed, but Anthony was of no account in them, no more than a mere chattel.

"Where did you get that funny pipe, Uncle Joe?" he asked, as Veal took the object from his pocket and began to fill it.

"Funny? There's nothing funny about it except to the ignorant. Many a man smokes a pipe like this out East."

"Oh," said Anthony, and was silent for some time. He was already hot and breathless. "Have you been out East a lot, Uncle Joe?"

"Java. Twenty-two years. Starboard a bit, boy. Right arm. *Right* arm. Me and your aunt were out there twenty-one years and eight months, on and off."

"Aunt Christine?"

"Yes. Your mother's sister. That's where she got the worm that killed her. Once you've got it, it's hard to be rid of it. Starboard again. Now ship your oar. *Right* oar."

They glided close beside an old barge which was moored in their path. Anthony expected the sides to grate.

They were well out now in the dancing water and could feel the thrust of the strong breeze. The sun was brilliant this morning without warmth. All about them were the sailing ships which another decade would see abandoned for ever. Four-masted barques with nitrate from America. Grain ships from Australia. Brigs loading with pilchards for the Italian ports. Schooners carrying salt to the New-foundland cod banks. Away in the distance was the St. Anthony lighthouse, white against the grey-green of the cliffs.

"But we always come back, we Veals," said Uncle Joe suddenly, wiping his moustache this way and that with the stem of his pipe. "There's been a Veal in Falmouth, boy, ever since there was a Falmouth. An' we're proud of it, see? A Veal was steward to the first Killigrew. Up in that ancient old house by the docks. His daughter had a natural son by William Killigrew. We trace direct back to him."

Anthony wondered what a natural son was, since hitherto he had thought that all children were natural.

"Straight as a die," said Uncle Joe. "Sons of sons all the way. Not many families can say that. And we've outlasted the Killigrews. They're dead and gone. That house and land should all be ours if right was right."

Across the water in the centre of old Falmouth a church was ringing its bells. The sound floated to them, gentle and iterative and sweet.

"We're the last Veals," said Joe. His pipe had gone out and his eyes for a moment were still, because they were focused on nothing. "Uncle Perry and me. We're the last Veals. And he's not married and I've no male issue. So that's the end of us, too."

Anthony rowed on. His mind went back to Patricia and her marriage. But he held his tongue. After that for some time there was no conversation between them.

As they at last neared the barquentine a dinghy approached them from the direction of the ship and a tall, well-set young man raised his blue cap very respectfully to Joe and called a courteous greeting as he passed. Joe responded with a brief nod.

"Who's that, Uncle Joe?"

"That's Ned Pawlyn, mate of *The Grey Cat*. No doubt he's off ashore to take Patricia out."

The boy struggled again with curiosity and this time was defeated.

"Patricia's married, isn't she?" he asked.

Uncle Joe's face went hard and narrow. He stared at a passing barge.

"Nobody's business if she is."

Anthony's face could not take on any more colour; instead it paled about the mouth.

"No. . . . I'm sorry."

"Nor is she by rights," said Joe after a moment. "Not if the law was as it should be. She married wi'out any consent. That should be enough to get it annulled. What did she want, marrying at her age. I'd nought against her having a good time. But her place is at home, as she rightly realizes now. Her place is with me, helping me. Who told you, anyhow?"

"It was – just mentioned," said Anthony, catching a crab.

"Well, it's no business of anybody's except hers and mine."

The dinghy had gone right off its course and he had difficulty in pulling it back. "I'm sorry if I shouldn't ought to have said anything, Uncle Joe. But why did she marry him if you didn't want her to and she didn't love him?"

Uncle Joe took out his pipe and pointed it at the boy. "Questions. Questions. Too young to ask so many questions. Perhaps you're going to be a lawyer. Pah!" He spat over the side. "Scum of the earth are lawyers. Wriggle here and wriggle there. Keep clear of them, I tell you."

"Yes, Uncle Joe."

"Why did she marry? you say. Because she's a woman and goes by opposites, that's why. But to you she's your cousin Patricia, nothing more and nothing less. See, boy?"

"Yes, Uncle Joe."

Veal's little eyes travelled past Anthony to the bulk that was looming ahead. "Now ship your oars. Gently does it. Don't wet my feet! There, that'll do. Now go up in the bows and ease her off as she touches."

They spent three hours on board and had a meal before returning. Anthony was surprised to find his uncle treated with extreme deference. Even the captain, a square hard man with mutton-chop whiskers, called him "sir".

Anthony played about the deck, pretending himself already at sea. He talked to the crew and watched the ships and tried to find out what every piece of rope was for and leaned over the side seeing what sort of a splash he could make with his spittle in the water below. The time passed like a flash; he had never enjoyed himself more despite the blisters on his hands.

Only for dinner was he invited to the captain's quarters, and the three of them ate together. Much of the conversation was of nautical matters he could not understand. Uncle Joe had quite recovered his good humour and joked with the captain, whose name was Stevens, about getting his nephew a berth in the ship as cabin boy. Joe ate very little indeed but drank a good deal of whisky. Anthony noticed how clumsily he held his knife and fork even before he touched the whisky.

Then before they left wines were brought up and several kinds tasted. The ship had just arrived from Lisbon with a cargo of port and was unloading here. When that was completed, Joe said, she was to take on a general cargo for Liverpool.

Some semblance of the truth was dawning on Anthony. The full significance of the matter was suddenly illuminated by a nautical magazine which lay open on the desk. Written across the top by some newsagent or supplier were the words, *The Grey Cat. J. Veal, Blue Water Line.*

He rowed his uncle home with increasing blisters on his palms and a proportionately increased respect for the old man.

When Anthony, sore and breathless and hot, at last brought the small boat back to its mooring and they had walked precariously over the mud by way of a broken wooden landing jetty, they found Mrs. Veal standing with arms folded at the side door, just as if she had not moved since they left.

"We're not drowned, you see," said Smoky Joe, wiping his eyes, which were watering a good deal.

"Caught a chill, I'll be bound," she observed from a small mouth above the unmoving mass of her figure. "And things waiting for you . . . Attention." She waved a hand.

"What things?" Joe was at once irritable.

"Pat's hubby here again."

"Don't call him that! Don't you know his name?" Joe walked into the kitchen and pulled off his scarf; he sank into a chair as if he had been doing the rowing. "Did you send him about his business?"

"In the lower restaurant now."

"Who let him in?"

"He came by the back. You can't expect me . . ."

"I'll soon get rid of him. Where's Pat?"

"Out with . . . I forget his . . ."

"Ned Pawlyn. She's always off with him. What does the man want? Fetch me a glass of whisky, Madge."

"Milk you should have."

"Whisky, I said."

Aunt Madge waved a hand helplessly and moved to a cupboard in the wall.

"More than that. Three fingers. Don't drown it. Hah!"

38

While Joe drank it Anthony reflected that in a queer way he had become quite fond of his uncle since they set out. The old man's bark was worse than his bite. And the boy warmed towards him because of his hostility for Patricia's husband.

Joe Veal stared at the empty glass, said "Hah!" again, then rose to go downstairs.

At a discreet distance Anthony followed

CHAPTER FIVE

Thomas Wilberforce Harris sat tilting a chair and reading *Punch* in the empty café. He was a young man of medium height, smartly dressed in black. On the table beside him was a silk hat and a gold-mounted stick. He was dark, with a strong nose, a strong neck and full brown eyes which gave the impression of seeing more than surface things. He was not good looking but his face had personality. He looked as if he might be both self-confident and self-doubting.

When he saw who it was who had entered he put *Punch* carefully beside his hat, untilted his chair and got up.

Joe strode across to him like an angry dog.

"What do you want?" he demanded.

Harris glanced behind Joe Veal to see if anyone else had followed him in.

"Can you let me have a meal?" he said quietly.

"Restaurant's closed," snapped Joe. "It's Sunday and against the law."

"There's no law against providing food for one's son-in-law."

This remark was evidently looked upon by Joe as the height of provocation. "You're no son-in-law of mine!"

"Well, the law, for which you have so much respect, says so."

"I'm not interested in that. By a trumpery trick you persuaded Pat to go through a marriage ceremony . . ."

The young man's eyes, which had been cool and reserved, flickered with a spark of anger.

"There was no trickery unless Pat practised it in pretending that she loved me. The marriage was entered into of her own free will."

Joe eyed him up and down with contempt. "No doubt you know the law. I'll give you credit for that. Well, she's changed her mind. She was too young to know it then, easily influenced. But she knows it now and there's no use your coming here with your patronizing airs."

"I want to see her first," said Harris.

"Well, you can't because she's out. Nor will she be back until dark. And you can't sit there. We're going to clean the place."

"Well, I'm not particular. I can wait in the kitchen."

Joe was about to deny him the right to do this when the sound of voices could be heard coming through the shop. Anthony ducked behind a curtain as Patricia appeared, peeling off her lavender gloves and laughing up at the big young sailor closely following her. There was silence in the restaurant as the voices passed the door and went into the kitchen.

"See here," said Joe. "Are you looking for trouble?"

Harris said: "No. Only for my wife."

"Because," said Joe, "there'll be trouble if you don't get out."

In the distance Mrs. Veal's monotonous voice could be heard talking to the young couple.

"Confound the woman!" said Joe.

Harris was looking at the little man with intent eyes. He seemed to be trying to sound the depth of his hostility.

"You gave me some very good turbot one time when I was here," he said. "With lobster sauce. There's a body about turbot that I like."

"You'll get no food out of me today," Joe said weakly.

There was a footstep outside and Patricia passed the curtain where Anthony was hiding. Following her at a distance came Ned Pawlyn. Patricia's face had completely changed from what it had been three minutes ago. Anthony watched the colour come and go in her cheeks.

Ned Pawlyn was a powerfully made young man with broad shoulders and long legs and a quiet walk, as if he was accustomed to moving along the deck and catching lazy seamen unawares. He had a deep slow voice with an attractive Cornish burr. His black straight eyebrows almost met over a nose nearly as strong as Harris's.

Harris coloured slightly when he saw his wife approaching.

"How are you, Pat?" he said, ignoring Pawlyn.

"Well, Tom," said Patricia.

"I very much wanted a chat with you," said her husband.

"What about?"

"I'd prefer to tell you that in privacy."

"You can say anything you wish to say here."

Neither of the contesting parties seemed quite as confident or as much at ease in the presence of the other.

"Why?" said Harris. "Are you afraid of giving me a few minutes?"

Ned Pawlyn bulked close behind the girl. "Should she have reason to be afraid?"

"Harris looked at him for the first time. "Do I know this gentleman?"

"Mr. Pawlyn," said Patricia. "Mate of *The Grey Cat*."

"How d'you do. What was your question?"

"You heard me the first time," said Ned.

"Well, since you ask, I think perhaps Patricia *is* afraid of having a few minutes' quiet talk with me alone."

"What're you getting at?" Joe said, looking as if he regretted not having his carving knife.

"As Pat persistently refuses me a private interview," said Harris, "it looks to me that she is afraid of being persuaded to return to her gilded cage."

"So you admit it was a cage?" said Patricia.

Tom Harris looked at her with his brown eyes.

"All people live in cages," he said. "Cages of good behaviour and decent manners. A cage is none the worse for being gilded."

"See," said Ned Pawlyn, "you talk too much, mister –"

Pat put a hand on his arm. "Let me manage this, Ned. Tom, I'm not coming to talk with you – not because I'm afraid, but because there is nothing to discuss. When I left you I told you I was not coming back. I haven't changed my mind and am not likely to. So that's all there is to it."

"Not quite," said Harris.

"What have you to say to that?" demanded Smoky Joe, plainly pleased with his daughter's attitude.

"Only that I might petition for a restitution of conjugal rights."

41

Anthony saw the girl's bosom begin suddenly to rise and fall.

"What d'you mean?" demanded Ned Pawlyn. "Talk English. Restitu . . ."

Harris looked at the other man pointedly. There was that flicker in his eyes again.

"I've stood your interference with very great patience, Mr. Pawlyn. May I ask what damned business it is of yours?"

"Look," said Ned, "if you care to step outside I'll teach you what business it is of mine." Pat laid her hand on the seaman's arm.

Harris nodded. "I know. Bare fists. The only argument you understand. But today I did not come here to quarrel." He picked up his silk hat and slowly began to brush it with his long fingers, for all the world, Anthony thought, as if he were reassuring the hat that no harm would come to it. "Tell me," he said. "Give me one valid reason among the three of you why I should not so petition. A wife's place is with her husband – unless he should be brutal or diseased or insane. The marriage ceremony was entered into freely – I might even say eagerly. There's no legal reason why I should be summarily deserted."

"No legal reason," said Pat quietly. "That's the whole point. You only deal in legal things. You don't feel things, I believe, until a seal has been put on them. Nothing is yours until it's sworn to before witnesses. Then nothing else matters. Very well, then, go and petition. See what a laughing stock you'll make of yourself!"

She raised her eyes and found his fixed upon her. She turned sharply away with a gesture of impatience.

"I didn't say I was going to – yet. I came here today to approach the matter in a friendly way, to ask you to return to me like an honourable wife. It *is* a matter of honour, you know."

Pat had gone white. "You twist everything round to your own way of thinking." She added: "Please go now."

"May I call again?"

She shook her head.

Harris rose and picked up his stick. There was a momentary quirk in one eyebrow. "No wife. No turbot. A disappointing afternoon." He went to the door. "I wish you all good day. Including the small boy peering through the curtain."

He went swiftly out. Mrs. Veal had come from the kitchen at this moment and was standing with short, fat arms akimbo in the doorway. Although she had several times openly favoured his suit, he went past her without a glance. In fact he seemed to withdraw his arm as if to avoid contact.

Clearly, thought Anthony, he did not consider any of them good enough for him.

CHAPTER SIX

Two days passed before Anthony had an opportunity of saying anything to his cousin. She had been rather moody since the visit and only brightened each evening when Ned Pawlyn called to take her out.

Patricia was taking some flowers to her mother's grave, as she did every Wednesday, and he offered to accompany her. They set off up the hill, at first through working-class streets, then down a hill past some fine residential houses to the cemetery, which was situated upon the hillside over-looking a lake. The lake was in the hollow of the hills and was surrounded by trees; at one end thick rushes grew and at the other a narrow bar of shingle separated it from the sea.

"What a lovely place!" Anthony exclaimed. "I shouldn't mind being buried here."

Patricia laughed. "I'd rather be alive at Smoky Joe's."

The grave was just inside the gate. When the old flowers were removed and the new ones arranged she said soberly:

"Let's go down and feed the swans. I always bring something with me."

So they clambered down to the lake and sat on its edge throwing bread and kitchen scraps to the big white birds, which knew Pat and came over to her at once.

An older and wiser person would not have mentioned the fracas of Sunday afternoon; but Anthony's was a nature which could not rest in peace while there was the possibility of misunderstanding with someone he liked.

"Look, Pat," he said. "I'm awfully sorry about – about

43

Sunday. I mean about me peeping through the curtain. I didn't intend – it was ..." As she did not speak he went on "I'd only just come out of the kitchen, and I heard the noise and ..." He was astonished with himself for telling this lie but was somehow forced into it by her silence and by his desire that she should think well of him. The words had come from him unawares.

She shrugged. "Oh, it doesn't matter. My affairs are free for all anyway."

"Oh, no," he contradicted. "They shouldn't be."

"Why?" she said after a moment. "Do you think I should have seen him alone?"

Thus questioned, he drew back quickly within himself like a snail which had touched something foreign and perhaps dangerous.

"I – I don't know. How can I tell? I don't know anything about it."

"No," she agreed moodily. "How *can* you tell."

There was silence, while the swans ducked their heads in the water and drank and waited for more food.

"It's funny," said Anthony. "I never even *saw* your ring, you know. I just didn't notice it until it was mentioned last Saturday...."

"Where d'you think I met him?" she said, taking off her picture hat and letting the wind and the sun play with her curls.

"... Don't know," said the boy.

"In the police court."

He screwed up his cap. "In ..."

"And who do you think introduced us?"

"Don't know."

"Dad himself."

Patricia emptied her bag into the lake.

Anthony's mind was struggling in deeper waters than any the pond could offer. "I thought Uncle didn't like him."

"Not as a *son-in-law*. Women aren't the only contrary ones, are they?"

The sun went behind a cloud and a breeze ruffled the waters of the pool.

"Of course, I was chiefly to blame," she went on after a pause, more brightly, as if she found some cause for self-congratulation in being in the wrong. "You see, it all began

44

like this. There was trouble in our restaurant one Saturday night; there sometimes is; but this was worse than
usual; a Dutchman got a knife stuck in him. I've always
told Joe; I've told him and told him not to let *anybody* in.
On a Friday and Saturday a lot of men spend part of their
time in a public house and then come into our restaurant
half drunk. I'd refuse them admittance. But Joe says, no,
they're all customers and have a right to buy what they can
pay for – and *he'll* keep them in order. That's all very well
most times, but if bad trouble ever starts it's too far gone
before he can stop it. And Uncle Perry shouts a lot of terrible oaths but he doesn't do much. Fridays and Saturdays
are usually the nights; you may have noticed the last two
evenings have been quieter."

Anthony nodded. "Uncle Joe said there was a Greek
ship in this afternoon," he volunteered.

"Well, this night in March a lot of men wanted to come
in together, and there were two or three among them who
were pretty drunk, and I happened to be standing at the
counter and I said to Dad, 'Say we're full up,' but of course
he wouldn't. Joe can't bear to turn away a penny. So in they
came. They were a lively lot in the lower restaurant even
then. Well, somebody started a quarrel, and before you
knew where you were everyone was fighting everyone else
– and by the time the police came someone had stuck a
table knife into a Dutchman who had nothing to do with it
at all. Two or three others had to be treated for broken ribs
and things."

"Did he die?"

"The Dutchman? No. But he accused a man called Fossett of having stabbed him. Mr. Fossett was a shipbroker
and practically Dad's oldest friend. But sometimes he
would drink heavily and he was a bit hot-tempered. Dad
didn't like the idea of him being accused: he's funny that
way when he makes up his mind about a thing, and he tried
to get all the blame put upon the Dutchman himself. Two
or three witnesses went into the box and testified that the
whole place had been sweetness and light until the Dutchman came in and that it was he who was the only drunk
one, and that he'd started an argument about the Transvaal
and then things went wrong. But that wasn't true at all."

"What happened?"

"Mr. Fossett got six months in the second division. Of

course, I never thought of getting him as much as that when I did it."

Anthony looked at the girl. "Did what?"

She pulled down a piece of stick and stirred the lake gently while the swans nosed about it expecting more food.

"You see, I was called as a witness, as I was in the restaurant at the time of the quarrel; but instead of testifying that it was all the Dutchman's fault as Dad expected, I supported the Dutchman's story, because he was telling the truth. He hadn't even been drunk at the time; he'd just come in for a quiet meal and was eating away when the quarrel broke all around him. It was Joe's fault for letting any rag-tag come in and be served; it was Joe's fault for being so grasping for every penny that it hurt him to turn a single one away. You know ... he wouldn't shut the restaurant the day Mother died. He even begrudged her having a doctor until near the end.... I thought this would teach him a lesson. At least ... I didn't reason it out as plainly as that at the time. I went into court feeling a lot and not quite knowing what to say, and then before I properly knew, I was telling the whole truth. I'd just got to."

Anthony spent some minutes wondering if even at nineteen he would have the moral courage to speak against his father in a court of law.

"And that was where you met – your ..."

She shook her head. "No. That was later. You see, other things happened then that I didn't expect. No sooner was that case settled than the police brought a charge against Joe for keeping a disorderly house. Of course, Joe was furious."

"Yes, I suppose he would be," agreed the boy.

"He quarrelled with almost everybody at that time. Even Uncle Perry had a job to stay on." She smiled wryly at this. "He turned me out of the house the night after I'd given evidence favourable to the Dutchman."

"What did you do?"

"Slept with Aunt Louisa in Arwenack Street. That was easily arranged because I lived with her during holidays while Mother and Dad were abroad. But it made things worse in a way because Dad can't stand his sister nowadays. Well, he quarrelled with his solicitors too about their conduct of the case, and when the police summons came along he put it in the hands of Harvey & Harris of

Penryn." She was silent a moment, pondering her own strange feminine thoughts. "Tom ... Tom Harris did very well for him in that: he was only fined ten guineas and costs. But he wasn't a bit grateful; he quarrelled with Tom because he hadn't got him off altogether."

The swans had become aware that this stirring of the water was a trumpery deception; one by one with slow imperceptible strokes they moved away, breasting the water square and smooth like a convoy of white East Indiamen.

"We ought to go," said Patricia rising. "They'll wonder what has happened to us." She picked up her hat and parasol. "Come on: I'll race you to the top of the hill."

Womanlike, she started off before he could even get to his feet. He rushed after her, but she was half-way up before he overtook her, laughing his triumph. Whereupon with the same curious lack of logic she at once abandoned the race and sat on the hedge careless of her frock and breathless and smiling.

But when they had restarted her mood changed again.

"You know, Anthony, mine was a funny sort of marriage. The way it happened, I mean. When I first saw Tom in court I admired tremendously the way he defended us. I thought him very good looking then. Of course he was in his element; I didn't realize that. But you don't marry a lawyer for the way he behaves in law courts any more than you'd marry a sailor for the way he sails his ship. I was silly; but there you are. He came to me when it was over and asked me to go out with him the next evening. I said yes. Joe started raising steam when he heard of it. I was living at home again when this second case came off, and we were good friends again; but me wanting to go out with the lawyer who, in his view, had just let him down was more than he could endure. So of course we had another quarrel and the more he said I wasn't to go out with Tom the more I went – and so it developed quickly."

Anthony said nothing, but he could well understand that much. Joe had been trying to govern someone with a bit of himself in her.

"So there you are," she said moodily. "That's the way it is, as you'll find when you're older. People never are what they seem. Nice people turn out nasty and nasty people nice. Tom has awfully pretty manners when he likes.
47

I – I thought I was in love with him. In a way for the time I was. A sort of infatuation, I suppose. I was absolutely in earnest, though it may not seem so now. After we were married things seemed to change."

"How did it change?" he asked, all attention.

"Oh, you – you wouldn't understand," she said, and again the conversation lapsed.

But now she was like a moth fluttering round a flame; at each remembrance she singed her wings and sheered away, but the flame still burned, attracting her back. She persuaded herself that there was pleasure in explaining to someone who did not matter. In fact she was glad to speak more fully than she had ever done since her return, to justify herself – but whether to him or to herself was a moot point.

"They live in a big house in Penryn, you know."

"Who do?" he asked, for he had been watching a yawl dipping out to sea.

"The Harrises. There's Tom and his mother and an aunt. He took me there for the first time after we were married. That was the first shock."

"What was?"

"Well, the house was big and old and full of big old furniture that looked as if it could never be moved. It's the sort of house you'd never expect anyone would ever dare to sneeze or giggle in. That didn't matter much of itself. Surroundings aren't very important, and you can be happy in a public house or a museum if you go the right way about it. But Mrs. Harris and Miss Harris and their surroundings were all of a piece. A – a stiff elderly maid let us in and another stiff elderly maid showed us into the drawing-room, and there were two stiff elderly old ladies waiting for us for tea. I hadn't – it had all been such a rush that I hadn't met either of them before, and I think Tom must have had a bit of a quarrel with his mother the morning before he left when he told her he was going to marry me. That didn't make for a good beginning. . . ."

"Didn't he tell her till then?"

"It had only been decided the day before. Then we went away for three days and came straight back to the house. I think now that Tom was in a hurry in order to *forestall* criticism. He thought that once we were married they would make the best of a bad job and put a cheerful face on it. But

I didn't want anybody to start looking on me as a bad job that had to be made the best of. That isn't the way to start married life. Anyway, they didn't try hard enough to deceive me. You see – you see, when I went there I felt very happy, bubbling over with good spirits. Their reception was a sort of smack in the face. It didn't take me long to see what the position was. They thought I wasn't good enough for Tom."

She stopped to push some grass through a gate to a pony.

"Of course I could see his mother's point of view. She wanted him to marry well, keep up the tradition, in the same house with the same furniture, be gracious, entertain the right people and live to be seventy-seven. In some ways she was nice, and could have been nicer if she'd tried." Judicially she repeated: "I could *see* her point of view, but she couldn't expect *me* to fit into it, could she? Sometimes she made a real attempt to be agreeable, and we got on fairly well then, though I was always thinking 'What an effort it must be for her!' and 'She doesn't really like me, she's only trying to,' and 'I wish I didn't mind being patronized, she doesn't really intend it as that.' "

They turned and walked slowly on.

"I wonder what it is that makes some people seem so afraid of coming unmelted. Tom has grown up in a house where every feeling and emotion has to be – to be muted and restrained, kept under lock and key because it's bad form to let them go free. Why are some people so scared of their dignity, Anthony?"

Anthony did not know.

"I was really thinking of Aunt Phoebe then," she said. "I *might* have got on with his mother if there hadn't been Aunt Phoebe. She ... I never could make up my mind which was the tightest about Aunt Phoebe, her mouth or her stays. Sorry if you're shocked, I keep forgetting you haven't had a sister. Aunt Phoebe disapproved of me from the start. I was socially inferior and hadn't been educated in the wooden-face school. I was too flighty and unstable. She didn't give me a chance before she started picking holes." Patricia choked as if the memory were not to be borne. "Naturally, the more holes she picked the more opportunity I gave her. You may say this isn't anything to do with Tom, but it is. You see, Tom couldn't understand us at all. He didn't seem to try. In his own house he was different,

49

seemed a part of it. It was *fantastic*. You can't be legal in a home, not if it's going to *be* a home. You can't weigh up things as if you were a judge, and then give so much credit to this side and so much credit to that. You may be able to *see* both sides, but you can't *take* both sides. If he'd come down on one side or the other, then I should have known where I was earlier.

"After three weeks it was about as bad as it could be. Then Dad was taken ill and I wanted to rush home and nurse him. Tom didn't want me to do that. He raised all sorts of objections that were just silly. He even offered to pay for a nurse for Dad, but I wouldn't have that. Joe wouldn't either, you may be sure. In the end of course I could see what it was: living with his family had convinced Tom that my manners needed a bit of tightening up – when I met a stranger I didn't say 'How d'you do-o' as if there were a nasty taste in my mouth; I went up and shook hands – and I'd committed the terrible sin of being found in the kitchen, talking to the tweenie. Anyway, I think he thought that if I stayed at Mount House long enough I should get like them, but Smoky Joe's was a bad influence for me. As if I'd lived anywhere else since I left school! He thought that if I went backwards and forwards between one house and the other I never would improve. So then I told him that I didn't want to improve by getting like him and his mother and his aunt, and that if he wanted someone like that I didn't know why he'd married me, and anyway the Veals had a longer pedigree than any Harrises he could find, and whether he liked it or not I was going to nurse Dad, and I wouldn't bother to come back and lower his prestige any more. . . ."

Towards the end of this statement her breath had been coming as quickly as her speech. They began to go down the other side of the hill. Anthony glanced at his cousin. In talking to him she had relived some of the emotions of that time. Until two days ago she had put all this behind her, tried to shelve it and forget it. Tom Harris's visit had brought it all up anew. She looked neither so young nor so happy as she had done a week ago.

"Was Uncle Joe very ill then?"

"Oh, yes. We thought he was going to die. He's better now. I'm watching his diet so that he takes regular meals."

"Is that why you're not going back to Tom Harris?"

50

"Oh, no," she said. "That doesn't make any difference. I'm never going back to him. I'm never going back."

Anthony looked down the hill and saw Ned Pawlyn coming up it to meet them.

CHAPTER SEVEN

It became a regular practise for Anthony once or twice each week to row his uncle out to some ship in the harbour. One week it was *The Grey Cat*. Then it was *Lavengro*. Then it was *Pride of Pendennis*. This followed by *Lady Tregeagle*. Then *The Grey Cat* returned from Liverpool. There were two barquentines, a schooner and a tops'l schooner, all around three hundred tons; tidy little craft busy about their owner's business. And the owner was J. Veal. How many, if any, more there might be trekking across the oceans of the world on the business of J. Veal, Anthony did not know.

Sometimes he sat in the little master's cabin and listened, less than half comprehending, to discussions on freights and port dues and insurance costs. He noticed that whenever the conversation was turned by one of the captains upon what they considered necessary repairs to their ships Smoky Joe had a talent for turning the conversation to something else. If they insisted that the repair or replacement was urgently necessary he always ended the discussion with, "Well, we'll consider it, mister, we'll consider it."

He never saw his uncle consult with anyone ashore, though Joe sometimes ventured forth in the morning on his own business with ship's chandlers, Board of Trade authorities and the like. Once Anthony pulled the cork out of the floorboard of his bedroom and saw his uncle in the office below counting a heap of gold into little piles. There were twenty or thirty such piles by the time he replaced the cork.

There is something about a spy-hole which has an irresistible fascination for a young boy, even the most honourable young boy, and Anthony on a number of occasions took out the cork and stared down on the greying head of his uncle as he was writing or sorting out papers or adding up figures in a huge ledger. Once a knock came on the office door, and the boy noted with what care Joe put everything away – this in the safe, that in a drawer – before unlocking the door to admit, as it happened, Uncle Perry. Uncle Perry looked round the room curiously and made some joke and laughed: it was clear that he had not often been in this room before; and Joe answered his questions tightly and disapprovingly as if to make it plain that he did not like to be interrupted.

On another occasion, hearing gruff and unfamiliar voices in the room below, Anthony saw the master and mate of *Lady Tregeagle* being entertained to a glass of rum and milk. This was the first time he had seen anyone invited into that private office. When they had finished their drink Joe brought out a piece of foolscap paper and signed his name on it, and they both signed their names after him. He did not however give them this paper but kept it himself; and when they had gone he sealed it up in an envelope and stood hesitantly in the middle of the floor for some seconds. Eventually he went to a small oil painting of an old lady on the wall and taking it down clicked it open on some sort of a hinge, so that between the painting and the back there was room to slip the paper.

Anthony tried to take a firm hold of himself over this matter of peeping. He seldom yielded to the temptation without feeling mean about it afterwards; also he had no lock on his door and knew that if someone were to come into his room while he was so engaged he would never live down the shame.

No word came to him during these weeks from his father. He had received one letter only since his mother's death, and he anxiously awaited another. He was quite happy in his new life, chiefly because of Patricia; but he longed to see his father. He longed above all to be in the company of someone to whom he personally belonged. He could not quite get over the feeling of not *belonging* here. It was as if he had been in the centre of a circle of friends, and suddenly he had lost that circle, and now he was attached to another circle, but was only at the extreme outer edge.

He did not come to know Aunt Madge any better than the day he first arrived. That small precise face built upon its column of chins seldom carried much expression beyond a certain vague distaste for the vulgarity of the world around it. The large, shapeless body, with its fondness for ornament – overburdened, one felt, as much by clothes as by flesh – seemed to dominate the kitchen without stamping the impress of a personality upon it. The weak, husky voice was what Anthony chiefly remembered when she was not before him, its habit of breaking off before its objective was reached, its capacity when angry of endless reiteration without being raised a semi-tone.

But he sympathized with Uncle Joe for having married her even though she was so unattractive; for she was a real commercial asset. With her to do the cooking, Patricia to charm the clientele with her pretty ways, and Joe himself to drive his hard bargains at the door, the supremacy of the restaurant was secure.

The only times Anthony was really uncomfortable were on the Friday and Saturday evenings. These nights might have improved since the law case, but they were still rowdy enough. The boy had few thoughts on the ethics of the matter, but he didn't like Patricia being in contact with a crowd of singing roisterers and he always felt a sensation of relief when Saturday drew to a close without having given rise to another mêlée.

This business of Friday and Saturday evenings was the only one on which Uncle Perry condescended to compromise his amateur status. When the fun got fast and merry he was usually somewhere in the middle of it with his laughing buccaneer face and Spanish-black hair. Sometimes he would be persuaded to sing, and he had a fine repertoire of comic songs with an occasional bawdy number thrown in. He would stand under the figurehead of the *Mary Lee Melford*, which had sunk off Maenporth, smile his attractive wayward smile, and sing his songs accompanied by the lame accordionist, while the crowded room roared the choruses.

One night by way of a change he chose the "Song of Tregeagle," and Anthony knew for certain the identity of the nocturnal carouser who still periodically disturbed his sleep.

"They heard the Black Hunter! and dread shook each mind;
 Hearts sank that had never known fear;

53

They heard the Black Hunter's dread voice in the wind!
They heard his cursed hell-hounds run yelping behind!
And his steed thundered loud on the ear."

The boy came to know much of Falmouth during these weeks, for he was constantly out and about, rowing Joe to a ship in the bay, accompanying Pat on shopping expeditions among the huddled narrow streets and courtyards, shopping on his own for Aunt Madge, roving round the town with Uncle Perry when Uncle Perry couldn't get his favourite baccy at the usual shop.

He came to appreciate and understand the pulsing life of the port. News would come through that one of the big nitrate ships was becalmed off the Scillies, and at once rival pilot cutters set off to race to meet her. Then one by one over a period of weeks the great grain ships arrived in the bay, standing well out in the calm sea, sails furled at last after a world passage of anything up to half a year's duration. Sometimes there were fifteen to twenty of them at once, awaiting their orders; then one by one as they received them they would slip away in the night, off to Queenstown or Liverpool or Clydebank or the Thames. The crews from these ships did not come ashore, but many of the masters and mates crowded into Smoky Joe's and sat there over their food talking of storm and stress which scarcely seemed believable with the quiet sea lapping the old stone wall outside; of scudding down the roaring forties, of heat and boredom in the doldrums, of rounding Cape Horn in the black of the night and losing men swept from the frozen yards by the giant seas.

Sometimes there were as many as two hundred head of sail in the roadstead and the bay, and among them all almost the only steam belonged to the Irish coastline boats. During busy periods keen-eyed old men sat in Woodhouse Terrace, the highest in the town, and scanned the horizon with powerful telescopes. As soon as a sail was sighted word went secretly down and the competing bumboats and tailors' cutters tried to slip quietly out of the port without arousing suspicion in the breasts of their rvals. Once the news became public it was a free-for-all race to the incoming ship to reach it first and bespeak it for revictualling and supplies.

Nothing more was seen of Tom Harris. He had apparently given up his erring wife as a bad job. As for Patricia, she pursued her light-hearted way, being taken out in turn by several good-looking young men, though the perceptive might have detected an element of determination in her gaiety.

The one obvious cloud in her life now was Joe. Joe appeared to be sickening for another bout of his old complaint. He carried on his unfailing routine without break, working in his office in the mornings and sitting the rest of the day behind the counter of his shop, fierce and intractable and dry. But although the spirit remained indomitable the flesh was weak: he could eat practically nothing, and his small terrier eyes had sunk deeper into a face narrow and hollow and grey. His appearance began even to affect the attendance at the restaurant on Friday and Saturday nights. People did not like to be jolly with a sick man serving their food.

Aunt Madge pressed him to take a couple of weeks in bed to see if that would help, and everyone joined her in urging him to see a doctor; but he refused to do either. If he took to his bed who would carry on the supervision of his numerous interests? And a doctor would only prescribe sickly potions which would do him no manner of good. Besides, doctors were expensive; they were the luxury of a rich man. One did not throw away one's shillings soliciting useless advice.

And doctors, he argued, could not rid him of a flukeworm. He knew what to take and was taking it. Plenty of purgatives and a starvation diet. When the attack subsided he'd soon pick up again.

In August the town was visited by Poulton's Players, a company of itinerant troupers who toured the south-west with their melodramas. This was an event of popular importance in the life of the community, Ma and Pa Poulton being respected figures and their return visits awaited with pleasure. Not for Poulton's Players the inconvenience of performing in strange halls with makeshift scenery and unpredictable lighting. Snail-like, Poulton's carried their house on their back in the shape of a tent, and this was erected on the Moor and the plays given before a select audience for which suitable seating accommodation was provided – easy chairs and couches for the patrons who came in evening dress from the big houses of the town, grading finely down to hard wooden benches for those who had not the money to afford better.

Patricia went to an early performance with one of her friends and enjoyed it so much that she persuaded her father to let Anthony go with her on the following night. Anthony had never been to a play in his life, and they set out together bubbling over with excitement at the thought of it all.

The Moor was centrally situated and they had only a short distance to walk. Patricia was wearing a blue dress trimmed with velvet which showed up her slender waist, and a feather boa. Her face was pretty and piquant under a small straw hat. They were talking animatedly as they walked, when Pat suddenly gave a little exclamation and was silent. The boy saw that on the other side of the street and plainly bound for the Moor himself was her husband.

At the moment Tom Harris turned his head and saw them; he stopped and crossed the street, hat in hand.

His manner was more friendly than it had been last time.

"I wonder," he said, "if you would care to admit to your society a member of the ancient borough of Penryn."

Patricia, after a moment's embarrassment, evidently decided to meet him on his own ground.

"Well, Tom," she said. "So *you're* going to the play too. I thought you would not consider it quite respectable."

"Oh," he said. "It is not so much *where* one goes as the company one keeps."

Anthony felt rather than saw the girl begin to flush darkly. "Then," she said, "I am sure you would not wish to be admitted to our society. Good night."

"On the contrary," he said, quickening his pace with hers. "I thought you might sit with me in the theatre."

"Thank you," said Pat. "I've promised to take my cousin. We'd prefer to sit alone."

"So this is your cousin," said Tom. "How d'you do?"

"How d'you do, sir," said Anthony, lifting his cap, not to be outdone in the frigid courtesies.

They climbed the hill towards the tent. From the summit of the "theatre" a flag fluttered briskly in the breeze.

"I suppose you know," Harris said, "that I've resigned my job."

Patricia looked at him quickly. "You've –"

56

He nodded. "I want a change."

She seemed to suspect some calculated manoeuvre on his part. "Why did you do that?"

They had come now to the crowd of people who gathered about the entrance to the tent.

"I said before I should like a word with you in private. Otherwise," he added "I might take the seat next to yours and spoil your evening's enjoyment."

She hesitated a moment longer, biting her lip.

"Anthony," she said, "will you buy our tickets, please. I'll join you when you've got them."

She passed him the money and he fell in reluctantly at the back of the queue, already aware that Tom Harris had begun to speak to the girl in a steady undertone.

The queue was slow in moving. There was some dispute at the booking window.

Then a voice in front of him said: "That's Joe Veal's girl over there."

Anthony glanced up quickly at the speaker. He knew him by sight, a tall man with a drooping moustache called Treharne, who kept the public house on the corner of the street. Anthony had often seen him standing at the door of his place, and sometimes he had been in to Smoky Joe's for a meal. Treharne belonged to that strange breed of people who always have confidential, advance information upon any subject which crops up for discussion. If the King has gone to Scotland they know why; if there has been unrest in the Welsh coal districts they know where; if a fine ship has run aground in a fog they know how.

"Who's she with?" asked his companion, peering. "He's a new one to me."

"Well, not to *her*," said Treharne. "That's Tom Harris, her *husband*, from Penryn, that's who that is."

The other man whistled. "I thought they were estranged. I thought they was separated."

Treharne speculated. "Hm, well, maybe he's trying to make it up. Lawyers usually have an eye on the main chance. She'll have a tidy little packet to her name one of these days soon."

"Yes, I s'pose."

"Smoky Joe'll be a very warm man, mark my words. He had a tidy nest egg when he came back here six or seven years ago, and since then he's made big money. Big money.

He's never spent a penny, y'know; and that restaurant idea of his was a gold mine. Then there's the shipping and one or two side lines. Young Harris will have to play her pretty careful; she's a 'andsome piece of goods but flighty, and there'll be plenty of other wasps round the jam-pot when she comes in for the money."

"Well, maybe they'll have to wait a bit yet. Old Joe—"

The man broke off as Treharne emphatically shook his head. Then he went on: "I didn't know Smoky was as ill as all that. . . ."

Treharne shook his head again. "Same thing as his wife, you know." He made the observation in a confidential undertone with the air of having received the news direct from the surgeon's lips. "It's all U.P. when a person gets that."

"Hm. I'm sorry. Is it . . . ?"

"Well, there we are. . . ."

Uneasily: "It surely isn't catching."

"Oh, I wouldn't say that. But I've noticed husbands and wives often seem to get it after each other, haven't you? Of course, mind you, mm – mm – mm – mm . . ."

"Poor old Smoky."

"Yes. Poor luck for him."

A moment later the men had passed on and Anthony found himself facing Ma Poulton in the box office.

He bought the seats and waited for Patricia to separate from her husband and join him. She did this almost at once and they entered the tent together. But Anthony's excitement and anticipation for the evening had dropped from him. Somehow the pleasure of the present had become submerged in a dread of the future.

CHAPTER EIGHT

Whatever the Poulton Players lacked in the finer points of acting as understood by the sophisticated few, they made up in verve and power and a conscientious determination to see that nothing was missed by the slower members of the audience. The play was called *The Last of His Line*; a title, the boy thought at first, with some aptness for the grey little tragedy which was taking place behind the drawn curtains of Smoky Joe's. But as the play progressed even the encounters of this evening were driven from his mind by the strange glamour of the footlights. For nearly three hours he lived in a world of Marquises and milkmaids, of mortgages and suicides, of love trysts broken and hearts with them, and of Christmas reconciliations to the sight of snowflakes and the sound of church bells.

He came out with his mind still staggering under the weight of enormous visual impressions. He was thrilled and delighted almost to the core of his being. But at the *very* core was a hard heavy weight which seemed to say: "This isn't what's happening to you; the part of the evening that's *yours* is what happened before you went in."

As they were leaving the tent Tom Harris joined them again. He asked if he might see them home, and although the boy felt that this was a usurpation of his own position he could see that Patricia was not unwilling to accept the offer. There were bound to be numerous drunks about at this time of night.

They walked some distance talking of the play. Anthony thought how much more reasonable they seemed in each other's presence now they were alone, except for himself. Then Tom Harris spoiled it by suddenly saying:

"Patricia, I want you to leave Joe's. I want you to come back to Penryn with me tonight."

She said: "I thought we'd finished discussing that, Tom."

"I don't know why it is," he said. "I can't give you better reasons than I've already given you. But I've a *feeling*. I don't like the atmosphere of the place. I want you to get out of it."

"I'm not coming, Tom. I've told you; I'm not coming."

They walked on.

"In a different way," he said, "you're just as obstinate as your father."

"If knowing my own mind is obstinacy, then I am. But what is obstinacy? Only the determination of another person to do what you don't want them to do."

"You're learning, Pat. You're learning the art of argument. But don't get too theoretical, I beg of you."

"I thought," she said, "you would like me to get all dry and precise and withered up like Aunt Phoebe."

"Why should I? Why should I compare the lily and the teasel?"

Against her better judgment she uttered a brief murmur of amusement. "That's just right for Aunt Phoebe. She's hard and dry and – and prickly and rustles when the wind blows."

"But even teasels have their uses. You're no botanist if you expect all nature to fit into one mould. If –"

"That's what's the matter with Aunt Phoebe," Pat said quickly. "She's no botanist."

He inclined his head. "A good point. But I'm to blame, not she. Nor you. *I* thought I was a botanist, yet I expected the lily and the teasel to grow in the same soil. Crabbèd age and youth ... Well ... I've learned my lesson. Now I'm suggesting that we try again on a different basis."

A long silence followed. Tom Harris knew how to argue his point. He carried too many big guns for the girl. Anthony felt that he should not have allowed the conversation to begin, that now it had begun he should exert himself to break it off. But he could not. He still laboured under the disadvantages of childhood. These were adults, arguing out their own problems between themselves. They had forgotten him. He could not muster the necessary self-importance to interfere.

"We can't turn life back," Patricia said in a low voice. "We can't just go back and start afresh as if nothing had happened, nothing been said."

"I'm not asking you to go back in the same way. I'm asking you to come back and live with *me*."

In the distance, through a gap in the houses, the St. Anthony light winked at them and disappeared.

"But you see, Tom," she said very quietly, "I don't love you."

They crossed the street. They were nearly home.

"Oh," said Tom.

"I'm sorry. I didn't really want to put it as bluntly as that."

They reached the steep little street and turned down it.

"How long have you known this?"

"Since – since soon after I came home."

"Any *particular* reason?"

"No. . . ."

They came to a stop just out of range of the lighted windows of JOE VEAL'S.

"Then I think," said Harris, "that you might perhaps
60

change your mind again. That I might be able to persuade you to change your mind."

"Now you're merely being odious," said Pat.

"I'm sorry," he said. "That wasn't my intention."

She said: "I must go now. Dad is still far from well. In any case, it's my duty to stay with him."

He took the hand she had offered. "Is it also your duty to go out with Ned Pawlyn?"

She quickly took her hand back. She stood very still for a moment. When she spoke again her voice was quite changed.

"I suppose that's the sort of remark I might have expected."

"Certainly it is; if those are the sort of men you go out with."

"Good night," she said. "Thank you for bringing us home."

He said, "Some of them may be good fellows; I don't know. But I took a dislike to Ned Pawlyn. I think I might come to dislike him more. The low forehead shows a lack of intelligence. I'm surprised that you should find him interesting."

She had left them and entered the shop. Anthony found himself alone with their escort. They looked at each other.

"Good night, Anthony," said Harris.

"Good night," said Anthony, raising his cap.

Then he too pushed open the door of the shop.

The light indoors was so bright by comparison with the feeble lighting of the streets that for a few seconds the boy could see very little. All he could make out was that Patricia was not there and that his uncle occupied his usual position behind the counter.

Then to his great astonishment he perceived that it was the wrong uncle.

He rubbed his eyes, but the man opposite him refused to change or disappear.

"Where's Uncle Joe?" he got out at last.

"Upstairs with a pain in his tum," said Uncle Perry. "Behold his deputy, as large as life and twice as efficient."

All the remarks of Mr. Treharne came flooding back into his head. He looked round again for Pat.

"Is he bad?" he asked in a voice instinctively pitched in a lower key.

"He'll be all right in an hour or two, me boy. Just one of his 'do's.'" Uncle Perry seemed in the best of spirits.

"Where's Pat?" the boy asked.

"Gone upstairs to see her Dad."

"Oh." Anthony glanced down at the savoury dishes set out on the counter. "Are there many people inside?"

"Business is a bit slack." Uncle Perry pushed back his hair and waved a carving fork. "Now, sir; what can I do for you, sir? What would you like tonight, sir?"

Anthony glanced round, but he was the only person in the shop.

"A little bit off the rump?" said Uncle Perry. "Guaranteed tasty and never been sat on; just the thing for you, sir." He picked up a carving knife and prodded each of the dishes in turn. "Now here we have a fine chicken. Chicken, did I say? Well, an old hen. May I offer you the guts of an old hen? Guaranteed to stretch *and* stretch. Very suitable for violin strings. No? Then a little roast swine? Can't I offer you some swine? The poor thing died last week, we don't know of what, so it *had* to be cured. Ha, ha! Or a duck's gullet? Help yourself, me boy, no waiting. Pay only if pleased. A five per cent discount for quiet eaters!"

Anthony tried to smile; then he tried not to smile.

"Uncle Perry; do you think Uncle Joe is seriously ill?"

'Ill? Belay there. We all get pains in the tum. You must have had pains in the tum. Were you seriously ill? Good grief, no." Uncle Perry took from under the counter a large mug of beer and drained it. Presently all that was left was a thin white froth upon his lips, which he carefully licked off with a large flat tongue. Then he parted his lips in a smack.

At that moment three customers entered. There were explanations; Perry laughed and joked with them and at last succeeded in selling them three plates of beef. *Ping — crash!* went the till. He sliced off the beef inexpertly, narrowly missing his thumb in the process. With the point of the knife he pressed the bell which summoned little Fanny. She came limping in.

"Three underdone beefs," said Perry. "Three beefs full o' blood for three customers short of it. There you are,

Fanny, my little pet. Why, what's the matter? Hurt your leg?"

"Twisted my knee," said Fanny. "Twisted it on them dark stairs. . . ."

"Elliman's Embrocation," said Perry. "Elliman's is the stuff. Makes excellent gravy. Rub it well in, my pet. Look, I'll rub it for you. An expert at massage. The Sultan of Kuala would have decorated me for what I did for his fourth wife, but I couldn't stay. Is it swollen? Let me see."

Fanny blushed and giggled and picked up the three plates and fled.

Uncle Perry opened another bottle of beer.

"They're all the same, me boy. They all like a little bit of fuss. From countess down to scullerymaid; black or white, red or yellow. Stap me if they don't!"

"The play was all about a Marquis tonight," said Anthony.

"Lor' bless me, yes, if you haven't been off gallivanting to a play tonight like a young lord yourself, while I've been working my fingers to the bone. To the bone." Uncle Perry scratched the back of his neck with the points of the carving fork and eyed the boy speculatively. "What did you think of it? Don't tell me. I guess you enjoyed it. Lucky young tinker. Not that this is much in my line, this food business. I wouldn't demean myself by touching it if it wasn't for obliging a brother."

"It was called *The Last of His Line*," said Anthony. "It –"

"Not that I couldn't turn my hand to anything if I chose," said Perry. "In 'Frisco in the winter of '89 for two weeks I helped a Chinaman to run his restaurant. Friend of mine, he was; I never believe in this colour bar."

"The play had a Chinaman in it," said Anthony. "At least, I think it was only a white man pretending to be a Chinaman, but –"

"Now there was a man for you," said Uncle Perry, tilting his chair back and putting his feet on the counter. His head disappeared for a few moments into the beer mug. "There was a cook. None of these fat, flabby joints sawn straight off a dripping bullock. He used to buy *innards*, me boy, *yards* of 'em, and serve 'em up as anything you asked for: grilled pigeon, lark's breast, noodles, bamboo shoots. And they all tasted different. And if there

63

was fungus growing on what he bought, so much the better; he'd make it into soup. He was a genius. None of this undercooked, *recognizable* stuff that'd turn anyone's stomach. No wonder your Uncle Joe's ill. No wonder he can't eat. Sitting here day after day with his nose bending over slices of sheep and diseased ducks. Poo, how they stink! They almost spoil a man's thirst."

"Thank you, Perry," said a voice. "You will not need to spoil it any longer."

Smoky Joe stood on the threshold of the little shop holding carefully to the door. He was fully dressed but his face was an ashen grey. His sharp eyes were watery and bloodshot and he spoke with difficulty. Behind him in the darkness of the passage was Patricia.

Uncle Perry put down his mug and put down his feet.

"Well, Joe, me bonny boy! I was just saying to our Anthony it was time you were down again. I knew you'd be down again soon. Welcome back to the old grindstone!"

"It's high time I came," said Joe.

"Well, I've been doing my best, Joe. Haven't I, boy? Not a dissatisfied customer. Is there, boy? I've sold half your beef and a bit of duck. *And* given the right change. To a penny. Behold Matthew at the seat of custom. Always ready to do my bit when the proprietor's off his food."

"With a mug of beer and your feet on the counter," said Joe between tight lips. "A fine business this would soon be with a drunken man at the till."

Perry blinked and pushed the hair out of his eyes. "Come now, Joe; that's a malig – malignancy. If you think I'm drunk you're barking up the wrong tree. Like the little dog Fido in the song." He laughed. "Why, if –"

"Let Joe sit down," said Patricia. "You don't seem to realize he's very ill. He should never have come down to-night."

"Well, it's not my doing that he's come," said Perry, suddenly sulky. "This isn't my business. God damn it! I might have been doing him an injury instead of a favour."

"No favour to me," said Joe, sinking into his chair. "I manage my own affairs –"

"When you're sick in bed, I suppose."

"When I am ill Patricia will manage them. She is my daughter."

"And I suppose you think I'm your brother and can be

treated like dirt! Well, you're mistaken! I'm sick of this household and its airs. I'll not stand for it another week. Being treated as if I was a no-account! You can sit on your chair and rot, Brother Joe; you won't get any more help from me!"

Uncle Perry brushed past Anthony and the shop door slammed.

Patricia put her hand on the counter and kept her eyes down. With slow, painful movements Smoky Joe settled himself into his usual position, rearranging the plates and the carving knives, rang the till and stared at the money in the various compartments of the drawer.

"Can I get you anything more, Dad?" Patricia asked.

"No. . . . But you'd best stay here with me a while yet. Maybe you'll be able to help." Smoky Joe slowly raised his head and looked at Anthony. "Isn't it past your bedtime?"

"Yes. We've been out, you know."

"That's no reason why you should stay up now, is it? Turning night into day will stop your growth. I'll be responsible to your father if you're pale and weakly when he sees you. Good night, boy."

"Good night, Uncle. Good night, Pat. Thanks awfully for taking me out tonight."

Patricia smiled as he passed her.

But he did not immediately go to bed.

CHAPTER NINE

As he entered the kitchen the heat and the familiar smell of it struck him like something he had known all his life. Here was the big square raftered room lit by gas which flickered uncertainly in the steam. On the left was the dark hole and the four steps which led down to the scullery and pantry. Welsh dressers lined one wall; the great table in the middle of the room was piled with dishes and jars and a pastry board; aprons were piled upon a chair; a cupboard door was open showing cooking utensils. Two cabbages and a bowl of scalded milk occupied another table. From the rafters, where they were not likely to catch in the hair, hung a string of onions, several fly-catchers and a

65

dozen tea-towels. Along the wall opposite the dressers the huge kitchen range roared and hissed.

Among all this confusion, presiding over it as if she were its chosen deity, Aunt Madge stood stirring a giant cooking pot. There was no one else in the room, and she stood there big and slow-moving and withdrawn, thinking her private thoughts, her hair piled, her features snub and insignificant, a boned collar, ear-rings, and a cameo brooch showing above the anonymous pink apron. She considered it vulgar to have a bare neck even when cooking.

She turned when she heard a footstep and looked over the top of her pince-nez to see who it was. Then she relinquished her spoon and took off the pince-nez to wipe away the steam.

"A carrot," she said. "I should like. The scullery. Fanny . . ."

He ran down the dark steps into the scullery and found little Fanny wading through a stack of dirty plates. He got the carrot and returned.

Aunt Madge took it and began to slice it into the pot.

"You're cooking late tonight, Aunt Madge," the boy said, reluctant to go upstairs, feeling too unsettled to sleep.

"We have an order," she said. "Men coming in. A ship. Who was that in the shop? Arguing . . ."

"Uncle Joe's just come down again."

"Foolhardy. Was he shouting?"

"No. You see, Uncle Joe . . . Uncle Perry was drinking beer behind the counter. Uncle Joe didn't seem to like it. Uncle Perry's gone out."

"Huff," said Mrs. Veal. "Too touchy. But Joe was very wrong. He shouldn't . . . So foolhardy. Must persuade him. A doctor."

Anthony walked round the kitchen. There were no confidences between himself and his aunt; nevertheless all that he had heard this evening seemed to come bubbling to his lips. It worried him and he could no longer contain it.

"I heard Mr. Treharne talking tonight," he said. "You know, up at the Ship and Sailor. He said – he said that Uncle Joe was very . . . might not recover . . . He said . . ."

Aunt Madge took out her spoon. "What were you doing . . . Ship and Sailor?"

"Oh, I wasn't there!" Anthony hastened on. "It was in a queue at the theatre."

66

There was silence. Aunt Madge shifted the pot a little off the stove and put on more coal. She opened the oven door and then shut it again without taking anything out. Anthony perceived that something was going on behind the pince-nez.

She took off her glasses and blew her nose. "People. So unkind ... Unkind to say such a thing. How does Mr. Treharne ... How does anybody know? Nobody, until he sees a doctor."

"I'm sorry, Aunt Madge," Anthony said. "I just heard him say that."

Mrs. Veal shifted back the pot and began again mechanically to stir it. "Married a year," she said. "I don't want ... to be alone again. Lonely all my life. Your uncle ... very kind. Though a little close. If he would take care. Give up drink and take care. I don't believe there's anything serious. That's if he takes care. But look at him. Won't have help. Hi've told him. Your Uncle Perry ..."

Anthony shifted uncomfortably from one foot to the other and tried to think of something to say.

"Well, perhaps he'll be all right again tomorrow."

There was a familiar rumble, and the dumb-waiter came up from the restaurant below. On it was a pile of used plates.

"For Fanny," said Aunt Madge. "Perhaps ..."

Anthony hastened to obey this request. Glad to be out of an embarrassing situation, he remained in the scullery for some time helping Fanny to wipe the dishes. When he emerged, hoping that Patricia would be in the kitchen, he was disappointed to find his aunt still alone.

The stew was simmering on the stove, and she had begun to roll out some pastry.

"Bed," said Mrs. Veal. "I thought you'd gone. High time."

She was making pasties for the party of men who were expected in an hour. Fascinated he watched her short plump fingers cut out the pieces of pastry and arrange the potatoes, meat and onions upon it, scatter a pinch of salt, then in a trice the pastry had been turned into contain the meat, and the nimble fingers had made a curious decorative pattern where the pastry joined.

"Aunt Madge," he said, "I wonder when I shall hear from Father again."

She worked silently for some minutes, and the pasties multiplied, ready to go into the oven.

"Bed," she said. "He should have stayed in bed. No reasoning . . . Where's Patricia?"

"In the shop, I think."

"Must go and see when these are done. See if he's . . ."

"Aunt Madge, how long does it take for a letter to come from Canada?"

"Eaten nothing all day. Can't go on like that. Canada? The one we had yesterday. Weeks . . ."

"You had a letter yesterday?" he exclaimed excitedly. "From Father! I didn't know. What did he say?"

Another pasty grew and came into shape. Her fingers were like machines.

"Schooling," she said. "Only about schooling."

"What did he say? You mean . . ." Excitement suddenly left the boy as air will escape from a pricked balloon. "Does he mean I'm to go to school here?"

Through her wobbly pince-nez she stared at the pasties as if trying to estimate whether she had made enough. Then she took up a few bits of pastry which were left and began to roll them together.

"One more. One or two more. . . ."

"Aunt Madge . . ."

She looked at him. "Not good enough. Father's duty to his son. *Make* a home. That's what I say."

"Aren't I to go out to him? Why mustn't I go?"

"Questions. Next spring, he says. School here this winter. We must see what your uncle says."

"Didn't he put in a message for me?"

"His love. He says conditions . . . no place for a boy in winter. Not quite right. Your uncle isn't fit to see about schooling. Inadequate, besides."

Anthony watched her for some minutes. All the pasties were put upon a shelf and slipped into the oven.

"Tomorrow," she said. "Doctor. Your uncle has too much on his mind. Won't allow others to help."

"Aunt Madge," the boy said, "do you think I could read Father's letter? You see, I haven't had one from him for ages. I wrote to him last week and the week before. If I could see what he said I should know more what to say."

She waved a hand. "Your uncle. Personally . . . boy's place is with his father. Should go to school in Canada.

Or he should come home. Evading responsibility. Your uncle must see a doctor. That Mr. Treharne . . . No right to spread such stories. So unkind. Get back to Joe and then he'd think perhaps it was true. Hi shall speak to Mr. Treharne."

"Has Uncle Joe got the letter?"

Patricia entered the kitchen. Aunt Madge peered at her.

"He seems better," said the girl. "What happened, Madge? How long was he like that?"

"Fanny," said Mrs. Veal, shaking her ear-rings. "Always dawdling down there. Dawdling over a few things. Everything left to me. Where's your Uncle Perry?"

"He went out in a rage. How was it —"

"*He* saw him. He just said: 'Perry, help me upstairs.' When I went up he hardly knew me. Just said his limbs were numb." Aunt Madge took out her handkerchief again. Her short fleshy nose disappeared into it. "But Mr. Treharne has no right. He only needs a few days in bed."

The girl looked perplexed. "What has Mr. Treharne to do with it? Did he help?"

Mrs. Veal went back to stir the stew. "Must have a doctor. Tomorrow morning. Can't go on. What time are these men coming?"

"Tonight? In half an hour, Joe said."

"The pasties won't be ready. Have to wait. Persuade him to go to bed. Hi can't."

"I'll do my best," said Pat. "I'm afraid it's a hopeless case, though."

She went back into the shop.

Aunt Madge tasted the stew.

"Another carrot," she said. "In the scullery. And Anthony . . . see what Fanny is doing."

What pressure was brought to bear upon Joe — unless it was his own feelings — Anthony never knew; but the next day the doctor was summoned. He was a tall, elderly man with muttonchop whiskers and he was upstairs for an hour.

When he came down a cloud had been lifted from the house. He had been not all discouraging, Pat said. Joe must spend at least a week in bed. Milk food was to be his only diet and he must neither smoke nor drink. Absolute rest and quiet; then perhaps a little change of air. He'd give him some ointment for his eczema and some pills to be taken after meals. There was no reason why there should not be a big improvement before the month was out. Joe lay in bed, looking smaller and more dog-like than ever in his nightshirt, and watched the doctor out of shrewd inimical eyes.

The business of the house was arranged to meet the new situation. To assuage her father's restless spirit, Pat promised to take over his vigil behind the counter; but she found this task even more tedious than she had anticipated, and two or three times each day she risked the Wrath by handing over charge to Perry. Perry was quite undeterred from doing this by any memory of the quarrel he had had with Joe. The morning after the quarrel he had turned up for breakfast at eleven o'clock, laughing his usual laugh and cracking his accustomed jokes as if nothing had happened. The memory of what had occurred had run off him like water off the champion swimmer he claimed to be.

On the fourth day *The Grey Cat* was seen lying in the roads, and Joe sent out his daughter to ask Captain Stevens to call on the morrow.

Anthony always enjoyed these visits to his uncle's ships but today was a special treat. Patricia could in fact row as well as any man, but she had no objection to sitting in the back of the dinghy and trailing a hand over the side if that suited her cousin better.

She was very simply but very charmingly dressed today, and Anthony wondered if the extra care she had taken was on Captain Stevens's account or was directed at his mate.

The effect was certainly more obvious upon the latter. They had been under observation as they approached, for Ned Pawlyn was down the short ladder to meet them, his clean broad face a-beam, the breeze ruffling his black hair.

"I could hardly believe my eyes," he exclaimed. "I said to myself, 'That can't be the Old Man; is it my eyes that's wrong? Or have I a fairy godmother?' Hold on, son; ship your oar; steady up; make her fast; that's the way. Now take my hand, my dear."

Patricia laughed at his eagerness. She stepped upon the gunnel of the boat, and then climbed swiftly and easily up the ladder with a flutter of lace petticoats. Anthony fumed a little at the unnecessary instructions which were offered him, but soon was climbing the side after the other two.

"Where's the captain?" said Pat. "Dad's not well and I have a message for him."

"In his cabin. When I saw who it was I didn't tell him of your coming. Well, and I'm sorry to hear about the Old Man; but 'tis an ill wind that blows no one any good. Otherwise I'd not have seen you before this evening. I couldn't have got away until then. Don't tell me you're engaged to do something else."

Patricia turned her face to the breeze and smiled. "The ill wind does not bring all good. With Joe in bed I must stay in and help. I am deputizing for him behind the counter."

Ned Pawlyn made a face.

"Then I'll help you there. I'll sit behind the counter too! I am sure I can carve a chicken better than you."

She shook her head, pursing her lips a little. "Joe wouldn't allow it. The only time you will see me will be when you are ordering your evening meal—"

"I'll order everything in the place," he threatened. "And eat it. And come back for more. You'll not get rid of me so easily as that—"

She laughed again, enjoying his easy good-tempered banter; but at that moment Captain Stevens came on deck and approached them.

"Mister Pawlyn; ye did not tell me we had a distinguished visitor."

"Beg your pardon, sir; I was so astonished myself—"

"I hope your father's well, Miss Patricia."

"Well, no, he isn't. I've brought you a message from him."

"Will you step down into the saloon, please . . .?"

Anthony was left alone with the tall, good-looking mate. There was silence for a time, for the boy was taking in all the shipping which lay around him. One of the great windjammers on the Australian run had arrived in Falmouth yesterday after the worst passage in her chequered history. Anthony had heard the story in snatches last evening when the master had had a meal at Smoky Joe's. She had limped into Falmouth after a passage of 197 days from Brisbane, having faced consistently adverse weather and having been partly de-sparred off the Portuguese coast near the end of her long ordeal. So instead of riding silently and proudly out in the bay she had accepted a pilot and come into the harbour to lick her wounds.

"Well, son, and how have things been doing at Smoky Joe's while I've been away? I hear that the threepenny gaffs are here again."

"Yes."

"You should go to Liverpool, son. They have proper theatres there. 'Tis not many days since I was at a handsome music-hall show." Ned Pawlyn began to describe it.

"Did you have a good voyage?" Anthony said, still looking at the battered windjammer.

"Eh? Voyage? Oh, it was all right. Head winds off the Caernarvon coast. Has that fellow Tom Harris been round plaguing your cousin's life out since I left?"

Anthony looked up at the mate. "Not really.... We've seen him once."

"Well, let's hope we don't see him while I'm ashore," said Pawlyn. "Else I shall be tempted to pull his tall hat down over his ears. I'd dearly like to have him aboard this ship for a voyage or two."

They chatted for some minutes until Patricia reappeared, escorted by the captain.

Anthony climbed over the side and got into the boat.

"Good-bye, Captain Stevens. Good-bye, Mr. Pawlyn."

"Good-bye, ma'am."

"I hope I can have the pleasure o' calling upon you tonight," said Ned.

Patricia smiled. "I hope you'll be hungry."

A moment later she had joined Anthony in the dinghy, and he was pulling away.

Ned waved from the side and the girl waved back.

None of them would have been quite so light-hearted had they known all that the evening was to bring.

CHAPTER TEN

While they were away Dr. Penrose had paid his third visit, and he seemed very cheery and much encouraged by Joe's improvement – so much so that when he had gone Joe announced his intention of getting up that evening. This went so far beyond the medical sanction that Aunt Madge and Patricia did their utmost to dissuade him.

But as usual he was adamant. This was Saturday night; there might be a big crowd; the whole place would need his supervision; besides, he felt better, the doctor had said he was better; this staying in bed was no more than the usual physician's fad, instructions designed to increase the doctor's importance so that he could charge an extra two shillings a visit. As it was, three visits in a little more than a week was pretty tight going; he should think Penrose thought they were made of money, coming so often and doing so little. Anybody could stand by a bedside and look important at so much a time. They were all the same; Penrose was no better than Dr. Barrat Clark with whom he had quarrelled over the bill for his wife's last illness. Had Fanny done enough potatoes for tonight? It was wasteful not to give customers enough potatoes.

He was helped into his alpaca coat and high white collar and assisted downstairs. They brought him a drink of patent milk food which he swallowed with many grunts and grimaces. Then before they were able to stop him his hand was fumbling with his bizarre old pipe and a match trembled and flickered at its bowl. A cloud of blue smoke hid his thin, wasted face, and when it emerged there was a different and more satisfied expression on it. Smoky Joe was himself again.

The restaurant began to fill up. There were many ships in the bay, the summer gales of last week having forced the smaller ones to run for shelter. The crew of the wind-jammer had also been allowed ashore, but so far only the three mates had arrived at JOE VEAL'S. The rest were celebrating their release in a succession of public houses.

Ned Pawlyn arrived about five-thirty, and when he knew that Joe was about again he pressed Patricia to go out with him for the evening. This she agreed to do, but only for a limited time, and they were back soon after seven. Pawlyn then went with her into the kitchen, anxious to help. Later in the evening nine of the windjammer crew, all Finns or Swedes and all in a merry state, arrived for supper. They ordered a slap-up meal and tramped into the upper restaurant; but finding the three mates there they turned round and tramped, laughing and talking, down to the lower restaurant where they would be free from the oppressive influence of authority.

Shortly after this Anthony had to take another milk drink into Joe and was told to stay while he drank it. All this week he had been anxious to ask his uncle for details of what his father had written, but there had been no opportunity to do so. Now, with some trepidation and spoken apologies for troubling the old man, he brought up the subject.

Joe peered at him with watery eyes over the top of the repulsive glass.

"I've only met your father once," he said, "so how can I tell what he means? Of course he's offered to pay for your schooling, for I haven't the money to spare. But I doubt if what he offers will cover the cost. And a young fellow like you eats up a pretty penny in the way of food; then there's clothing and what-not. We'll have to see."

"Doesn't he want me to go out to Canada at all?"

"I went prospecting once in my young days," said Joe. "It isn't a time when you want somebody *attached* to you. You've got to be free. You've got to travel light and travel rough. He says he'll be in Winnipeg in the spring; maybe you'll be able to join him then. But you can't just do nothing here all winter; he sees that. Your aunt'll see about a school, see which we can afford on what your father's sent. 'Tisn't a lot he's sent; we've got to cut our coat according to the cloth. Can't be ambitious on a few pounds.' He put down the empty glass and shuddered. "Pah! Pobs ... Babies' food. No stuff for a grown man. That's what this life does for you: when you're young you feed on milk; then when you grow up you grow to know what's good; when you're old you have to go back to milk again. . . ." He hastily re-lit his pipe.

Two customers entered. They were the bosun and sail-maker of the windjammer, both Germans. The sailmaker was an inoffensive, pleasant little man; but Todt, the bo-sun, square-built and fair-haired and mean, although one of the best sailors afloat, was hated in his ship. They parleyed for a few minutes in guttural tones, then paid for their meals and went in. Following almost on their heels came three more men off a Penzance tug which had brought in a damaged brig that afternoon. Two were weather-beaten west-Cornishmen; the third, who had had

74

a little too much to drink, was a red-haired Scottish engineer. While they were discussing what they should have, a single customer entered. It was Tom Harris.

He stood back while the other men were being satisfied. There was not so much of the dandy about him tonight, Anthony thought; he was wearing a cap and a tweed suit.

Joe had bristled at the sight of him, but he said nothing until they were alone. As the other three men disappeared he put down his carving knife and fork and took out his pipe to wipe down his moustache with the mouth-piece.

"What do you want?"

"I'm glad to see you up," said the younger man in an uncontroversial tone. "I'd heard you were unwell."

"Never mind that," said Joe. "What do you want?"

"A meal. It's not Sunday today." Harris glanced along the counter. "This is a clever way of running things. There's something about an array of cooked meats and fowl and other tasty dishes that appeals to the glutton in us all. The sight of them together –"

"I don't want any of your advice," Joe said, trembling with weakness and annoyance. "If you've come to see Patricia you'll be disappointed."

"I want a meal," Tom Harris said. "Nothing more. I'm in Falmouth for the evening and have come to the place where I can get the best meal. It's a matter of business. I think it's against your principles ever to refuse a customer, isn't it?" He took out a sovereign and put it on the counter.

"I can look after my own principles, thank you," Joe muttered. "I don't want a legal opinion on them." But his eyes wandered to the gold coin.

There was silence. Tom looked at Anthony and smiled slightly.

"Are you full?" he asked. "I can wait."

"It's just a trick to see Patricia. I know you. It won't do you any good."

"She's under no compulsion to see me. It's quite outside my control. Is that pheasant you have there? I should like some of that, with a little steamed fish before it. Come, take the money and give me what change you please."

"I've my fixed charges," the old man said aggressively. "You needn't think I profiteer on anybody. Have you come here to spy?"

Tom Harris looked mildly exasperated.

"My dear sir, your daughter happens to be my wife whether we like it or not. I'm not likely to wish to bring you into disrepute while that's the case."

Smoky Joe picked up the coin and rang it on the counter. Then he put it into the till and slid a half-sovereign and some smaller change across to the younger man.

"Lower restaurant," he said. "You'll get your first course in a few minutes."

Joe's reason for directing Harris to the lower floor was that he knew Patricia to have been helping on the upper one, which had rapidly filled up. What he did not know was that, with the immediate rush over, Pat had gone down to the lower one to begin her own supper at a table with Ned Pawlyn.

When Tom entered they had just been served at a small corner table near the window. His eyes went as if by a magnet towards them, but his expression did not alter and he walked across to the other side of the room and took an empty table next to that occupied by the nine Finns and Swedes.

When Patricia saw him her colour changed, as it always seemed to do when he appeared unexpectedly, and Pawlyn, following the direction of her gaze, uttered a growl of dislike.

"What's the matter with the fellow?" he said. "Always skulking around. Don't he know when to take 'no' for an answer?"

"He's not here at *my* invitation," said Pat. "I told him last week; I was quite straight about it. He said . . ."

"What did he say?"

"Oh, it was nothing important. Let's forget about him." She suddenly realized it would have been dangerous to mention her husband's objection to Ned Pawlyn in front of Ned Pawlyn. "Dad should never have let him in. He must know that it's embarrassing to me to have him calling here."

"What he needs is a lesson in how to take 'no' for an answer. I'd dearly like to give it him. He'd stop skulking if he felt the weight of my boot."

"Hush, hush. Eat your supper like a good boy and talk of something else."

The meal progressed. Tom Harris was served and ate

his meal very slowly. So did Patricia and Ned, for they were talking and joking between themselves. The girl paid more attention to the sailor than she had ever done before, in order to show Tom her complete freedom and independence. Ned was enchanted to find he was making progress at last.

Tom finished his second course and ordered cheese and coffee. This ordering of more food when the other dishes had been eaten was something 'not done' at Joe's. David, the young lascar waiter, was nonplussed and went into the kitchen to ask for instructions. Presently he returned with a large piece of bread and cheese on a plate, but no coffee. Tom gave him a shilling and lit a cigarette.

All through the meal one of the Swedes at the next table, a big, blond, pasty-faced man, had been giggling at Tom Harris. There was nothing specially funny in the solicitor, but the Swede was in such a state that anything would amuse him. The episode of the coffee and cheese was altogether too much. His laughter shook the room, then he choked and knocked over a glass of beer and all his comrades fell noisily to smacking him on the back and laughing and arguing among themselves. The German bosun, eating an enormous plate of roast pork near the door, put down his knife and fork and shouted at them a command to make less noise.

His voice was as ill-tempered as his look. The air was filled with cat-calls in reply.

> "Falla Båtsman! . . ."
> "Inga bra, bawsted! Inga bra!"
> "Satan och Satan; kyss me, Satan!"

When it seemed that there might be a scene, several newcomers entered the room and the worst of the noise died down. But the pasty-faced Swede still went on giggling.

Then the lame accordionist struck up a tune and several people hummed and whistled the chorus. After a few minutes some of Uncle Perry's friends pushed him forward from his corner. With a selfconscious grin he took up his usual position beneath the figurehead of the *Mary Lee Melford*, pushed back his hair with two fingers and began to sing.

77

> *"There was a youth, a well-loved youth*
> *And he was a squire's son;*
> *He loved the bailiff's daughter dear*
> *That lived in Islington.*
> *Yet she was coy and would not believe*
> *That he did love her so;*
> *No, nor at any time would she*
> *Any favours to him show."*

Tom Harris finished his cigarette and stubbed it out. He was well aware of the amusement he was giving the Swede, but he ignored the man with good-humoured tolerance. All the same, the consciousness of being laughed at, together with the circumstance of seeing his wife flirting with another man, had frayed the edges of his temper.

There was applause when Perry finished. He grinned again and turned to the accordionist, wiping his good-humoured, feckless, indolent face. Tom Harris got up to go.

Perry began the verse of a popular song of the eighties. Tom took his cap from a convenient hatstand while the Swede went off into a fresh burst of giggling. The solicitor went across the room to the table where his wife was sitting and spoke to her. Ned Pawlyn, in an instant changed like a dog from playful pleasure to prickly dislike, sat and glowered at him but did not speak.

Perry reached the chorus, and all those who had finished eating, and many who had not, joined in the rollicking song.

Explosions of violence in public places usually occur without the least warning to the majority of people indirectly concerned. Ill-temper, enmity, malice, have flourished unawares in their midst. No one has seen or suspected anything. Two, four, half a dozen people may be quietly reaching a point of white-hot anger while all about them others read or eat or are entertained quite unaffected. Only when these emotions reach flash point are they communicated to spectators through the medium of action. Of such insensitive clay are we made.

It is as if gunpowder has been quietly scattering itself about the room. No one notices, no one cares. All tramp where they please, kicking or stumbling with impunity. Then someone drops a lighted match.

The room was noisy but peaceful. Square and low and raftered and full of smoke, with its ancient bow windows looking out upon the winking lights of the river and harbour, there was a faintly Continental air about its decorations as well as its company. Perry, with his bold, lazy, brigand's face, stood under the painted figure-head singing his song while an old man, with a wooden leg and a bald head shining in the gaslight, accompanied him upon his battered accordion and many of the company joined in. Near the service hatch and underneath a picture of Admiral Pellew in action against the Malay pirates, two Germans, with the air of starving men, were rapidly finishing off large plates of pork. In the corner window-seat a respectable, staid-looking young man in a neat respectable tweed suit was conversing with a pretty girl and a dark-haired sailor. In the middle window-seat was a mixed party of six and in the other corner window-seat two hard-bitten Cornishmen were arguing good temperedly with a red-haired engineer. Stretching across the width of the ancient brick fireplace was a long table containing the nine Norsemen from the windjammer. The rest of the tables were all filled. There were model ships on shelves and ships in bottles, and dark smoky oil-paintings of ships hung on the yellow-painted walls.

Into this comfortable cosmopolitan scene a lighted match was dropped. It flashed and flared suddenly at the corner table by the window. The man in the respectable tweeds was speaking to the girl and the sailor lolling on the opposite side of the table made a remark. That was the match. The man in the respectable tweeds abruptly leaned across the table and smacked the sailor across the face with his open hand, the sound being heard clearly and sharply above all the other noise. In a second the sailor was up, had grasped the other man by the throat, and pulled him across the table regardless of the plates and the cutlery and was trying to force his head down.

CHAPTER ELEVEN

The singing persisted only for a few moments against this unfair competition. First the diners stopped. Then Perry stopped. Then the cripple stopped; and everyone's attention was on the scuffling couple in their midst.

Ned Pawlyn had never in his life known what it was to be so grossly insulted as by that open-handed smack. A straightforward punch he would have accepted with far less malice.

For a few moments he went berserk, pulling his struggling opponent across the table by sheer muscular strength before Harris could break free. Then, while Patricia shrank back against the wall, he pursued the half-strangled Harris round the table, hitting him almost as he chose until the solicitor staggered back into the table containing the two Germans and sat on the knee of Todt the bosun. At this there was an unholy shriek of laughter from the drunken Swede.

Todt swore and dragged his pork away from a tweed elbow and thrust Harris to his feet again. Harris stood up and drew breath. There was a look in his eye which Pat had never seen before. He took off his coat and dropped it on the floor. Then he went out to Pawlyn with a will.

It is possible at this stage that had Perry stepped forward with an air of authority and thrust himself between the two the clash would have ended there, or at least been transferred to a more suitable venue out of doors. But Perry was a man concerned in avoiding his own troubles, not one to interfere in other people's. And Patricia, who should have run upstairs for her father, found she could not move. She was like a witch who had been playing with forbidden potions and was now aghast at the spectre she had conjured up.

The next table to suffer was that of the six in the window, and this time it was Pawlyn who was retreating with Tom closely following him. The table went with them and the girl at the end screamed shrilly as she was nearly pushed through the window. The men at this table were all youngsters; one of them put his hands on Pawlyn's shoulder but he was shaken off and brushed aside. The table continued to slide back, and the red-haired Scotsman found himself suddenly hemmed in by strange people who seemed to want to push him off his chair. He got to his feet and shouted and began to push back.

At this moment pressure was relieved by a turn in the nature of the fight. The two men grappled and went reeling back into their own table. David the waiter appeared on the stairs, gazed open-mouthed and fled.

Neither of the two men now seemed to have any advantage. They were both far too angry to remember any boxing they had ever been taught. What Tom Harris lacked in hardness of hand he made up in determination and staying power. There was something about the shape of his neck when his collar came off which suggested he would be a hard man to have done with, for all his respectability.

One of Ned Pawlyn's eyebrows had begun to bleed, and to clear his sight he tried to break away. But Tom was still holding, and in the next scuffle he succeeded in getting two more punches to the same eye. Then Pawlyn butted Tom and sent him staggering. He arrived back once more on top of Todt, and the chair beneath them, which Smoky Joe should have discarded nine months ago, gave way and collapsed on the floor.

A jeer of satisfaction went up this time not only from the drunken Swede but from all his less intoxicated companions.

Todt cursed and rolled over and kicked Tom Harris furiously in the back. He was about to kick him again as he got to his feet, but at that moment a bottle sailed through the air and smashed against the wall above Todt's head. He was showered with beer and broken glass.

His attention diverted from Harris, he rose to his feet and looked where the bottle had come from. As he did this the red-haired Scotsman, irritated by the press about him, cuffed one of the inoffensive youngsters on the ear and in so doing upset his own table.

David the waiter had been up to summon Smoky Joe. Joe, his hands wavering and clumsy, rose from his seat, locked the till, gave a key to the youth to lock the shop door and directed Anthony to run for the police. Then Joe picked up his carving knife and proceeded, supported by David, to the scene of battle.

But before they reached the head of the stairs they were met by a stream of people anxious to get out. With an irritated angry wave of his carving knife Joe directed them towards the kitchen, then went on. Half-way down the stairs he halted.

This was worse than the uproar of six months ago. Stopping it was obviously beyond even his moral powers.

Certainly it was beyond the physical power of a single carving knife. Not two were fighting now but eighteen or twenty. In a bedlam of overturned tables and broken crockery men were fighting desperately with each other as if the mortal enmity of a lifetime had bubbled over and was blistering their souls with hatred.

There were four Swedes and five Finns and two Germans and two Cornish sailors and a red-haired Scotsman from Ayr and two young shop assistants who had never been to Smoky Joe's before and would never come again, and a Cornish mate and a Cornish solicitor and three or four odds and ends who had been unwittingly embroiled. The one-legged musician had retired into the most isolated corner of the room. Perry Veal stood by the fireplace shouting horrible curses and threats and eating a piece of cake.

Even now the thing might have ended as suddenly as it had begun. While light persisted reason was not far away. There would be a point when the first impulse to violence had exhausted itself and most of the men would be glad to draw breath.

Unfortunately at this point the three mates of the wind-jammer, having heard the noise, came hurrying down from the upstairs room. Joe greeted their arrival thankfully; he waved his carving knife towards the struggling figures and shouted quaveringly. A tall young Finn heard the shout and glanced up; he saw the mates and knew well the feel of their hard fists. So as they came down the stairs he reached up and turned off the three gas-taps of the chandelier.

Darkness fell on the room.

Patricia found herself deprived of sight. She wanted to scream; the sound choked in the back of her throat. She stared into a darkness which had not yet even assumed shape; outside there were the winking lights of the harbour shipping; these grew brighter in the corner of her retina; but ahead and around was nothing at all. Only her ears told her that the darkness, far from putting a stop to what she had last seen, had added its own secretive encouragement. The scuffling and grunting of men, the shouts and threats, the crack of dishes and the thud of furniture ebbed and flowed about her. She could press no closer to the wall, could shrink no further into the corner. Once a man thumped into the wall beside her. Then a chair fell against her legs and a bottle rolled off it.

Suddenly a man rose beside her, touched her hand and arm, following it to the shoulder. She drew in her breath.

"That you, Pat?" said the voice. It was Tom.

"Yes," she said, feeling sick.

"Is there any way out of this place but by the stairs?"

Anger and hostility followed relief. He had begun everything; but for him there would have been no trouble at all.

"Well?" he said, his voice rough and low.

"Ned!" she called. "Ned! He's over here, by me."

"He won't answer you just yet," Harris said grimly. "What sort of a drop is it from this window?"

She would not answer. Someone, she thought it was one of the shop assistants, had got into a panic and was shouting in a shrill voice; "Bring a light! There's somebody dead! Bring a light!"

By now shapes and different degrees of darkness were coming to the room. Dim light reached down the stairs from the shop above.

"You little fool," said Tom. "Haven't you the sense to come out of your sulks at a time like this?"

He had never spoken to her in that tone before. It made her desperately determined not to help him.

"It's like you to run away," she said, "now that you've caused all the trouble."

He had opened the window and was peering out. He withdrew his head. "There are knives about," he said. "You're just as likely to get one as I am. Come on."

"Where's Ned?" she demanded.

"Under the table. Safe enough, but he banged his head." He put his hand on her arm.

She shook herself free. "Let me alone!"

He gripped her elbows with hands which had no time to be respectful. He pulled her to the window.

"Will you jump or shall I drop you?"

"Let me go! Ned! Ned!" she shouted.

Someone struck a match in the room behind her, and immediately it was knocked out. "Bring a light!" screamed the voice. "Bring a light!"

She found herself sitting on the window-sill. Fear of falling made her cling to it. Then he was beside her and

before she had time to say any more they had fallen together.

The ground came up so quickly that it seemed to hurt
more than if they had had some way to fall. She bruised
her hand and twisted her ankle on the hard cobblestones.

As she sat up the first impression was of peace and cool-
ness and that great emptiness of the open air which, after
leaving a room full of people, seems to echo with the faint
sounds of a thousand miles of space. The whisper of water
came to her ears, reminding her that the tide was in.

He was already up and bent to help her to her feet.

"I can't get up," she said. "I've hurt my ankle."

Only the second of these statements was strictly true.

"I'm sorry," he said. "If you'll put your arms round my
neck I'll lift you."

"Leave me alone," she said. "I can get back to the house
myself."

"You're better out of it at present. The police will be
here any minute."

"Well, I want to go back. Dad will need me."

He bent and with a big effort picked her up – for it is no
easy task to lift a woman from the ground level when she
offers you no help at all.

Once up, the carrying was quite simple.

"Where are you going?" she said. "I tell you Dad needs
me! He'll want my help. He's been ill!"

"I know that well enough." He walked on, to the edge
of the wall and began to go down the stone steps to the
water. She was afraid to struggle lest they should both fall.
She could not imagine where he was going. Did he intend
to take her out in a rowing-boat at this time of night and
argue with her in the middle of the harbour?

At the bottom she found that the tide was not as far in
as she had imagined; there was room to walk along the
base of the wall among the flotsam of this morning's tide,
which was what he now did.

"I don't know what you think you're doing," she said,
finding it hard to think of the dignified protest.

He did not reply, and she stared at his profile in the
darkness. His hair was over his forehead like a new Uncle
Perry.

"Dad's been seriously ill," she said. "If he has a relapse

you'll be to blame; it was his first time out of bed; I didn't think you'd ever do what you've done tonight, Tom."

"It's time we all started thinking afresh," he said.

About a hundred yards from where they had descended a big square shape loomed up. It was a large boathouse belonging to the Royal Cornwall Yacht Club. Harris was a member of this club and as he reached it, stumbling once or twice over the seaweed and the loose stones, he turned towards the back of the house and found a small door.

"Can you stand a minute?" He put her on her feet, keeping one arm round her waist while he found the key. Then he unlocked the door and carried her inside.

They bumped against a boat, and he set her down upon some sort of a seat against the wall while he stood by the door and lit an oil lamp which stood there. Then he shut the door and the light from the oil lamp spread itself slowly.

Patricia found she was sitting on an old couch which had evidently begun its days in the club room and was ending them here. The house was full of the usual paraphernalia of its kind: oars slung from the ceiling, rowlocks hung on nails, pots of paint and fishing tackle on shelves. There was only one small boat in residence, for the sailing season was not yet over.

He came across to her carrying the lamp. He was still in his shirt sleeves, and one sleeve was torn and his waistcoat had lost all but one button. There was blood drying on his forehead and a big black bruise on the left cheek-bone.

"I'll go to the police and make a statement in the morning," he said; "but you're keeping out of this, Pat. I'm not having you in the courts again. We can stay here for an hour and then I'll take you back."

She stared at him again curiously, trying to fathom the change which had come over him tonight.

"I don't care about the courts," she said. "It's not fair to keep me here when Dad needs me."

"He's got a wife. There's nothing you can do except become involved with the police."

She sat there in mutinous silence.

"Is your ankle painful?"

"Yes," she said.

"There's a tap somewhere. Perhaps I could bathe it."

She did not reply. He sat looking at her for a moment, then rose and picked up a bucket and walked over to the double doors, seeking the tap.

She watched him carefully until he was the furthest distance away, then sprang up and ran to the little door.

She reached it before he even heard her. She would have been through it before he could move but the door stuck. She pulled at it madly; there was a catch on it somewhere which she could not see; there it was; her fingers fumbled; that was it; the door opened; she was out; but on the very threshold of freedom his hands closed round her waist and pulled her struggling back again.

Patricia was the reverse of an ill-tempered girl, but she was hot-blooded, and tonight's experiences had jagged her nerves. In his arms she was suddenly beside herself with frustration and anger. She twisted and hit him in the face and kicked him with her pointed shoes. It was a bad policy. With a display of faintness she would have disarmed him and taken control of the situation. But such a reaction reawakened the devil in him which had been roused for the first time that night.

He pinned her arms to her sides and began to kiss her. The sting of her kicks were a bitter flavour added to the sweetness of her face.

She wriggled like an eel and fought herself half free. He laughed and exerted all his strength to hold her. She tried to bite him, and he avoided the mouth while it was open and kissed it as soon as it was closed.

"You beast! You beast!"

"This," he said, ". . . possession – ten points of the law."

She tried to scream, but every time he squeezed the breath out of her; and presently it began to dawn on her that she was fighting a losing battle. Now she went suddenly limp and helpless. But the trick was played late. He only seemed to take her limpness for deliberate acquiescence.

Scandalized, she began to struggle again, but more weakly, for her strength was partly gone.

So it came to pass that Patricia, who had begun the evening flirting with Ned Pawlyn, ended it in the company of her husband. Had Tom Harris been more of a brute the encounter might have gone further than it did. Patricia, for once in her life, was really frightened, for she did

86

not misread his intention. Love can so change that it becomes instead a fusion of hatred and desire. That was what Tom Harris found.

But unless the change is absolute, it can injure but it cannot wilfully destroy. That and something in the fundamental relationship between civilized man and woman finally stood in his way.

Not, however, before she had paid in good measure for her deceit and resistance.

He turned quite suddenly and left her there on the old couch, bruised and breathless and silent. She had never been so shaken up since she was three.

CHAPTER TWELVE

Policemen are not often found when and where they are most needed. Anthony had to run half a mile, as far as the parish church of Charles the Martyr, before he came on two standing defensively in the recess by the steps.

Market Street and Church Street were not pleasant at this time of a Saturday night; the boy was astonished and rather frightened by what he saw. Sailors were sitting on doorsteps singing, women were arguing shrilly outside public houses, and drunks lay about in the gutter waiting for the wheelbarrow men to come along and take them back to their ships or to some convenient doss-house.

By the time he reached the policemen he was so much out of breath that he had difficulty in explaining what was the matter, but rather suspiciously they decided to accept his word and hurried with him back to Smoky Joe's.

When they reached the scene of the trouble they found that order was just being restored. The Chief Mate of the windjammer had succeeded in lighting the gases again, and the fight had been broken off. Casualties were about to be examined for serious injury. Contrary to the statement being shouted in the darkness, nobody was dead, but four were unconscious, and this made an impressive picture. The most seriously injured was Todt, who in addition to a broken arm had been hit over the head with a bottle. Then one of the young shop assistants had been hit by the

Scottish engineer and had fainted clean away. The tall Finn who had turned out the gas had been put out of reach of further mischief by the second mate, and the drunken Swede with the giggles had gone under with drink and was snoring peacefully with his head in the fireplace.

The second mate had a knife cut on his cheek and one of the Cornish sailors was bleeding from a similar cut in the forearm. Ned Pawlyn was on his feet, supporting himself against a chair and looking furiously round the room. One of the girls with the shop assistants was in tears. Uncle Perry had finished his piece of cake.

The long process of inquiry stretched out to infinitely tedious lengths. During it Joe Veal sat upright in a chair, his mouth set in a line beneath the grey-black moustache. He did not move and hardly spoke except now and then to shoot out a word at this witness or that. Aunt Madge stood beside him, her pince-nez wobbling with indignation from time to time. In this crisis Joe had gone back to his whisky, and no cajolings could persuade him to renounce it for milk food.

The upshot of all these painstaking inquiries, so far as the testimony went, was that the disturbance had been begun by one Thomas Wilberforce Harris, a solicitor of Penryn. It seemed that this man, under the influence of drink, had forced his way into the restaurant much against the wishes of the Proprietor, Mr. Joe Veal, and having seated himself at one table for a time, had then gone across to a table where Edward Pawlyn, mate of *The Grey Cat*, had been peacefully having a meal and had tried to pick a quarrel. Edward Pawlyn had refused to take him seriously until he leaned forward and hit him across the face. Despite all efforts to calm him, Thomas Wilberforce Harris had continued to fight. Failing to rouse his chosen opponent to the proper pitch, he had then set upon the six young people eating in the middle window table, and pushed their table across the room and knocked one of their number unconscious with a foul blow in the stomach. He had then thrown a beer bottle at Heidrich Todt, bosun of the *Listerhude*, rendering him unconscious, and had finally begun to aim any crockery he could lay his hands on at the nine Norsemen eating by the fireplace.

This was about as far as the matter could go at the moment. The only circumstance which troubled Constables Smith and Behenna was that this Thomas Wilberforce Harris, having, as it were, stirred up trouble on every side, had somehow with diabolical ingenuity succeeded in making his escape in the darkness, leaving all these peaceable people fighting furiously among themselves. However, being not without experience in matters of this sort, they made no editorial comment.

And presently, when all the names and addresses had been taken and all the statements had been written down, one by one the witnesses were allowed to go. After that, in their own good time, the policemen also went; and there were left only Smoky Joe and his wife Madge and their nephew Anthony and brother Perry and David the waiter and Ned Pawlyn, standing and sitting in various attitudes amid the dust and the ruins.

The instant they were alone Ned Pawlyn snapped:

"Where's Patricia?"

"That's what I want to know," said Aunt Madge.

"So we shall," said Joe, between tight lips. "So we shall."

"Do you know where she is?" Pawlyn asked.

"No, I don't. And don't bark at me!"

"They went out through that window," said Perry. "I saw them. Blast my eyes, what a mess!"

Anthony went to the window. "There's no sign of them. It's not a big jump to the ground from here."

"The bastard may have kidnapped her!" Pawlyn exclaimed. "I wish I could get my hands on him again."

"Are you looking for me?" said a voice from the stairs.

Patricia had come from somewhere in the interior of the house. She was neat and tidy and cool – outwardly cool. But somewhere in her appearance there was a difference. Her eyes were too bright, the corners of her lips not quite sure of themselves.

"Where have you been?" Ned demanded. "We were all worried. The police have only just gone."

"Are you all right, Dad?" she asked.

"No credit to you if I am," he snapped.

"I know," she said quietly. "I'm more than sorry –"

"What happened?" Pawlyn asked. "Did he force you to jump through the window? I was out for a minute or two and when –"

"Get back to your ship!" said Joe. "This is a family

affair. We don't want outsiders in it. David, get this place cleared up. Perry, make yourself useful."

"Yes, we went through the window," the girl said. "Then . . . he wouldn't let me come back until it was all over. He – he wanted to keep my name out of it."

"He'll find his own name in it tomorrow, by God!" said Ned Pawlyn. "The police will be round at his house first thing –"

"Your place was with your father," said Joe. "I thought I came first."

"So you do. But . . . he wouldn't let me . . ."

"D'you mean he held you by force?" Ned asked.

"I've told you," said Joe, "to get back to your ship! Otherwise you'll lose your job. I'll not have every Tom, Dick and Harry interfering in my affairs. Good night."

"Well," said Ned, "I –"

"Now I'm going to bed. Madge, give me your arm."

Patricia came forward quickly to take his other arm. For a moment it seemed that he was about to refuse, but he accepted her help.

"Pat," Ned said. "Can –"

She gave him a queer constrained smile.

"Not now. Tomorrow."

The trio moved slowly up the stairs.

"Well," said Uncle Perry when the procession was out of hearing. "A pretty peck of pickles we've stirred up tonight. A good thing one of us kept cool about it. I remember when I was in Jo'burg, much the same sort of thing happened. You need to be able to keep your nerve at a time like that."

Ned Pawlyn looked at him. "Oh –" he said, using a vulgar word, and left them.

Midnight was long past before even Anthony found his way to bed. He could not sleep. For some reason he kept thinking of the occasion when Mr. Lawson, the master of his school, called him out of the class and said, "Your mother is ill, Anthony; she would like you to go home at once." He remembered the way in which he had snatched up his satchel, first making sure that his homework was inside, and then gone bounding off down the lane that led home. Certainly he had been anxious, but he did not expect anything serious, and almost outweighing the anxiety was the pleasure at missing most of an afternoon's school. Then, he remembered, he reached home and through the window he could see three people standing talking gravely in the drawing-room. One was Dr. Braid, one was the next-door neighbour, the third person, a woman he had never seen before in his life. At that moment he wondered where his mother was, and it seemed as if a cold hand clutched at his stomach. For minutes he stood on the door-mat and was afraid to go in.

The incidents of that afternoon were a watershed which divided his life. Before that he had been a child; after it he had become half adult, acting for himself, answering for himself: things that happened to him now remained with him, were confided to nobody. There was an end of frankness.

He had been pitchforked abruptly into an adult world. Nobody really troubled about him; they were not concerned what he thought, and therefore they were not concerned with what he learned. *They* did not hide things.

He remembered the foreshortened figure of Uncle Joe counting up his little piles of gold. He saw again Uncle Perry slipping through into the restaurant with a couple of bottles of gin under his coat. Other happenings too; things occurred which he could not quite understand, for the explanation of which he did not yet possess the adult key.

Over and over again he remembered the expression on Patricia's face as she came down the steps into the restaurant, returning from they knew not where. Her face was beautiful then rather than pretty in its strange suppressed wildness; she kept her eyes down so that they should not be seen.

He remembered also an incident of two days ago when Patricia had rolled her sleeves up almost to the shoulder to do some washing in the kitchen, and he had seen Uncle Perry looking at her pale, slender arms, and he had glanced away and suddenly perceived that Aunt Madge was watching Uncle Perry. And Aunt Madge had said: "Joe thinks *The Grey Cat* might be here tomorrow. Nice for you that will be, Pat . . . Ned Pawlyn."

Once or twice he dozed off to sleep, but woke with a start as if there had been voices in his ears. He seemed to hear his uncle say: "There's been a Veal in Falmouth ever since there was a Falmouth; an' we're proud of it, see? Straight as a die. Sons of sons all the way." And he seemed to hear Perry laughing and his words: "*Houd vast*, now, so we've taken another hand aboard. Greetings, boy! I could do with a second mate." Then there were the stumbling drunken footsteps making their way to bed and that queer haunting song: "They heard the Black Hunter! and dr-read shook each mind; Hearts sank that had never known fear-r."

...He woke suddenly with the sense of a frightening dream still upon him. He thought he had heard strange unpleasant sounds somewhere below. The noises were still in his ears. The room was pitch dark and he had no idea of the time; he only knew that the dream had struck down the defences of his courage and he was afraid. The menace was the greater for being unseen and unguessable. Everything was at its lowest ebb in this dark hour; he shivered and turned over and tried to bury his head and body under the tangle of the bedclothes.

So he lay while the dream like a slow tide of horror ebbed gradually away. Dank pools of it still lay in his mind. Fear of death, fear of illness, fear of sex, fear of the whole hollow cavern of life, these lay on his struggling reason. A light would have helped, but the matches lay on a table by the window and he could not bring himself to jump out, to leave the semi-security of the bed and venture among the unknown dangers of the room.

Time passed and he felt warm again, and warmth brought a return of drowsiness. He was just dropping back into the comfort of dreamless sleep when he started into wakefulness.

This was no dream. The sound was coming up from the darkness below.

The menace of a dream is usually harder to combat than the reality because its outlines are vague and fearful. But sometimes not even nightmare can stand against the brutal hard clarity of waking fact. A man may dream of the cut of a knife and wake in perspiration. But that is nothing if he feels the knife itself.

No sooner was Anthony kneeling up in bed than he heard footsteps climbing the uncarpeted stairs which led to his room.

Frozen, he waited. They came slowly but with a hidden suggestion of urgency, as if haste were intended but not achieved.

A light showed through the cracks in the door and someone began fumbling with the door handle.

"Yes?" he said, his voice cracking.

The door opened and someone came in. A wavering candle showed up the ambiguous bulk of Aunt Madge.

"Yes?" he said again when she did not speak. He saw that she was trembling.

"Dressed," she said. "Get dressed. Your uncle; very ill. We want you . . . go for Dr. Penrose."

CHAPTER THIRTEEN

By the half light of a gibbous moon Anthony picked his way through the deserted streets of the town. He was thankful that this mission led him in a different direction from when he had run for the police. At four o'clock in the morning the main streets were probably as empty and silent as any others, but the earlier memory of them remained.

In white night things and a white dressing-gown Patricia had come down the stairs with him.

"You know the way we always go to Mother's grave? Well above the cemetery a lane leads out towards the sea. There are four houses on it; Dr. Penrose's is the last. You can't miss it."

"Is Uncle Joe . . . Has he–"

"He's ill again, Anthony. I feel so awful about it, as if it was my fault. The doctor said he mustn't have worry or excitement."

Anthony had overcome his shyness sufficiently to touch her hand. "It wasn't your fault a bit. I'm sure everything will be all right. And I'll run like anything."

This promise he was now proceeding to carry out. Up the hill, padding silently in his rubber shoes, his breath coming sharply, he moved among the shadows, one moment slipping through darkness, the next crossing one of the brilliant shafts of moonlight, which lay in bars athwart the narrow street. Soon he had reached Western Terrace and the going became easier. He dropped down towards Swanpool.

In the moonlight the cemetery looked unfamiliar and ghostly. All the white tombstones trailed black cloaks of shadow. They were like an army marching up the hills, an army of invaders fresh landed on the coast and marching to attack the town.

Every few yards along this lane the boy glanced over his shoulder to see if there was anything behind. Once he stopped and sheered to the other side of the road. But the object which barred his path was no more than the shadow cast by a misshapen hawthorn tree.

Once past he was comforted by the thought that on the return journey he would have company. He reached the doctor's house and pulled at the bell. At length his summons was answered, and in about ten minutes he was on his way back, walking and trotting beside the tall physician, whose breath came in grunts and whistles in the cold moonlit morning.

They reached Smoky Joe's almost without conversation; Dr. Penrose seemed a little petulant at the inconsiderateness of a man who could take ill at such a time of the night. Anthony led the way upstairs and then was shut out of the lighted bedroom. For a few moments he hung about on the landing listening to the murmur of voices within; then he slowly went down.

Little Fanny, red-eyed and sleepy, sat by the stove on which a kettle and a pan simmered. She looked up at Anthony's entrance and said: " 'As 'e come?"

Anthony nodded. "Have you heard how Uncle is?"

"Miss Pat was down just now. She didn't say much."

Anthony took a seat on the opposite side of the stove and the conversation lapsed. Fanny began to doze.

"What's that?" Anthony asked suddenly.

She jumped. "Uh? What? What's what?"

"I thought I heard someone talking downstairs."

"Oh? Oh, yer-rs. That's Mister Perry. 'E's still clearin' up the mess what was made. 'E's not been to bed at all."

Silence fell again. Fanny's small tattered shoes were stretched towards the warmth, toes touching. Her mouth fell slowly open.

The boy got up and tip-toed out. Better to help Uncle

Perry than sit and do nothing. Sleep was impossible until the doctor had left.

Down in the restaurant a single gas jet cast its anaemic light upon the ruins. For a moment Anthony could not see his uncle and supposed him to be brushing up the floor. But further inspection showed him to be sitting at the little corner window table where all the trouble had begun. He was resting from his labours.

Anthony's rubber soles made no sound until he stepped upon a piece of glass. Uncle Perry jumped a visible inch and glared at the boy.

"Belay there! Damn me, I thought it was a ghost! Never wear rubbers, boy; they're an invention of Old Scratch himself."

Anthony saw that there were three bottles on the table, and two were empty. Uncle Perry had been resting from his labours almost since they began.

"Sorry; I thought perhaps I could help. I ... don't feel like sleep."

Perry was not long in recovering his temper.

"Don't go away; don't go away. Of course, you don't feel like sleep. No loving nephew would at a time like this. Nor do I; no more do I; that's why I'm down here trying to think of something else. I've worked myself to a standstill. Have a taste of rum?"

"No, thanks, Uncle Perry. I'll – just wait down here till the doctor goes."

"So you've been for him? There's a good lad. I said you would. I said, 'Young Anthony's got the fastest legs of any of us. Why ask me?' I said, 'I'm good for nothing tonight. I'm out of sorts myself. I'm worried about Joe,' I said. 'It's the anxiety that's getting me down.' I'm a – an abstemious man, Anthony; anyone'll tell you that, but the anxiety over Joe is getting me down. I'd got to do something, so I came down here and began clearing up."

Anthony perceived that he had mistaken the nature of the relationship between the two brothers; evidently the way they barked at each other sometimes only disguised their real affection. He forgave Uncle Perry for getting drunk.

He shivered, having cooled off from his run. "It's a bit cold down here."

"Get a glass," said Perry. "Ever tasted rum, boy? That'll

warm your lights. Go on, there's nothing to be afraid of."

The boy brought a glass and sipped at the liquid Uncle Perry put in it. He thought he had never tasted anything so vile: sweet and sticky and hot in the throat. When it was gone he shivered worse than ever.

"It's the starting that matters," said Perry, pushing back his hair. "It's the first drop that counts. The first teeny drop. Once you've taken a sip there's no turning back, no innocence any more. Life's like that; I tell you, boy, take it from me. You drink a glass of rum or have a bit of lovey-dovey, and where does it lead? Nobody knows; you've started something and've got to follow it; one thing leads to another; see what I mean? It isn't that a man's bad – nor that he's good – it's just following a lead. Often it's just being good-natured; nothing more than that; no intentions of any sort, and then where are you? They say who rides on a tiger ... But which of us isn't in that fix? Can I get down? Can you get down? We're all on our own tigers which – which we've fed for a bit of sport or brought up from being a cub; and – and now we wish we hadn't ..."

The rum was warming the boy. Sleepy in spite of himself, he gazed out across the harbour. There were two lights on the water, that of the setting moon and that of the dawn. The reflection of the moonlight was like tinsel silver, twinkling, without colour, except a suggestion of coffee brown in the water not immediately caught by it. The dawn light was a pure cold blue glimmering on the water like a shield.

"What's that?" asked Uncle Perry, peering towards the shadowy stairs.

"I didn't hear anything," Anthony said after a moment.

"I thought maybe it was the doctor. I thought it was him or somebody else. I thought it was. But there you are, mistaken again." He drained his glass and the lock of hair fell back from his forehead. This morning hour seemed to have caught Perry in a strange mood. He was not his usual jovial buccaneering self. Even Perry had his moments of doubt.

"Shall I go up and see?"

Perry tapped the boy on the shoulder. "I know how you feel. I know what it's like to be young. You think you know everything at that age. But the older you grow the more you see your mistake. The world's a snare, boy, make no mistake of it. *And* everybody in it. Everybody's different. Like – like the trees in a forest. Some's crooked; some's straight. Some's healthy; some's got moss on 'em. Some'll stand any storm; others'll fall at the first puff. Some's got fruit that's good to pick; some hasn't. *And* you can't tell. That's my meaning, boy: you can't tell. Not the cleverest person in the world can tell what's behind a face. They think they can, but they can't. It's been a shock to me ... Many times it's been a shock to me. It shakes your nerve. You don't know where you are. Then before you can say knife you're riding somebody else's tiger ..."

Silence fell. Uncle Perry's disjointed allegories were too much for Anthony. Eyes pricking, he watched the shadowy light grow in the east, slowly gaining ascendancy until it penetrated into this room, showing up new outlines of disordered chairs and tables, whitening a pile of broken crockery, driving before it the dismal defeated light of the flickering gas jet. Unnoticed, Uncle Perry's face had also emerged, wan and bloated and strained. When he poured himself a drink the bottle neck went *tat-a-tat* against the side of the glass.

The doctor had been here a long time. He could not have gone for they would have heard his footsteps.

Day was coming. Clouds high in the sky had begun to flush. They reflected a terra-cotta stain upon the opal blue of the harbour. Seagulls had begun to wheel and cry.

Suddenly there was a footstep behind them. Uncle Perry knocked over his glass. They had both expected to see the doctor, but it was Aunt Madge.

The monumental calm was shaken. "Very tired," she said distantly. "Brandy or something ..."

"Well?" said Perry, and his mouth twitched.

"About the same. Dr. Penrose is doing all he can. Touch and go, he says ..."

Perry wiped his forehead. "Poor Joe."

"Brandy or something," said Aunt Madge. "I feel .. can't stand it."

Perry put some rum into Anthony's glass. "This'll do."

She kept pausing to wipe her eyes while she sipped it.

"What does he say?" said Perry anxiously.

She waved her glass in sudden irritation. "Joe's right: doctors *pretend* to know. Anthony ... should be in bed."

Perry slumped back in his chair. "I've had an awful night . . ."

"You? You've done nothing. There's . . ."

"It's the waiting. All of you up there and me down here. Me thinking of poor Joe and doing nothing to help. Not able to do anything; you know, Madge, it isn't so easy as you think when a brother goes down like this – stricken down in his fifties; when we were kids; it reminds you of that time; we used to go out in a row-boat together; used to fish for dabs; used to bathe up the river; he was a big boy then, or so he seemed to me; there was six years, you know; that's a difference when you're kids; now it don't seem much; those days I never dreamed there'd come a time when I should sit here while Joe lay upstairs; it shakes you up more than you'd think, more than I thought. Blood will tell, you know; blood's thicker than water; you don't think so till it comes to the test; at a time like this. Honest to God, Madge, I'd – I'd rather . . ."

Aunt Madge had risen to her feet again. She looked down upon Perry from an altitude, remote as a snow-covered peak, frozen and impersonal and secretive. "How do you think I feel? Ill myself. Husband. Lonely. Got to carry on. Not sit there. Some have got to do. To act. Not sit there over a glass. Where should we be if everyone sat over a glass? Where should we be if I'd done nothing all this night? Anthony . . ."

The boy got up sleepily and stood beside her. "All right."

"Let him stay here," said Perry argumentatively. "He's company for me. If you're going I'll have no company; it's too late to go to bed now; we can sit here. I'll light a fire. I'll get Fanny to light a fire and we'll sit down here; it'll help to brighten things up; then when it's light we'll go on with clearing away the mess; somebody'll have to clear the mess; if the boy goes to bed now he'll sleep till midday. We might need him before then. You don't want to go to bed, do you, boy?"

"Not if I can help."

"There's the boy. We'll stay down here together, Madge, if it won't affect you. We'll be anxious to know –"

"Anthony," Aunt Madge said, as he was about to reseat himself.

He straightened up again.

"Quite light now," she said. "You can clear up, Perry. But —"

A voice came from upstairs. It was Patricia calling her.

"Aunt Madge! Aunt Madge!"

Ponderous in her haste, the older woman left them. With a premonitory chill Anthony watched her climbing the stairs. There had been something in Patricia's voice which told its own story. Joe Veal, for all his tenacity, had this time met an opponent who was going to get the better of him. Standing in the battered restaurant with the first full light of day creeping among the final shadows, his nephew knew this as surely as if he already heard the toll of a requiem bell. He knew it, and he was afraid.

From behind him came a *tat-a-tat* as Uncle Perry shook more rum into his glass.

CHAPTER FOURTEEN

The death of Smoky Joe and the other events of that August night had consequences which completely changed the lives of those concerned in them.

Everything came to a standstill. To the boy, who had known only the busy routine of Joe Veal's when it was in full working order, the silence which fell was peculiarly oppressive. It was as if he had been in a railway terminus and there had been an accident out on the line and the station had suddenly emptied. In such a case he would no doubt have wandered at will, through the turnstiles, past the ticket office, through the luggage departments and back upon the deserted platform. So now he found himself at a loose end, sitting in one or other of the empty restaurants, mooning through the kitchen passing into the larder, where quantities of uncooked food gradually became offensive, standing in the shop behind drawn blinds allowing his fingers to play with the keys of the automatic till.

Not that there was no activity at all on the closed premises, but none of it concerned him. Everyone had more *time,* but no one had any *attention* to spare him, not even Patricia.

There were the endless visits from old customers and

friends who came round with suitably grave faces and talked and drank cups of tea in the kitchen. There were the relatives: Aunt Louisa from Arwenack Street, a small tight woman with varicose veins, received with statuesque dignity by Aunt Madge. There was a cousin from Percuil and a second cousin from Mawnan Smith. By virtue of their relationship they stayed much longer than anyone else, sitting back purse-lipped in a corner while others came and went. By tactful stages they steered the conversation round to money matters and Joe's belief in blood ties; but Aunt Madge said Joe was very reserved about his private affairs, Joe's financial arrangements were a closed book to her, she'd left everything to Joe, all that would have to come out later, when the proper time came they'd be told if there was anything for them. With that they had to be content.

Then there were the men in silk hats and black suits with shiny elbows who came and went furtively with a sort of shop-soiled grief. They spent some time in the lonely room with the blinds drawn in the front of the house and later returned with something bulky which was manoeuvred with difficulty up the crooked stairs.

Joe might have been flattered had he been able to see and appreciate the gap his disappearance left in the lives of his relatives and how much they felt his loss. Patricia went about the house with her face full of tears: they were there impending but would not fall; her eyes were like flowers which had cupped the rain. Uncle Perry was hardly seen at all: he was up in his bedroom and only appeared for an occasional meal, puffy and pale, or when he wanted another bottle. Even little Fanny sniffled about her duties.

As for Aunt Madge, she said she could not sleep, and appearances bore her out. During those first three days of gloom and waiting, when the whole house seemed oppressive with what it contained, she sat nearly the whole time listlessly in the one armchair in the kitchen, dozing before the fire and waking suddenly with a jerk to stare about at the familiar scene as if she did not believe it was still there. She seemed to need company and she seemed particularly fond of the kitchen. Even the closest relatives were never invited upstairs.

It was as if the shadow of mortality had brushed close

beside her and she needed the reassurance of all the most familiar things of her everyday life. Anthony wondered how, just from a physical point of view, she could stay in one room for such a long time without moving.

On the day of the funeral there was a marked improvement in her bearing. She came down in an impressive dress of fine black silk with great cascades of lace pouring down the front like the Zambesi Falls and began to busy herself making sandwiches for the mourners when they returned. For the first time she seemed conscious of the full dignity of her position as the Widow of the Deceased. The three-day siege was nearly over. The last night was gone.

One of the black-coated gentlemen arrived early, and this time she went upstairs with him. Later she came down with an expression on her plump face of having triumphed over a weakness.

When she came into the kitchen she put on a pair of big black ear-rings and said: "Do you wish to see him?"

Anthony waited a moment and then realized that he was the only other person in the room.

"Who?" he said in surprise.

"Uncle. It's the last chance. Hi thought you might."

"Oh, no," he said. "Thank you." Things moved up and down his spine at the suggestion.

"His nephew . . . I thought you might."

"No," he said. "I'd . . ."

"It's as you like. Haven't you . . . black tie?"

"No, Aunt Madge. This was the nearest."

"Go and get one." She felt in her bag. "Due respect. Round the corner and down the hill. Thought you might have liked to see him. Very peaceful . . ."

He picked up his cap and ran quickly out to buy his tie. The wind and the spattering rain were refreshing to his skin but still more refreshing to his spirit. They seemed to say to him, "You are young; life for you is here outside; not in there; not in there; life is sweet and wholesome."

He dawdled about in order to prolong his freedom. He watched a cutter slipping gracefully out of St. Mawes Creek. He saw a fisherman returning from a morning's sport and tried to count the fish in his bag. He stopped at the street corner to talk to a boy he had come to know. They talked about wholesome interesting things, about a catapult, a dog which hunted rabbits, a farmer and an

101

apple tree. At length he could stay no longer; people would be arriving in another few minutes; he must go back to the hushed voices and the drawn curtains and the smell of moss and chrysanthemums.

Aunt Madge was sitting in her favourite chair. She glanced up at the clock as he slipped in.

"Been playing," she said. "Not nice to be out and about today. Not seemly. Thought you might have liked to see him for the last night. Nephew and all. I thought you might. But it's too late now."

There was some expression in her eyes which suggested she begrudged him his escape.

That night he had another unpleasant dream.

He dreamt he had been down feeding the swans at Swan-pool, and on his way back who should be waiting for him at the cemetery gates but Uncle Joe. They walked home together, Joe smoking his foreign-looking pipe. As they walked along he was trying to persuade Anthony to do something which Anthony was reluctant to do: the boy could not afterwards remember what, but it seemed a matter of urgency to the old man. While they argued they kept meeting people Anthony had never seen before, thin grey people all going in the opposite direction. Many of them seemed to be moving without walking, like figures in a rifle gallery. Uncle Joe said: "These are all my friends; we're all of a family now." As they passed one woman Anthony peered under the hood of her cloak and saw that her head was shrivelled to the size of a clenched fist.

They reached the restaurant. The Joe Veal sign had been torn down; the shop door hung on one hinge and the place looked empty and dark as if nothing had moved in it for years.

Uncle Joe put something into his hand. It was a chrysanthemum flower.

"This is where I live," the boy said. "Won't you come in?"

"No," said Uncle Joe. "I'd best be going Home."

He left him there and Anthony stood alone with the flower in his hand staring at the dark and empty shop. Then he looked down at the flower and saw that it had crumbled to moss.

He dropped it quickly and put his foot on it, feeling the

squelch beneath his heel, then stepped up to the threshold of the ruined shop. He knew that he must go in in order to go to bed; but he knew also that something was waiting there for him among the cobwebs and the darkness.

He entered the shop.

Something moved at the back of it. He turned to flee, but his feet were as if bogged in quicksand and the shop had become enormously big and the door of escape a small oblong of light in the distance. He tried to concentrate his attention on the effort of moving his feet but each step he took carried him no further away.

With his eyes wide open the scene did not change. He sat up in bed and it was still there. He was still in the shop; his bed was in the shop and he had been sleeping there. The thing still moved by the stairs and he could still see the lighter oblong of the door with the hump of the automatic till.

He rubbed his eyes, his mind tearing off the fetters of nightmare even more slowly than it had done four nights earlier. He knew he had been asleep and dreaming, but he was still in the shop, still terrified. He knew that if he went outside he would be able to pick up the piece of moss that Uncle Joe had given him. That had just as much reality as the bedclothes he plucked.

The realization that the oblong of the shop door was really the oblong of his bedroom window finally brought him to safety. He lay back in bed breathing his relief out slowly from between closed teeth. He should have laughed; anyone as old as he was should have been amused at the perverted vitality of the dream. But you never could see things like that in the dark, however much you might do so in the following day's sunshine. Besides, the stirring and rustling had not stopped.

He raised his head and listened. There it was again. But he was completely mistaken as to its character and direction. This was someone moving about in the office below him.

Determined not to give way to the reasonless fear which had beset him when he heard Aunt Madge coming up the stairs, he listened quietly for a time while the square of light at his window grew and spread into the room. Just daybreak. A few mornings ago he had sat with Uncle Perry while a life ebbed slowly away. Daybreak. No reason why somebody should not be moving about in the office. People could get up at what time they pleased. It was just the sort of noise Uncle Joe made: the shutting of drawers, the occasional scrape of feet, the movement of heavy books. Strange to think that Uncle Joe was no longer interested. But was he not? Who was to say that it could not be so? Supposing he was moving about down there, still attending to his affairs.

Anthony climbed cautiously out of bed. As he did so the sounds beneath him ceased. With the hair prickling upon the back of his neck he slid silently under the bed and pulled out the cork spy-hole.

The early light falling through the narrow window lit up the office greyly. Some books were piled on the desk, and papers lay in disorder on the floor. But the room was empty.

As he replaced the cork the unmistakable smell of Uncle Joe's tobacco came to his nostrils.

The old man had kept the threads of his various business undertakings so jealously within his own hands, had so refused to delegate responsibility, that the unravelling of them was like fumbling with a tangle of string to which one cannot find an end. In his time he had had dealings with every solicitor in town, and Mr. Cowdray, whom Aunt Madge called in, knew little more of his affairs than anyone else.

But in a sense, too, Joe's one-man business resembled a clock which has been wound and will run of its own accord for a time although the owner is gone and the key lost. Goods were delivered; letters arrived from ships' chandlers and shipping agencies; a cargo appeared for *The Grey Cat* and she proceeded to take it on board and would shortly depart for Hull. *Lavengro* arrived with a cargo of pit-props from Norway and the purchaser was ready waiting for them; bills and receipts arrived and could be filed or settled. Aunt Madge and Uncle Perry – who had recovered his good spirits – and Mr. Cowdray worked hard together to keep the clock still ticking.

A few days after the funeral the relatives of Smoky Joe, together with Mr. Cowdray, who was plump and untidy and wore a heavy beard to conceal a birthmark under his chin, assembled in the upstairs parlour to hear what there was to hear about the settlement of the estate. The parlour faced north and was therefore hung with dark red wallpaper which took away most of the light that filtered through the thick lace curtains. On the floor was a red carpet with blue flowers and a blue border showing ridges of wear by the door, and the furniture consisted of an upright rosewood piano which no one had ever used, a red plush music stool, and crimson plush furniture which emitted an ineradicable smell of dust. The mantelpiece carried an ornate overmantel with numerous small shelves and a gilt mirror.

Present were the cousin from Percuil and the cousin from Mawnan Smith, the sister from Arwenack Street and the brother from across the landing, who, incidentally, seemed to want to open the proceedings with a joke and a toss of his black hair. Aunt Madge and Patricia sat side by side on the sofa; and Anthony had slipped in almost unnoticed and pricked the backs of his legs on a horsehair stool.

Mr. Cowdray opened with an explanation of the difficulties which confronted him in clearing up the estate. He talked ponderously and leisurely from behind his beard, and no evidences of impatience on the part of the sister from Arwenack Street or the cousin from Mawnan Smith were sufficient to hurry him by so much as a syllable or cause him to miss out a single rusty clearing of the throat. Nor was he influenced by Perry's good-natured desire to make a party of the occasion. As if he were addressing a jury on a clear case of tort, he went on and on, making each point with the maximum of effect and the minimum of brevity. Perry caught Anthony's eye and winked wickedly, then it roved round for fresh eyes to contact. But all the others were too conscious of the solemnity of the occasion to meet such a challenge. If they were aware of it, as it must have been difficult not to be, they avoided it as the good little boy will avoid the bad little boy thumbing his nose on the way to church.

Aunt Madge was a mountain of unrelieved black, installed with closed eyes on the larger end of the couch. A breath moving from time to time among the darker recesses of her bulk was the only evidence that she lived. Beside her Patricia looked slender to the point of frailty, taut like the stem of a daffodil and as easily snapped.

So far as any final settlement of the estate was concerned, Mr. Cowdray went on, the work entailed might stretch over many weeks. But it was felt – he personally felt, and he knew Mr. Veal's widow felt – that to give at once a broad outline of the disposition of the bequests would be the fairest to all concerned. He did not propose to read the Will, but would just state the facts, and of course anyone could examine the documents afterwards –"

"I think you should read the Will," said Aunt Louisa sharply. "What do you say, Peter?"

There was a faint stir. Louisa's harsh voice had disturbed the reverential dust.

Peter from Percuil looked uncomfortable and pulled at one end of a drooping moustache. "Reckon I don't mind one way or th'other."

Mr. Cowdray glanced at the widow but she did not open her eyes. "Very well, then, if you wish it – hrrr-hm! – naturally no objection myself." He opened his bag and took out a sheet of parchment. "Actually, quite a short document; Mr. Veal was not a man to waste words; that is so far as I knew him; he deposited this Will with me, but I had not previously had business transactions . . . ."

"When you've been about the world a bit," said Perry, "it teaches you not to waste anything. Words, time or money. Joe was a regular one for seeing nothing went to waste. That's Joe all over." He chuckled. "Well, read it out; I'll bet old Joe's got a surprise or two up his sleeve."

" 'This is the last Will and Testament,' " read Mr. Cowdray stiffly, " 'of me, Joseph Killigrew Veal, of Falmouth, in the County of Cornwall. In consideration of the fact that for forty-seven years he has proved unpunctual in all his dealings and appointments, including the day he was born, I give and bequeath unto my brother, Perry Veal, my gold watch and ten pounds for its maintenance. Unto my sister –' "

"Well, I'll be stung!" exclaimed Perry. He threw back his head and laughed in a sort of unmalicious indignation. "If ever there was an old –"

"Perry . . ." said Aunt Madge, opening her mouth but not her eyes.

"Go on with the will," said Louisa.

"Hrr – hm . . . 'Unto my sister Louisa . . .' Yes. 'Unto my sister Louisa I give and bequeath forty-six pounds ten shillings and eightpence, which is the return of a loan made to me thirty years ago plus compound interest added to the year 1905, a return for which she had persistently pestered me. To my dear sister I also bequeath such records of the family as survive, dating back to 1690, and the family Bible, which I trust she will make more use of than I have.

" 'To my cousin Peter Veal, of Percuil, I give my piano, my edition of Chambers' Encyclopaedia, and twelve pounds, one pound for each of his twelve children. If any of his children should predecease me, let him lose proportionately. To my cousin, Polly Emma Higgins, of Mawnan Smith, I bequeath my cottage and two fields situated near that village.

" 'To my daughter Patricia, in view of the fact that she has seen fit to marry against my express wishes and against my specific threat to disown her if she did so, I leave five hundred pounds as a free gift and no further interest in my estate. To my wife, Madge, I bequeath the residue of my property absolutely. And I appoint my said wife sole executrix of this my Will, and revoke all previous Wills – mm – mm – mm . . .' " Mr. Cowdray's voice descended into the depths of his beard. For some time it stirred and rustled in the undergrowth and then was still. He raised his eyes and his eyebrows as if to say, "There you are; there it is; I disclaim all responsibility."

CHAPTER FIFTEEN

Anthony's eyes flew unbidden from face to face. As the only person not directly concerned, he alone had the leisure to appreciate the situation. But appreciate was not the word, for he felt a burning sympathy for the girl on the sofa. While the solicitor had been speaking of her Patricia had gone so pale that it would not have been difficult to imagine her slipping to the floor in a faint.

The boy was furiously indignant with his uncle. Although he was not old enough to put the matter in an ethical frame he felt the bitter injustice of leaving such acrimonious remarks to be read after one was dead and free from query or reproach. No one had the right to make a bitter accusation, to leave a smirch where it could not be answered or removed. That was not playing the game. Especially was it unfair when the accusation was groundless. Patricia had left her husband to nurse him and had been with him to the last. There had seemed no enmity between them. To her alone he had been prepared to delegate little business items during that last fortnight in bed. She—

"When is that Will dated?" Patricia asked.

"April the twelfth of this year."

"Thank God!" the girl said.

The boy's forehead wrinkled a moment, then he remembered that in April had occurred the estrangement between Smoky Joe and his daughter, first over the court case and then over her marriage. She had—

"I call it perfectly scandalous!" said Aunt Louisa, fiddling suddenly with the bits of fluff on the armchair. "I do really. I've never heard anything like it. He goes out of his way to insult all his blood relations and then leaves everything to his — wife. 'Tisn't right. 'Tisn't right at all." She looked up suddenly, her eyes like darts. "And I don't mind telling you I'm not at all content with it!"

"Now Louisa, now Louisa," said Perry. After the first brief spurt of indignation he seemed to be taking his own lack of fortune in his usual philosophical manner. Everything with Perry was easy-come, easy-go. "Put about. It'll do you no good bringing your head up to the wind. We've all of us suspected what Joe thought of us, and now, bigod, we know! Well, it's cleared the air, but it don't alter the Will, do it? I get my gold watch and you get your family Bible. And that's the end of it."

"I'm not so sure." Louisa allowed the words to escape from between tight lips. " 'Tisn't only for myself that I care, though I care for myself sure enough; but it's Patricia. Look at the way he's treated her!"

"Don't bother about me, Aunt Louisa," the girl said, her fine eyes dark. "I wouldn't touch any of his money now if I had it."

"But something can be done about it surely!" Miss Veal transferred her gaze, which had been fixed for so long upon Aunt Madge, to the bearded solicitor. "Look, Mister Cowdray. This Will you've been reading ... it was made in a fit of raging bad temper when Joe, when my brother was estranged from his daughter. In another month they'd

108

made it up again and were as friendly as you like. Can't that be taken into account? What about his earlier wills?"

Mr. Cowdray shook his beard. "Each Will has a clause revoking previous testaments. Unless he has made a later one this must stand, Miss Veal."

"Well, what of a later one? What about that? Has any search been made for one? Has the house been searched? Or he may have deposited it with some other solicitor. I refuse to accept this until a full search has been made.

"I've looked," said Aunt Madge, speaking for the first time. She closed her eyes again. "Everywhere . . ."

"That may well be, but –"

"Aunt Louisa," Pat said quietly. "If you're saying this for my sake, don't bother. No doubt Dad gave me what he thought I deserved. Well, if he thought that, I am quite content to accept it."

"Are you indeed!" said Miss Veal, her nose going pale with excitement. "Well, I'm not. You should be ashamed of yourself, Pat! I thought you had more spirit. Why Joe – your father – must have been worth fifteen or sixteen thousand pounds if he was worth a farthing. It may be much more. That's no right to go out of the family. That's Veal money and should stay Veal money –"

"Mrs. Veal," said Mr. Cowdray sombrely, "happens to be his wife, you know."

"His wife! Who two years ago was his cook! That's no true wife. His true wife is dead and buried, Patricia's mother. You don't make a wife of your servant. Besides, where did she come from? Nobody knew her in Falmouth till she came as his cook. She's no Veal –"

"*Houd vast,*" said Perry, patting her arm. "You're working up for a squall, sister. It'll do you no manner of good to spill a lot of bad blood. The law's the law and that's an end of it. Learn to face your disappointments with a smile like me. I can't pretend that I'm pleased with my share but there's nothing to do about it. We're both in the same boat and it's no manner of good standing up and whistling for the wind –"

Aunt Louisa withdrew her arm impatiently. "Your concerns are your own, Perry. You make your own peace with your conscience and I'll make mine."

"That's what I'm telling you, sister. Leave Patricia to mend her own affairs. I'm sure she'll not lack for a home, will she, Madge? There, I knew not. And besides, she's married to a rich and handsome young man who'll see that she's well taken care of. Now if I were you –"

"The black sheep," said Miss Veal distantly. "You've always been the black sheep, haven't you, Perry? If you must know, I'd trust *you* no further than I could see you. I'm not here to cast insinuations, but maybe you think you'll not come off so badly after all –"

Aunt Madge's eyeglasses wobbled at last.

"Hi've tried," she said. "Politeness. Manners. How long am I to stand this? My own house . . ."

"Your own house, indeed! It's Patricia's house by every manner of right, and Joe's no licence to disown her. I'll warrant there's a later will than this – if it can be found."

"Insinuating . . ."

"My dear Miss Veal – hrr, hm – I beg you to calm yourself. It is not at all unnatural for a man –"

"And what have you to say to this, Peter; and you, Emma? Joe was not in his right senses when he made this Will. Will you help me to contest it?"

Peter pulled at the end of his moustache. "Well, can't say that I'm altogether satisfied. But if we get mixed up in the law all the money'll go to the lawyers. It was like that when I went to law over that cow. It isn't what they get for you, it's what they take from you . . ."

"We don't want that to happen," said Polly Emma hastily. "We certainly don't want that, for sure. As for me, I can't say as I expected much more than I've got. I've seen little of dear Joe for these pretty many years, and husband was saying only last month that I did ought to call. But when he's that ill, I said, it looks like asking. It looks like begging, I said, going round and calling special on my dear cousin after all these years, when he's that ill, I said."

"Insinuating," said Aunt Madge, towering over Aunt Louisa. "Don't like. Own home . . ."

"Nothing but a cook," said Aunt Louisa, bantam-like. "A cook from nowhere, to wheedle into his good books. Where *did* you come from? I'll see it doesn't end here!"

"By rights," said Peter, "he should have left a little something for my eldest. Eldest was his godson. He'll be eighteen in January month, and a little something might have set him up in something. Never a present has he sent in all these years, though Christine remembered it now and then. A little –"

"Well, I'm sure we never bothered him," said Polly Emma, "except that husband would pass the time of day if he saw him in the street. I think well-to-do folk don't like to be bothered. But Albert is that way, you know; proud as proud, and not liking to go licking people's boots."

"Any action," said Aunt Madge, quivering. "Any action you think fit . . ."

"Well, there are other solicitors in the town besides Mr. Cowdray, and I don't mind telling you I intend to consult one. I should consider it a sheer neglect of my duty if I did not. And I may tell you that not only me but all the town will be of the same opinion, that – that undue pressure –"

"My dear madam – hrrr, hm – you may take any action you think fit. You are legally within your rights to do so. But I may inform you that your brother has made himself *persona non grata* with every one of my colleagues in this district, and is unlikely to have deposited a Will with them. I may also say –"

"Maybe we're not so partic'lar about these things, Emmie Higgins," said Peter, "but when we asked Joe to be Billy's godfather, 'twas intended as a mark of respect, not anything more. Lizzie and me don't go round licking of people's boots – neither his nor yours, see?"

"Oh, dear me, I'm sure I beg your pardon, cousin," said Polly Emma; "it was a figure of speech that was intended. It's not for the like of me to criticize other people. But, of course, what I say and what Albert always says is, if the cap fits, wear it, you know. That's what Albert always says. And it seems to me that when people are too quick to take offence –"

"Everybody in this town will feel just the same as I do. Public opinion is something you *can't* ignore –"

"Vain loud voices," Aunt Madge was heard to say. "House of mourning . . . Not yet cold . . ."

"If takin' offence is to be mentioned, what about when your Albert was in St. Mawes soon after Lizzie had been ill with pneumonia . . ."

Anthony, still withdrawn, again the only spectator, suddenly realized in a flash of inspiration what was missing at this gathering today. It was the presence of Tom Harris.

111

One might say or feel hard things about Tom, but he would at least have kept the meeting in some sort of order. He would never have allowed himself to be dragged into the arena, to be pulled into the thick of the quarrel, as Mr. Cowdray had done. His presence alone would have prevented this awful squabble. Give him his due. Anthony thought; give him his due, Pat, he's a cut above all these. Well might she sit there with her brown eyes down and a pulse beating in the white curve of her neck.

Strangely enough, it was the boy himself who provided the first effective check to the wranglers. In boredom he got up from his prickly stool and walked to the window and stood looking out. Something in his attitude there by the window, his hunched shoulders, his hands in his pockets, seemed to be an unspoken commentary upon the unseemly arguments going on behind him. One by one the quarrellers fell silent, stood about in sudden self-consciousness and constraint.

Miss Veal picked up her bag, felt for a handkerchief and blew her nose loudly.

"Well, you know my views. I was brought up to be blunt and I've been blunt all my life. I believe in honest dealing. That's more than some people do. What I've said to your face I'll say behind your back. You know what action I'm going to take. So there's nothing more to be said. I'll bid you good afternoon. Are you coming down the street, Peter?"

The thin man looked from one to another of his relatives and hesitated.

"Yes, I reckon so," he said at last.

"And you, Polly Emma?"

"Thanks, dear, I think I'll wait for the trap. Albert is calling for me in the trap."

Aunt Louisa went across and kissed Patricia on the forehead.

"Don't worry, dear. Don't worry at all," she said firmly.

"She won't if you don't," said Perry.

But his sister ignored the remark and walked with dignity from the room.

There were still two hours of daylight left, and Anthony presently escaped from the house and ran down to the derelict wooden jetty which led out into the harbour from the wall of the quay. This jetty was submerged when the tide was in, and was one of Anthony's favourite haunts. He could sit here and watch the water lapping up through the cracks, covering one slippery black board after another, and he could imagine himself stranded on a desert island – or trapped in a cellar under the Thames while the river rose.

Fancy was a pleasant companion after the grim and dusty happenings in the house, and his mind turned to his imaginings as a parched man to water. To be free of the chains of reality, to slip them off and wander at will, to be independent of time or space or hunger or heat, to make life up as you went along, to fashion life as you *wanted* it, romantic and exciting and bright with the obvious colours, no second thoughts, no reservations, no avarice, no frustrations, no hidden complex motives, no adult deceits: a world of good and evil where each was plain marked for what it was, in which good always triumphed and the ill-fortunes that you suffered, however tragic and toilsome they might be, were edged about with the silver thought that you could change them at will.

Anthony felt that he wanted to re-write the world. It was not right that there should be death for good people, and permanent unchangeable sadness and incurable illness, and strange muffled hatreds which hid themselves for years under a cloak of everyday behaviour. Or, if there had to be death, then it should only come to good people when they were very old and tired and when all their children were grown up and had children and grandchildren of their own. And especially there should be no bitterness which went beyond the grave, no tawdry squabbling over a dead man's goods, no remarks which made insinuations and left a stain.

Tonight the tide was going out so he could not play his favourite game. He had hoped to find his friend Jack Robbins somewhere about the quay.

The harbour itself was unusually empty for this time of day, and there were few big ships in. A solitary oarsman was rowing out from further up the creek and would pass close beside the jetty. A flight of starlings were wheeling and fluttering just above the rippling surface of the water, making dark shadows as they swooped, turning and manoeuvring with military precision, climbing the cloudy sky in a dense flock and then suddenly straggling out like children dismissed from drill. A group of them came to perch upon the roof of the house, arriving in ones and twos with a sudden swift dart and a flutter. One minute there was none, then they were all there like pegs on a line, chattering and arguing, turning their tails to each other and edging up and down. A moment later, as it seemed by a single instinct, they were up and away again, their short wings fluttering the air above the boy's head.

He watched them out of sight beyond the clustered climbing grey roofs of the old town, then turned to see if the tide had gone down sufficiently to allow another step.

As he did so he recognized the solitary man in the boat. It was Tom Harris.

CHAPTER SIXTEEN

He had not been seen, for the rower had his back to him, but before he could make up his mind whether to call out or to make his escape, Tom turned his head and nodded and smiled. He began to pull on his right oar, which would bring him nearer to the jetty.

Presently they were within speaking distance. Tom glanced up at the tall grey house with the bow windows of the restaurants looking out over the harbour.

"Hullo, Anthony. I'm just going over to Flushing. Like to come?"

"Yes, rather!" said the boy, and then hesitated. "How long will you be gone?"

"I've only to collect some fishing nets. Should be back in an hour."

For a second longer Anthony hesitated, wondering if, by continuing to associate with this man, he was being disloyal to Patricia. But during these last days Patricia had hardly spoken to him; she had never once mentioned the night of the fight; she had been preoccupied with her own concerns and had left him to his. Besides, she had never forbidden him to speak to Tom; how was he to know her mind?

With these sophistries he was content, and he stepped eagerly into the boat when Tom paddled it nearer. In a moment he was seated in the stern, enjoying the unusual experience of being a passenger and happy to ripple his fingers through the water and watch his cousin-in-law do the pulling.

Harris did not look as well as usual. There was still a slight swelling over one eye and a piece of plaster on his chin, but it was not these relics of battle which were responsible for the change. His eyes were tired and there was a hint of puffiness about his cheeks as if he had slept badly or been drinking.

Still, he engaged Anthony in conversation brightly enough – conversation which was adroitly steered away from dangerous subjects. The distance to Flushing was short, and there were no awkward silences on the way.

Flushing is a little old town built down to the very edge of its quay, and all day it quietly mirrors its grey slate and sash windows in the blue-grey waters of the harbour. Anthony was left to take stock of it while Tom went in search of his fisherman. Very soon he was back carrying a roll of net and they pushed off on the return journey.

Tom said: "Have you started school yet?"

The question no doubt was innocently meant, but its answer would entail considerable explanation. However, Anthony could hardly deny him this, having already accepted his companionship. He told the other how he had come to be here in the first place, that he had been expecting to join his father almost any day but that there was now some sort of delay, that just before Uncle Joe died there had been talk of sending him to school in Falmouth but that his death had put a stop to all plans. Soon, he supposed, as soon as everything was settled up, he would be going somewhere, if only for a term or two.

He stopped, aware that he had been getting near a proscribed subject. But Tom did not hesitate.

"Have they read the Will?" he asked.

Anthony crimsoned, trying hard to make up his mind what to say. If he replied as he should he would give offence to a man for whom he had begun to feel a sneaking liking. But if he told ...

"Don't answer me if you don't want to," Tom said. "You're under no obligation to tell me. But of course I shall know all the details in a day or two. They can't withhold information from someone directly concerned."

115

The matter hadn't struck Anthony that way.

He said awkwardly: "They read it this afternoon."

"Were you present?"

He nodded, still hoping that the subject might be allowed to drop there.

"How was the money left?" Tom said.

Underneath his casual tone there was a note of keenness, of anxiety.

"They ... It ... nearly all to Aunt Madge."

"And Patricia?"

"Five – five hundred pounds. Look, Mr. Harris, I –"

"Tom is my name. Were there any other important bequests?"

"No ... Aunt Louisa was angry; she talked of doing something, fighting the Will ..."

For some moments Tom had only just been keeping way on the boat. He seemed to have lost interest in his rowing. His brown eyes were fixed on the distant cliff line which had begun to haze over with the setting of the sun. He seemed to see more there than Anthony could.

"It's only what I expected," he said at length.

The boat began to drift. The boy shivered.

"I ought to be getting back. They'll wonder where I am."

"Well, I'm glad it's turned out that way anyhow," said Tom.

The boy stared. He could not make head or tail of that remark. Tom's questions had seemed to suggest only one thing, the obvious thing: that he had hoped all the money would come to Patricia, so that he would stand a chance of getting some of it himself. Tom's eyes had been specially keen when he put the questions, if not with cupidity, then with what? Slowly it began to dawn upon him that if Tom had plenty of money of his own it would suit him better that Patricia should not also be independent. There would be more chance of inducing her to return to him if she was without money or prospects.

Anthony had felt a little disillusioned at Tom's inquiries. Pumping *him* did not seem quite playing the game. At this development he did not know whether to feel relieved or further disillusioned. He wished most earnestly that he had never come. He wished that he had been left alone with his own make-believe.

"Anthony. Will you do something for me?"

116

The boy looked across at the man. Their eyes met, and then the boy looked down at his finger-nails. Tom Harris had a very direct gaze and, meeting it, one could not believe him capable of the worst forms of trickery. It was the way you looked at a thing, the boy supposed. If *he* was in love with Patricia – well . . . if he was *married* to Patricia – and she had left him, would he not welcome any lever which might persuade her to return? All was supposed to be fair in love and war. Would he want to see her independent?

"First," said Tom, "I'd like you to give her this letter."

He stared at the envelope offered him.

"But then she'll know I've been out with you."

"There's no crime in that. But I might have met you in the street."

He slowly accepted the letter and put it in his breast pocket.

"Thank you. The second thing is something rather bigger, Anthony. It may come to nothing, but then . . ."

He stared at the glow among the clouds. The sun was already down. Soon it would be dark. The light was moving off the water, moving away as if someone were gently rubbing it out.

"I trust you," Tom said. "There's something very frank and honest about you, and I feel that young as you are, you wouldn't willingly let anyone down. Well, I can't come to the house; you know that and the reason for it. Patricia is alone in the world now – except for, except for a stepmother and an uncle who don't really count. I'm anxious about her and about what she'll do. I should like to be by her side to help and – and to advise. As I can't be there, I want to feel that there *is* someone there, someone I can trust. I want you to be that person."

Anthony murmured something inarticulately. He was warmed and pleased by Tom Harris's words. Everyone is gratified at being paid a compliment, but with Anthony the sensation was something more. Ever since his mother died he had been one apart, and desperately lonely. He had moved among ordinary people and behaved in an ordinary manner, but he had had no sense of belonging. Even Patricia, who had been so kind, had not *needed* him. He had been in her life but not of it.

"It may not be very easy," said Tom, "and there may

not be much you can do. You're only young and no one can expect you to reach big decisions on your own. But I do feel you can help me just by being there."

"What do you want me to do?"

"When you get in," Tom said, "and think this over you may feel that all I've asked is that you should spy upon people to my advantage. But I don't want you to look at it that way. I don't care anything about my own advantage, I'm only concerned with Patricia's – though I'd like her to come back to me, of course. But she's young and hot-tempered and impulsive, and this is a testing time. I want you to come and see me now and then and talk to me. Come to see me in Penryn. It's only fifteen minutes' walk and we can have a cup of tea together and talk about how things are going at Veal's. Will you do that?"

"Yes," said Anthony.

"Good man." Tom slowly resumed his rowing.

"How shall I find where you live?"

Tom gave him instructions. "If you have any difficulty ask for the Harrises. Everyone knows us."

Tom Harris seemed only to want a thing and you were prepared to give it him. Perhaps it was in such a mood that he had persuaded Pat to marry him. But the first stirrings of criticism were already awake in Anthony's mind.

"I don't know what Pat will say if she ever gets to know."

Harris looked up thoughtfully.

"I think I know what she'd say. That you were a traitor to your own family carrying tales to me, wouldn't she?"

Anthony nodded.

"Well," said Tom, "it's not a pretty position for any of us. But I don't think in the long run that you will ever regret helping me. And I think you've a fairly good sense of right and wrong. It's entirely up to you what you tell me and what you don't. I have no means of judging whether you are telling me everything or only a part, but I'm prepared to leave that to your good sense. Only remember that I'm trying to help Pat. Even if she wants to free herself from me altogether, I still want to help her."

"That's what I want," Anthony said stoutly.

"Then it's a pact?" Tom rested an oar beneath the other elbow and extended his free hand.

They shook hands. Anthony was glad then that it was

118

going dark, for some sort of emotion had brought tears to his eyes. If Tom was appealing to his sentimentality he was not aware of it.

They were almost at the jetty.

"One last word," the other said. "I want you to promise me that if anything really important should happen you'll come to me at once. Whether it's day or night doesn't matter. Slip away and come straight to me."

Anthony felt that he was constantly being asked to concede fresh ground. He had yet to learn the first lesson of all conspirators, that there is no such thing as limited co-operation.

"How do you mean, important?"

The boat grounded gently in the mud.

"I'll leave that to you," Tom said abruptly. "Nothing so far as I know is likely to happen. But if anything should, well, you'll easily recognize it as something that I would be anxious to know."

Now that it was time to go Anthony felt reluctant to leave the intimacy of this newly founded partnership. It seemed to him that he had taken on a good deal with far too little to guide him. The terms of definition were still so vague. That so much should be left to his own initiative and judgment was flattering but a little oppressive. He knew many questions would come to his mind as soon as he got indoors, but now, while there was still time to ask them, he was tongue-tied.

"No second thoughts, Anthony?" Tom's teeth gleamed white for a moment. "Great men never indulge in them. Remember, I'm relying on you. And again, many thanks."

The boy climbed out of the boat and smiled back into the dusk. Then he leaned upon the bows of the boat and pushed it gently into the water.

"All right, Tom," he said, and watched the shadowy figure turn to row away. Then he himself turned and picked a path among the mud and the seaweed towards the dark bulk of the house.

Only Fanny was in the kitchen. She was reading *Home Chat,* and her feet, toes together as usual, were on Aunt Madge's favourite footstool.

"Hullo," she said. "Where've you been? 'Ad your supper?"

"No . . . Is there anything left?"

"A pasty. 'Tisn't 'ot, but there's plenty of meat in it.'"

He picked up the pasty and absently took a bite, his mind still busy. Instinctively he drew nearer to the fire, for his hands and feet were frozen.

"Did they ask for me at supper?"

"No, I didn't 'ear 'em."

"Where's Miss Patricia now?"

"Gone out. Mr. Pawlyn came round."

The letter was burning a hole in his pocket. The brilliant idea came to him that instead of handing it direct to Pat he would slip it under her bedroom door. Then she might not even think of asking if it was he who had put it there. He couldn't quite understand what had driven him to promise Tom what he had done. Pat would look on it as plain treason. He was torn between two loyalties.

"And Aunt Madge and Uncle Perry?"

"In the parlour."

"I think I'll take this to bed," he said. "I'm tired."

"Coo, it's early yet. Don't go readin' in bed and leaving your candle burning an' setting the 'ouse afire."

"Getting bossy, aren't you?"

She pulled a face. "Well, that's what *she* always says to me."

He went out into the hall, ducking instinctively to avoid the fly-paper, and paused a moment to stare into the darkened shop. All the lower part of the house was unlighted: the shop and both restaurants and the various storerooms. A week or two ago the place had been thronging with people and Uncle Joe had been sharpening his knife behind the counter and bargaining with customers for the various cuts off the joints. Life and bustle. Darkness and decay. Better the light and the heat and the noise. Anything better than darkness. Anthony hated and dreaded it.

The memory of that dream crept into his mind like a thief, and he turned abruptly away from the shop and began to mount the stairs. So vivid had been the dream that even now he could almost hear that furtive rustling in one corner of the shop.

On the first landing a tiny oil lamp burned. A single pearl of light in all this darkness, no larger than a drop of water in a cavern. Beyond, round the corner, another flight of stairs, narrow and gaunt, led to his room,

But first the letter. He took it out and turned it over. There was no writing on it at all. Perhaps Tom had been afraid that if she saw his writing she would destroy it unopened. He crept past the door of the parlour, from under which emerged a thin bar of light, and came to Pat's room. The sound of murmuring voices had reached him for a moment like something warm and cosy as he passed the parlour. He wished so many of the floorboards did not creak; useless to be light-footed and stealthy when the whole house complained at every other step.

Greatly daring, he turned the handle of Pat's door and pushed it a few inches open. He had never been in here before. (Strange how many rooms in this house he had not yet been in.) A faint sweet smell of femininity came to his nostrils. It thrilled him; everything that was dainty and pure and untouchable went with that smell, the essence of womanhood and beauty and grace. Reverently he tiptoed to the dressing-table, put the letter upon it and, suddenly afraid of being surprised, turned and hurried out again.

The door made a noisy click as he closed it, and he stood in the darkness of the passage for some seconds listening to the beating of his own heart. But the two in the parlour had no reason to be suspicious of noise; faintly he heard their voices again. Uncle Perry seemed to be doing all the talking. But then Uncle Perry always did.

He reached the door of the parlour and paused, hesitating whether to go in. He would not really be welcome; he would be in the way; their talk would not interest him. He was about to move on when he heard Aunt Madge's voice raised.

"No, Perry; I won't . . . definitely won't allow . . ."

He heard Perry's masterful buccaneering chuckle, then silence fell, to be followed by a little high-pitched laugh. The boy did not know where that laugh came from. It might have been uttered by Aunt Madge, though it didn't sound like any noise he had ever heard her make before. But then he had never heard her laugh. You wouldn't have thought it possible; you wouldn't know what to expect.

"Too soon . . . not decent . . . How dare you? . . ."

Perry's laugh went slower and deeper and subsided to a little throaty chuckle. Then the other laugh broke out again, but short and breathy and sustained upon a giggle. It was as if delight and outraged dignity were fighting for supremacy in it, and dignity was losing ground.

Anthony turned and ran up the stairs to his room. He knew that if he had had the courage he might have opened the door of the sitting-room and walked in.

But he knew he would not have done that for all the jewels of Asia.

Book Two

CHAPTER SEVENTEEN

On a mellow day of late September proceedings were opened at Falmouth police court whereby one, Thomas Wilberforce Harris, solicitor, of Mount House, Penryn, was charged with assault and battery upon the persons of Edward Pawlyn, of Mevagissey, and Franz Todt, of Hamburg. The case had been held up because the beer bottle which came into contact with Franz Todt's head had done more damage than was at first supposed. He was, however, now well enough to come into court with his head swathed in bandages and an expression of justifiable resentment on his milestone of a face.

Harris had elected to be dealt with summarily and was represented by one of his partners, a tall man with a deceptively gentle manner. The gravamen of the charge against Harris was that he had come down into the restaurant in a quarrelsome drunken mood, had gratuitously picked a quarrel with Pawlyn and, not content with taking on one good man, had also contrived to commit a battery upon Todt.

Harris pleaded guilty to having begun the quarrel with Pawlyn, but not guilty of having struck Todt. People in the court felt that history was repeating itself and wondered if Harris would get six months in the second division like Mr. Fossett in the last case.

There were a large number of witnesses, and although they had all seen what had happened before someone turned the gas out, nobody had seen anything at all after. Very soon it became clear to anyone with a moderate knowledge of the law that the accused was in little danger of being found guilty on the second charge. However morally responsible he might be for making the opening move in the affray, there was no proof that he had assaulted Bosun Todt in any other way than by accidentally sitting on his knee. Indeed, the weight of evidence suggested that if any blow at all had been exchanged between the two men it had come from the German, who took exception to his supper being interrupted.

The quietus was given to this part of the case by the third mate of the windjammer, who had stayed behind to give evidence. Under cross-examination he admitted that there had been bad feeling during the long and very arduous voyage home, and also that when he arrived on the scene of the quarrel, just before the lights were put out, Bosun Todt was fighting with several of their own men. These men, it was ascertained, were no longer under the jurisdiction of the court, being with their ship, which was now in the Baltic.

At this stage Mr. May, Harris's partner, submitted that there was no case to answer in law, and the Stipendiary Magistrate in charge of the court agreed with him and dismissed the charge.

There remained, however, the first charge, to which the accuse pleaded guilty; and the magistrate gathered his papers together and prepared to deliver a weighty homily on the folly by which a young man of a highly respected local family, of good education and holding a responsible position in the affairs of a neighbouring town, should find himself in this deplorable position. But just as he was about to begin Mr. May rose again and in a quiet voice said that he had one further witness to bring forward, one whom he produced with considerable reluctance, but who insisted upon entering the witness stand and giving testimony in this case. He called Mrs. Tom Harris.

There was a stir in the well-filled court, and Patricia was to be seen making her way down the centre aisle. Tom half rose from his seat, then glanced at Mr. May in annoyance.

Every person in the court, with the possible exception of the two foreign witnesses, knew something of the history of the whirlwind marriage and the equally sudden separation. There was a general peering and shifting and craning, and a rising murmur of voices was to be heard until the rap of the hammer checked it and brought a return of silence.

"You are Mrs. Patricia Harris, wife of the accused?" Mr. May said, when the formalities had been gone through.

"I am." She spoke in a low voice. She was dressed all in black with a small black hat worn rather forward on her head and a veil hiding her expression. But in order to give her evidence she had lifted the veil. In these last few weeks since her father's death she had matured, grown suddenly and quietly adult. Her features had fined off, the chin had
126

lost a little of its roundness. She had done her hair a different way, which emphasized the pale curve of chin and neck.

"You were present in the restaurant on the night in question?"

"I was."

"Will you tell the court, Mrs. Harris, in your own words, what happened?"

Patricia put down her small black muff and looked at the magistrate.

"Your worship, I must first explain that I am the daughter of the late Mr. Joe Veal who owned the restaurant at the time. I had – left my husband some weeks before this happened, and he came to see me at the restaurant, where I was living. He was not drunk. I have never seen him in any way under the influence of drink. When he came –"

The magistrate looked over the top of his spectacles.

"Why was this witness not produced before?"

"Your worship," said Patricia, "because everyone wished to spare me the pain of appearing in court. There has been that intention from the beginning – my husband, Mr. Pawlyn, all of them wished to prevent it becoming known that the – the quarrel was – over me. But . . . I have insisted, because it – it is not fair that all the facts should not be known. Not from any – not from any . . ."

"Take your time, Mrs. Harris," said Mr. May gently.

Patricia put her gloved hands together in an effort to steady her nerves. That other time, when she had appeared in court and given testimony damaging her father, had been nothing to this. Then her personal, private life had been in no way involved. She had been in a spirited, reckless mood, not at all enjoying the experience but keyed up to do what she had suddenly, impulsively resolved. But now she hardly knew how to keep her hands or her lips steady.

With a great effort she went on:

"A few months ago, I separated from my husband *permanently*. Once or twice he has visited me, asking me to return, and I have refused. Mr. – Mr. Pawlyn is an old friend whom I knew before I married and who always calls in when his ship is in port. My husband objected to my associating with him. I claim the right to associate with whom I choose. On the – that night I was having supper in

127

the restaurant with Mr. Pawlyn. Tom – my husband – came across and spoke to me. He was absolutely sober and I think had no idea of making trouble. But a few words were exchanged between them and then ... then Mr. Pawlyn called Tom an offensive name – and it was then that the – that my husband hit him."

"Your worship," said the prosecuting solicitor, "I completely fail to see in what way this witness is going to affect the case. The accused has already pleaded guilty to assault and battery."

"Go on, Mrs. Harris," said the magistrate.

She hesitated. "I – I think that is all."

Mr. May had no questions to ask, but the prosecutor at once came to his feet again.

"How did you know that your husband was not drunk, Mrs. Harris?" he asked.

". . . He wasn't. He was quite sober."

"You've just told us that you have never seen your husband drunk. How would you know, then, if you saw him?"

"Well ... he was not unsteady – or – or ... I've seen too many drunken men not to be able to tell."

"Certainly he was not unsteady: look what happened to the restaurant. But a man needs just the right number of drinks to become quarrelsome – or to have been drinking steadily for some time. Since you had not been in his company, how could you tell?"

". . . I'm quite certain that –"

"Mrs. Harris, what was the offensive word Mr. Pawlyn used to your husband?"

There was a titter at the back of the court.

Patricia fumbled with her muff. "I don't wish to repeat it. . . ."

"As bad as that? Or have you forgotten?"

"No, I haven't. Your worship, I'll write it down if necessary."

"She'll write it down, if necessary, Mr. Prior."

Mr. Prior did not pursue the subject.

"Do you wish to return to your husband?"

"No."

The man looked at her with his head on one side.

"Not?"

"Certainly not."

128

"Are you sure that your testimony today is not given with a view to effecting a reconciliation?"

"Certainly it is not."

"Are you still – friendly with Mr. Pawlyn?"

"Yes."

"A little damaging for him, isn't it, to come forward like this?"

"I don't know what you mean."

"To say nothing of your own reputation?"

"I can only tell you the truth. Your worship, I can only tell the truth. There was never anything at all between myself and Mr. Pawlyn. I have no wish to return to my husband. I don't want to at all. But I don't want to see him go to prison for something that was only partly his fault."

"Quite so," said the magistrate sympathetically. "Have you any other questions, Mr. Prior?"

"No, your worship. But I submit that this young woman's testimony is entirely useless. She has proved nothing which was not already admitted and disproved nothing that the prosecution alleges. The case surely remains unaffected by it in any way."

"You may leave the stand now, Mrs. Harris," said the magistrate.

Patricia had promised to meet Ned Pawlyn after the case and spend the rest of the day with him. But when it was at last over she would gladly have made some excuse and gone straight home. Always, it seemed to her, when she became involved in the law her testimony had to be damaging to the people whose interests were closest to her own.

But Ned Pawlyn, whatever his private feelings, was waiting for her when they came out of the court-room, and in a few moments he had led her past the staring bystanders to where a closed landau was waiting.

They got in and drove off.

A long silence fell between them. The day was unusually warm and sunny for the time of year, with the temperature in the sixties. The month might have been August were it not for the angle of the sunshine slanting through the trees and casting the long shadows of houses across the dusty road.

At last Ned could contain himself no longer.

"Bound over to keep the peace for twelve months," he

said explosively. "That's what becomes of being tried local. And the law looks after them that's in the law. If it had been me that had been in the dock I should never have got off with less than twenty-eight days."

Patricia leant back and looked out at the slow panorama of lane and tree and river.

"It was my fault," she said.

"I don't care about myself," he said; "but it seems to me it was a pity you had to come in as you did. I wondered why you went out of court with that Mr. May. I don't know enough about those things to say whether they would have twisted things round to suit him in any case, or whether what you told made all the difference; but you know what they'll say about you now . . ."

"No."

"About us, then. They'll say that you and me –"

"I know, I know, I know! What does it matter?" she said suddenly, angrily. "What does it matter what narrow-minded people say?" She was taut beside him. "I couldn't help it. I'm not good at conspiracies, especially if I benefit. I didn't want to get him off; but it wasn't fair for him to be judged on only one side of the story just because you're all too delicate to let me be involved. Don't you see? *I couldn't let that happen.* I'd have been under an obligation all my life. And an obligation to him. What happened was as much your fault as his – and – quite as much mine as either. I'd got to tell the truth. Now it's all out and he's free and it's all over. Let's not talk about it. Forget it. Forget it."

He saw that she was near tears.

"Sorry, Pat," he said. "It was what we were both thinking about, wasn't it?"

"I'm sorry too," she said, suddenly quiet again. "I'm sorry to have – to have turned on you in court. I always seem to be – up against my friends. I don't want to be. And you're always so very patient and kind. . . ."

Silence fell again; but this time it was one from which the electric charge had been dispersed.

"Where are you taking me?" she asked, after they had passed through Penryn.

"Anywhere you like. I thought the drive would do you good. I thought while you were giving evidence, I thought: what she could do with after this is a drive, just sitting back and nothing to do. And I thought I might get you away

130

without meeting *him*. I slipped out before you and got this cab. I thought we could go as far as the Norway Inn and have tea there. I know the man who keeps it."

They were beginning to climb the overgrown winding hill out of the town. The horse had fallen to a walk.

"You're very kind, Ned," she said, touched by his solicitude. "I don't deserve it. I wish I . . ."

"What?"

"Oh, nothing."

Only scraps of conversation passed between them for the rest of the drive, down the other side of the sharp hill, through the valley where the sunlight lay in wasp bars across the road and the trees were showing their first tinges of autumnal yellow. In places the rank vegetation of the hedgerows had grown lushly out to flop across the road and catch at the carriage as it passed. This was the old coaching road, but since the railway came it had fallen into disuse. Ridges of grass grew between the dusty and uneven ruts.

They drew up at the inn, and Ned told the driver to wait and they went inside and ordered tea, which was served in a low, shadowy little private parlour.

Patricia lay back in her chair and drank tea and ate a split with jam and butter on it to please Ned. She was more than grateful to him for his tact and consideration. So pleasant and restful was it to lie back here and say little and feel that for a time you were away from prying eyes. She knew well that Ned was right in his appraisal of the situation, that she would only get notoriety and ill fame for the part she had played this afternoon. She knew that tomorrow *The Falmouth Packet* would be out, and the fullest possible report would be given of the events of today. The paper would probably sell out in no time, for everyone would be anxious to read for himself the exact account of Tom Harris's trial and what Patricia Harris – *née* Veal – had actually got up in the court-room and said about herself and Ned Pawlyn.

Her position in Falmouth had been a little difficult ever since she left Tom. There were some who said she deserved a good whipping for turning her back on a well-to-do young gentleman who had done her the honour of marrying her. This view was strong among those who would have liked to marry him themselves or had eligible daughters.

Marriage vows were not to be treated like waste paper; what would the world be coming to if everyone acted in such a fashion? Besides, it was a wicked bad example for all the young folks growing up. Pat Veal, they said, had shown her upbringing and her parentage: the Veals were a queer lot nowadays – all except Miss Veal of Arwenack Street. Young Mrs. Harris must be carefully and systematically cut.

Then after the contents of the Will became known she noticed the onset of another change. Young women who had come in for a good deal of ready money, considerable property and a complete shipping line were somehow more entitled to their impulses and foibles. But young women who had been practically disowned and left penniless would be well advised to eat humble pie and go on eating it. If they did not do so, then so much the worse for them.

Now, after this afternoon, the town would be well confirmed in its worst views.

Not that it mattered, she told herself. What did anything matter any more? They would go their way and she would go hers. She did not yet depend on their patronage.

"You know we're leaving by the morning tide, don't you?" said Ned.

She nodded, but the information chilled her afresh. Ned was a good friend who had stood by her in everything. His friendship did not waver with changed circumstances. He was one of the few who were worth knowing.

They were quite alone in the little parlour, and the last sun had left the room. It was dark and quiet and smelt of damp earth from some ferns in the window.

"Why don't you come away with me?" said Ned.

She looked at him startled.

"How do you mean?"

He grunted. "I don't mean in *The Grey Cat,* of course. I could cut that and stay behind. What I mean is ... Well, I can't ask you to marry me, because you're already married. But why not come away with me somewhere? Later on Harris will get tired of hanging on and will divorce you. Then we can do things legally. But ... that may be a year or two. Come away; let's leave the country altogether. You can't stay in Falmouth. Everybody'll talk and talk. You can't live on what you've got. Well, I've not much, but I can earn. I can earn enough for two. We can go to Australia,

132

start a new life. Nobody'll know us there. It'll be dropping all this and starting all over again. What d'you say?"

It is doubtful if Ned Pawlyn had ever before said quite so much without a break. Patricia stared somewhat startled at the sudden vista which opened before her. She had never contemplated such a thing; but she suddenly found the prospect not without its attraction. Two months ago she would have dismissed the idea with scarcely a thought. Then life in Falmouth, for all the break-up of her marriage, was good. She enjoyed the life of the restaurant; besides, she was so young that she looked into the future eagerly and without fear. But now ... the restaurant was closed and Aunt Madge was making as yet no effort to open it. Even if she did, she, Pat, would not feel the same proprietorial interest in its success. And she had lost her father and the respect of most of her neighbours. If Uncle Perry eventually found somewhere to retire, as he still talked of doing, the household might boil down to no more than herself and Madge; and although she had no special complaints to lodge against Madge as a stepmother, there was no pleasure in looking forward to having her as a sole companion. (Besides, Madge had made no secret of her view that Pat's proper place was in her husband's house; when Pat first returned she had always been going on at her about the sanctity of marriage vows: on and on in her best water-weareth-away-stone manner. Though in fairness, Pat had to admit that she had never suggested it since Joe died.) But what alternative was there now except either to return to Tom or to live with Madge? With only a few hundred pounds she could not set up in a little cottage of her own.

Here was an alternative suddenly before her eyes.... Australia was a new conception: a big hot land of rolling sheep farms and miles of ripening wheat. Life there with Ned might be adventurous and new. Men had made big fortunes out there in the last few years; why not Ned? She pictured herself as his partner and companion all through life, living in a wooden shack, then later in a big ranch house, sitting on a veranda with a warm, sweet wind blowing in from the miles of grass land, and perhaps two or three children tumbling about at her feet.

"What d'you say, Pat?" Ned repeated.

Slowly her eyes came back to the drab little room and to

the dark-browed eager young man opposite. With Ned. That was the point. With Ned. Slowly the vision faded.

"It's sweet of you to ask me," she began.

In a moment he was kneeling beside her, one arm resting upon her knees.

"I needn't go tomorrow," he said. "Stevens can get someone else. There's a ship leaving for Brisbane one day next week. We can make a long honeymoon of it."

She felt that she wanted to refuse him, but she did not seem to have the strength left. And, although the vision had faded, there remained a thread of self-knowledge in her mind which told her that this was what she was really cut out for: not to be a lawyer's wife, not to live as a grass widow in a narrow circle of relatives and friends, not to live in a provincial, respectable, genteel comfort, but to launch out with the man she loved, risking hardship and overcoming difficulties, finding adventure and frustration and fulfilment.

"I'll think it over," she said. "I'll think about it, Ned, truly I will. If –"

But he knew that such a favourable moment was unlikely to return. Tomorrow things might look different to her. But he knew that if he could coax a promise out of her tonight she would stick to it tomorrow and the next day.

And, if nothing happened, he was due to sail on the morning tide. In a few hours he would be gone.

He bent towards her and found her face closer to his than it had ever been before. It delighted him and he kissed her gently on the mouth.

Her lips were yielding; they did not respond but they were not unfriendly. He kissed her again, and the success went to his head. He put his arms about her and drew her towards him and tried to kiss her again.

And then suddenly he found that she was resisting him, unmistakably resisting him. They strained for a moment or two and then he let her free. She rose to her feet quickly and went to the window. He could see her breath coming quickly, misting the pane.

He went and stood beside her, put a hand upon her arm.

She turned. "Please, Ned," she said quietly, and her face was white. "Please, Ned; take me home."

CHAPTER EIGHTEEN

Amid the opal clouds of dawn *The Grey Cat* slipped out quietly into the bay. Anthony was awake and craned his neck from his window to watch her shake out her sails one by one like a white flower unfolding its petals at the touch of the sun. He was sorry to see her go, for he liked the burly mate with his long legs and his quiet, slouching walk and felt sympathy with him in his obvious devotion to Pat. Since his pact with Tom, however, he had experienced a sense of constraint in Ned's presence and had tended to avoid him. He felt as if he were accredited to an unfriendly power and did not want to abuse his diplomatic privileges.

It was a beautiful morning with the early autumn sun dispersing a scarf of mist which clung to the low hills on the other side of the harbour. Anthony was the first stirring in a house which had curiously cut adrift from its old routine since Joe died. In the old days Perry had been the only member of the household to stay late in bed, but with the incentive of business removed Aunt Madge was now not rising until about half-past nine, and little Fanny, a reluctant waker at the best of times, usually succeeded in putting in an appearance a bare ten minutes ahead of her, like a saucy frigate in front of a ship of the line.

Patricia was usually the first about, with Anthony close behind her, but this morning he was down much earlier. When he happened to go outside he saw what somone had written in white on the pavement outside the shop and on the shop window, he felt there was a reasonable hope, if he was very quick, of being able to remove the writing before Patricia came down.

Although he had not been at the police court, Aunt Madge and Uncle Perry had discussed it in front of him later in the evening, and he realized that the inscriptions had some reference to what had passed there. The writing on the window said: "SAILORS ONLY." That on the pavement was more explicit, and ran: "CALL IN ANY TIME YOU ARE IN PORT."

There was another reason for haste, for it was now full daylight. The street was at present deserted, but people would soon be passing this way.

The shop door was not open, so he had to carry a bucket round from the kitchen door and up the steps at the side. He realized he had brought nothing to work with and ran back for a cloth and a scrubbing brush.

He began on the window, and at once found that the stuff used was not whitewash, as he had first thought, but paint, and it had been dry several hours. The letters would be removable only with great difficulty. He could barely reach the top of the letters, but that did not matter so long as he made them unreadable.

He had been at work about five minutes when Warne's milk cart stopped at the corner. Fred Warne, the big, over-grown son, came down the narrow, sloping street carrying a milk churn. He stopped at the sight of Anthony and set down his can.

Fred Warne was the result of a marriage of first cousins and was not among the brighter intelligences.

"Whar'ee doing that fur?"

Anthony stopped a moment and shrugged his shoulders.

"L-O-R-S," spelt Fred laboriously. "O-N-L-Y. That don't make sense. Who's been writing on the pavement?"

"Don't know," said Anthony.

"Out early this morning," said Fred. "Don't b'long to see anyone stirring round 'ere s'early as this. Not since the Ole Man died. What are 'ee out s'early fur?"

Anthony began to sweat with the effort of his work. Fred Warne watched him with a slightly open mouth. There was silence while the L O disappeared.

"Call-in-any-time-you-are-in-port," Fred read out, putting his tongue round his mouth in between words. "What fur should anyone want fur to write that, eh?"

"Isn't it time you delivered the milk?" the boy suggested.

"Reckon you're opening again," said Fred, suddenly struck with the idea. "Reckon that's what 'tis. 'Tis a bit of a joke fur to attrack people. Did Widow Veal ask fur that there notice to be splashed on the pavement, eh?"

"Your horse is straying," said Anthony, glancing up the road. "Look . . ."

Fred scratched the fair stubble on his chin.

" 'E cann't do that fur 'e's tethered to the lamppost. Reckon that's another joke, eh?" He burst into hearty but contemptuous laughter.

"You'll waken everybody."

136

Fred shifted on to his other foot and leaned a hand on his milk churn. "Well, 'tis daylight. Didn't people ought to be woke up when 'tis daylight, eh?" His hearty laughter brayed out again. A small child came to the end of the street and stared down with his finger to his mouth.

"Call-in-any-time-you-are-in-port," said Fred. "I'll tell fathur 'bout you opening 'gain. Maybe you'll be wanting more milk again, eh?"

A window opened above their heads. With a sinking feeling the boy saw Patricia looking down.

"Anthony! Whatever are you doing?"

"I thought," said Anthony. "I thought I'd – I'd clean the windows. They were dirty and I thought it would be –"

"What's that writing? Move the bucket, will you? I –" She broke off and her face went a sudden white.

"Shall I tell fathur you be goin' t'open up again, eh?" called Fred.

She quickly shut the window.

"Don't seem to like it, eh?" said the milk boy. "What's the matter with she?"

"Mind your own business!" Anthony suddenly snapped, losing his temper. "Get on with your milk round...." He stared at the shop window. The R S had gone. ONLY did not convey much. He glanced at his water, which was now a greasy grey.

"You just be windy 'bout something," said Fred Warne. "Getting snappy an'–"

But the water had been suddenly emptied on the pavement, swilling almost over Fred's feet, and Anthony and the empty bucket were gone.

In the kitchen Anthony came full tilt into the girl. He swerved past her and hurriedly clanged the bucket under the kitchen sink and turned the tap on full. She came and stood beside him without speaking while the bucket filled; he could see one white sleeve of her dressing-gown trembling against the table.

The tap was turned off and he grabbed the bucket.

"Leave it, Anthony," she said, speaking rapidly but with some difficulty. "What does it matter? Leave it. Don't – show that – we care ..."

"It'll be gone soon," he gasped, and rushed out up the steps and round the corner to the front of the shop.

The small boy and a strange man and Mrs. Treharne,

the publican's wife from the corner, had joined Fred Warne. An effort of will was needed to go out and ignore their questions and their sly looks and get down on your knees and begin to scrub for dear life. Learning from experience, Anthony concentrated on the important words: CALL, TIME and PORT.

Three youths going to work at the docks now joined the gathering, and then a shrewish little woman from a cottage next to the public house who, having had the situation explained to her, gave it as her opinion that after all folks generally got what they asked for in this world, but that boy didn't ought to be the one scrubbing it off, the one to do it should be *her* that was in the fault.

All the time he was at work the audience remained, though in the nature of things it was a fluctuating one. Even with such a pleasant and original spectacle to view and discuss, people in the early morning were generally up at that hour to some purpose, and work called the faithful to their several tasks. But others came to take their places.

When the thing was at last done, Anthony took up his bucket and brush and, ignoring the last questions and humorous remarks, slid quietly round to the back of the house, leaving the solitary word ONLY still upon the shop window as a mark of the defamer's hand.

Breakfast that morning was a joyless meal. Patricia had gone upstairs and did not reappear, Perry as usual was still asleep, so Aunt Madge presided in due solemnity with Anthony beside her and Fanny occupying an obscure seat at the end of the table. Without the lightening effect of the two other adults Madge was like a blanket, and conversation ran into blind alleys. The only time Madge was ever talkative was when she had a grievance.

The morning passed, and it was not until lunch time that Patricia came quietly down the stairs and took her seat at the table. She smiled faintly at Perry's humorous sallies, but bent over her meal in silence until little Fanny had carried off her own meal into the scullery.

Then Pat raised her head. "Madge," she said, "don't think I'm not happy here; but I'm going to get a job."

Her stepmother put up a plump, white hand to pat the pad in her hair.

"While I'm alive ..."

"Yes, I know, my dear, and thank you. But I can't stop

138

here on your – charity all my life. Besides, forgive me, but I don't want to. I've been trying to make up my mind for days – ever since the Will was read. This morning has decided me –"

"Pah! What's there in that to take on about?" said Perry, patting her knee. "You've no need to pay attention to a few old gossips. They mean no harm. Everyone gossips. Even me. Even Anthony, don't you, boy? It will die down in no time. Now in China –"

"What," asked Aunt Madge, turning up her eyes, "did you think of doing?"

The girl puckered her smooth brow. "I've hardly got as far as that yet. There's so few things a woman can do. But I'll find something."

"People will think," said Aunt Madge, blinking. "People will blame me. Your Aunt Louisia. They'll say . . ."

"In China," said Perry, "there's a sign language, you know. If they draw one little figure under a roof, that means harmony. If they put two little figures that stands for marriage. If they put three little figures that means gossip. It's just the same wherever –"

"I don't see why they should say anything against you," said Patricia. "I'll tell Aunt Louisa it's nothing to do with you. I'm a free agent and –"

"Not the solution," said Aunt Madge; "not the solution Hi should have . . . A good husband . . ."

Pat's firm young face did not alter. "I can't, Madge. I don't want to go back to him. I want to live my own life, stand on my own feet . . ."

"Whereas in Japan," said Perry, "there isn't the same inducement, as you might say."

"Not nice," said Aunt Madge. "A young girl to go out . . . earning her own . . . Later. This restaurant. We shall open again. Shan't we, Perry?"

"Yes, duck. Anything you say. I remember in Yokohama, there's a geisha palace. I've heard it said that they thrash the girls' bare feet with bamboo canes if they aren't obliging to customers. Which just shows that there's two sides to every story." He pushed his hair out of his eyes. "There's one side, and there's the other side. Like young Pat wanting to go out and earn her own living. Some would say it was all right, and others –"

"I shall try in Falmouth first," said Pat. "But if nothing

turns up here I shall try somewhere else. I'm fairly good with my fingers and there might be an opportunity at somewhere like Martins or Crosbies."

"No cause to hurry," said Mrs. Veal. "Your father. Dead only a little while. I don't think . . . would have liked . . ."

But this time she had definitely chosen the wrong appeal. Patricia said: "I'm not concerned with anything my father would have liked."

Aunt Madge rose slowly, and her pince-nez wobbled a little on the top of the monument. She took away Perry's plate before he had quite wiped up all the gravy and began to stack the dishes.

"In that case . . . nothing further . . . Nothing Hi can say . . . One goes one's own way . . . regardless. Naturally I . . ." She mumbled on for some moments and her voice mixed up with the clack-clack of the plates.

"What's for after?" Perry asked, trying to smooth things over. "Lemon pud? D'you like lemon pud, boy? Don't tell me, I believe you hate it. It always reminds me of an African native I knew once. His head had been burned in a bush fire and all his hair was gone –"

Pat got up from her chair and went up to Aunt Madge and kissed her soft loose cheek.

"No offence, Mother Madge. Nothing against *you,* you know. Besides . . ." After a pause she went on: "Besides, it may be weeks and weeks before I'm off your hands in any case. So cheer up."

The pause had been occasioned by the kiss. As she withdrew her lips Anthony saw a peculiar expression cross the girl's face and disappear. It was as if she had had a sudden twinge of pain or distaste . . . or it might even have been one of presentiment.

After dinner, in the privacy of her own bedroom, Pat stared at the reflection of her flushed face. She felt bitterly rebellious and bitterly unhappy. With this morning's tide Ned had gone, perhaps for weeks, perhaps not to return. Now she was alone, desperately alone.

She did not regret her refusal of last evening; she felt she had done right; but that did not comfort her loneliness now; rather did it accentuate it, for a woman does not think the worse of any man for being in love with her and wishing to marry her, and these last few days Ned had been her only companion, the only one she could trust and to some extent confide in. Anthony, of course, remained, and in a way his friendship was the most reliable of all because his devotion was without any thought of personal profit. She would not forget his work this morning when, but for him, the writing might have been there until midday for everyone to see. But you could not talk to an eleven-year-old boy in quite the same way as you could to an adult.

She wondered, as she had wondered several times during the last week or so, what it was in her character which made her rebel against so many of the things which the average person, the average girl, accepted as a matter of course. Was there some perversity in her nature which prevented her from living a normal life? Above all, in all her actions of the last six months, was *she* in the wrong? Pat had a reasonable belief in her own judgment, but she could not help but think of the Irishman who said all the regiment was out of step but himself.

In the first place she supposed she should have put affection for and obedience to her father above an abstract love of justice in the case of the wounded Dutchman. Then again filial piety should have prevented her from going against her father's wishes by marrying Tom. Or, if she had married Tom, she should have accepted such dispositions as he had made for their married life meekly and without criticism. Other women did. When you accepted a man in marriage you did so for better or worse; you automatically transferred your fidelity from one man to another. Henceforward husband came before father. It was like changing situations. In either case the man was not open to criticism.

Or was this a jaundiced view of the matter? Were they truly right and she wrong? Perhaps the rest of the regiment were not entirely mistaken in their views. Between a man and a woman who loved each other there was often a sort of sex loyalty which went beyond mere personal judgment. There was something rather admirable in the type of patriot who in a crisis said, "My country, right or wrong." So, in married life or in family relationship, was there not something equally admirable in the woman who . . .

Yes, she thought; in times of crisis, yes. But there was nothing so admirable in the patriot who said, "My country,

141

right at all times." The best type of patriot was surely the man who would always stand by his country in a pinch but reserved the right to his own judgment when the pinch was over. Why then could a woman not reserve a similar right?

The point was, of course, to define exactly what was a crisis. She had certainly not seen the incident of the Dutchman as such at the time, but from the immense consequences following it she was prepared to admit her mistake. And the analogy of a crisis did not quite work out in her relations with Tom. A sudden incompatibility had emerged, had hardened, and she had come to see that it was insurmountable. In such circumstances, was the patriot justified in leaving his country?

She unpinned her crisp thick hair and let it fall about her shoulders; then she began to brush it with a measured sweep which she often found soothing. But nothing seemed to have the right effect this afternoon and presently she gave up and sat on the bed.

She supposed that the fate of all rebels was loneliness. In a sense she had felt herself to be a rebel all her life, she had felt always a reluctance to bow heedlessly to the things other people bowed to. Without conceit, she had known there was a difference between herself and most of the people she had met. She moved quicker and thought quicker. Often in conversation she had found herself running on ahead like a child before its grandparents, coming back to pick them up, then running on again. And often she chafed at the delay. But always she had cherished, as a sort of most-prized possession, a sense of personal freedom. That it was a spiritual rather than a material freedom did not seem to matter. It had been there for her to fall back on in the privacy of her own heart.

Not until this year had the material dependence come into conflict with this independence of spirit; but once the struggle was joined it had seemed vitally necesssary to her that there should be no compromise.

And so far there had been no compromise. But she felt that she now had arrayed against her all the forces of precedent and public opinion. The struggle would be long and hard, and she was not enjoying it. She wanted only to be happy and free and to live on terms of friendship with everyone. Essentially there was no one less quarrelsome than she was if life was only prepared to concede her a measure of liberty and self-respect.

She got up impatiently, picked up a towel and went to the bathroom, where she bathed her hands and face in cold water. Back in her room, she put on a different frock and put up her hair. In opening one of the drawers to take out a brooch she saw the letter which she had found on her dressing-table a week ago.

She picked it up and unfolded it, stared at it a moment with a queer sense of guilt as if by even regarding it she were being disloyal to herself.

Dear Pat [it ran]:
I have made a number of attempts to begin this letter and each time have torn it up to start afresh, faced with an extraordinary sense of difficulty in trying to express my true feelings about Saturday night.

First, let me make it clear that I'm more sorry than I can say if the disturbance I started in any way hastened your father's death. He did not like me because I was a lawyer and because I wanted to take you away from him. But I could sympathize with him most sincerely in the second particular, and I only felt deep sorrow on hearing he was dead.

But it is not so much of that as of what came afterwards that I want to write – of what passed between us.

Regret – the word springs to one's mind and conveys nothing. Nor would it be true to use that word alone. Oh, yes, regret enters into it. I should regret it for ever if hope for a reconciliation between us had been further squandered by what happened. But if reconciliation was already past, then there was nothing to lose, and some pagan pleasure makes a mockery of all the polite emotions. Shakespeare wrote of taking a woman 'in her heart's extremest hate, with curses in her mouth, tears in her eyes. . . .' I know what that means now.

But unfortunately I still love you, and love, I found, is not satisfied with the fruits of conquest – rich though they may be. So even conquest was not for me.

For excuse, if excuses are wanted, remember that you lied to me. There: is that a pretty plea? You had been with another man, giving him your companionship, and I had not seen you for weeks. Then when we were alone

143

for a few minutes you lied to me about your ankle and would have been safely away but for the self-locking door.

Perhaps we should not have married. Love doesn't always go with affinity – sometimes not even with liking, for you certainly seem to dislike me with a will.

As I told you, I'm resigning my partnership in Harvey & Harris. I feel I want a change, and feel I must get away from this district now. If we have to be separated then I want the separation to be a wider one.

I should like you to know that if ever you are in need of help and feel you can accept mine, I shall be more than happy to do anything I can.

Believe me,
Ever your
Tom

For some time after reading the letter Pat stood before the dressing-table playing with a string of pearls which had been her mother's. She had dropped the letter back into the drawer, but now she picked it up again and stared at the envelope, turning it over as if in speculation.

With a sharp, painful impulse, she grasped the letter and ripped it across and across. With the need to destroy it still on her she struggled with the pieces, but her fingers were not strong enough to tear it again.

As sharply as she had begun she dropped the bits back into the drawer and turned to the window, staring blindly out. Tears formed in her eyes and she blinked them away. They formed again and this time overflowed upon her thick eyelashes and presently began to drip upon her cheeks. It was the first time she had cried since her father died.

CHAPTER NINETEEN

Patricia's attempts to find work for herself did not meet with conspicuous success. She had never realized before what small opportunity there was for an intelligent, energetic girl to earn her own living, to become self-supporting in a decent respectable business-like way. One had to be a nursery governess or a sempstress or a milliner, working endless hours for a starvation wage. It was as if the world had entered into a conspiracy to prevent the independent young woman from breaking away from the herd, so that she found herself hemmed about and compelled to conform. For the first time Patricia found herself becoming a rebel against the whole structure of a society which condoned this state of affairs.

Towards the end of the third week she was surprised to receive a letter from an old school friend in Truro.

Dear Pat [it ran]:

I don't know if Maud Richards is mistaken, but she told me yesterday you were looking for something to do. Perhaps you'll forgive me for being nosy, but do you know that a Miss Gawthorpe who runs a private school here, is looking for an assistant? I don't know what the qualifications must be; Miss Gawthorpe was telling Mummie the other day that it was not degrees she was particular about – probably she doesn't want to pay for them – but chiefly she needed 'a young lady of good appearance' who could help her manage the younger children and take them in a few elementary subjects.

In case this appeals to you her address is Green Lane, Truro. I don't suppose you could get back to Falmouth at night, but it would be nice having you living near here.

Affectionately,

SYLVIA KENT

In haste Patricia wrote to the address supplied, using her maiden name and glossing over such facts in her life as seemed likely not to appeal to a lady of Miss Gawthorpe's calling. Three weeks ago she would have scorned the idea of sailing under compromise colours, but disappointment rubs off the sharp edges of integrity, and she had seen too often the change which came over a prospective employer's face when she explained the fact that she was married but separated from her husband.

Three days later a reply came asking her to call, and she left for Truro by an early train.

Miss Gawthorpe was large and formidable but not shrewish. She was clearly the sort of person who formed her judgments rapidly and she seemed at once to take a liking to Pat. The salary, although poor, included meals and sleeping accommodation at the house, and Pat saw that she would just be able to manage. In any case she was

145

so delighted at the offer that no thought of quibbling entered her head. She arrived home bursting with the news that on Saturday next by the four o'clock train she was leaving Falmouth to take up her new duties.

Nobody looked very happy at the news. Widow Veal, as she was now generally called, had had a trying day with Mr. Cowdray. So many details of the estate still needed settling, and Aunt Louisa, true to her promise, was doing her best to put all possible obstacles in the way of their being settled. She had some papers connected with the land Joe had owned, land inherited from his father, and these she could not be persuaded to part with until legal action to recover them was actually put in motion. Lengthy letters were still passing almost daily between Aunt Louisa's Mr. Crabbe and Aunt Madge's Mr. Cowdray.

But despite all efforts to the contrary, the time steadily approached when everything should legally become Aunt Madge's, and Louisa Veal persisted in her efforts in the light of faith rather than reason. About a week after the reading of the Will another Will had been produced by a solicitor at Helston, dated five years earlier and leaving the bulk of the property to Joe's first wife, "in trust" for his daughter Patricia; and this had encouraged Aunt Louisa in the belief that there must be a later Will as well as an earlier one. No man, she felt, who had so vented his spite at a sudden quarrel could so criminally neglect the decencies as to fail to register the reconciliation in a like manner.

Her latest idea was that she or her representatives should be allowed to search the house for such a document, and this Aunt Madge statuesquely refused to concede. It was against all right, she was heard to mutter. The idea offended her to the core. She would sooner die, she implied, than let that woman come into her house again, picking over her personal belongings like a carrion crow. Mr. Cowdray, growing sick of the endless altercation, suggested that he might be able to make some capital out of the concession if she were to permit it as a gesture. He might even wring some promise from Mr. Crabbe that, if such permission were granted, he would persuade his client to drop the quarrel.

But so far Aunt Madge would not move an inch. The position was at a deadlock. When Aunt Madge was at a deadlock she looked it. For the last two days life had congealed in her and words emerged from that little pursed mouth reluctantly, like slow drops of wax from a melting figure.

So her reception of Patricia's news was a preoccupied and a grudging one. She seemed to feel first that she was too busy to be bothered with Pat's affairs and later, when the news had sunk in, to feel a grievance against the girl for adding one more trouble to the sum of her burdens.

Aunt Madge was getting fat. She had put on weight noticeably in the weeks since her husband died. One day when she sat down to supper Perry had jocularly remarked: "Stap me, Madge, but if you go on at this rate you'll be a big woman when you grow up!" But he did not repeat the joke. Sometimes lately one might have thought that the irreverent Perry went slightly in awe of his sister-in-law. He broke out from time to time, but on the whole, especially where the decencies of mournings were concerned, he increasingly took his cue from her. Since the long bout of drinking at the time of Joe's death Anthony had not seen him drunk once, nor had anyone's sleep been disturbed by hearing *The Black Hunter* sung in a wavering voice as its owner stumbled to bed in the small hours.

As for Anthony, Patricia's appointment struck him almost with the force of a second bereavement. As the term was getting on and no more mention had been made of his going to school he had begun to hope that his affairs would be entirely overlooked until after Christmas. From the time of Ned's departure he had had a good deal of Pat's company and in it had found a real compensation for his disappointment in not joining his father. But if Pat went – with Pat gone – his life would be so dreary as to be scarcely supportable. Even school might be preferable to the emptiness of the days which lay ahead. When the time came for her to leave, as it did all too soon, he stood with his uncle on the station platform and tried his hardest to put something of his dejection into words, but found to his own annoyance that he could only stumble and mutter before her and hope that his face expressed what his tongue could not.

Patricia had her own private intentions. She did not feel that Madge or Perry had any real affection for the boy, and if his father still failed to send for him and if she was happy in her new situation, she thought there was a possibility of persuading her stepmother to consent to his being sent to the school at which she taught. Accommodation might be found in the house for him and he might even be able partly to work his passage by doing odd jobs.

But all that lay in the very doubtful future. Any of a dozen obstacles might emerge to prevent it, and she had no intention of raising hopes on such a flimsy foundation.

"You'll hardly notice I'm gone," she assured him. "I shall be back at the week-ends and it's only a short time to Christmas when I shall have three weeks' holiday. So there's no need at all for you to look despondent."

"No," said Anthony. "It'll be quiet, though."

"Well, make it noisy, then. Uncle Perry will go on walks with you, won't you, Perry?"

"Ugh," said Perry. "I'm past my walking days. Though at his age I could do fifteen or twenty miles without turning a hair. I well remember in the Uganda —"

"It's time I got in. You'll write to me, both of you, won't you? I really don't know why you both need look so glum. I'm the one who ought to look glum, leaving home and ... Oh, well, this is the time when ... I shall be glad when this is over!"

There was a slight tremor in her voice. She put a hand on Perry's shoulder and kissed him on the cheek. He kissed her in return twice rather noisily, and pinched her arms and eventually released her. Then he pushed back his hair and laughed to disguise the pleasure he had got out of it.

The guard whistled.

Patricia turned on Anthony. He put out a hand woodenly, but she drew him to her and kissed him, not on the cheek but on the mouth. For about a second the world lit up for the boy. Then she stepped into the carriage and a moment later the train was drawing noisily out of the station.

"Well," said Perry, "a rattling good job your aunt didn't see that, eh?" He laughed one of his old infectious laughs as they left the station, but his mouth twitched a little as if he had bitten on something that wasn't there.

"Why?" asked Anthony, still warm inside.

"Oh ... You wouldn't understand. What it is to be young." Perry sighed and stared a second at the tall boy by his side. "Wish I was young again. Innocent as a new-born infant. Clean as a baby's whistle. That's what I like to see."

"Perhaps I know more than you think," said the boy.

"Ah. Good luck to you if you do. Then why ask me silly questions?"

"Well, I don't see why Aunt Madge should object to us saying good-bye to Pat."

"Us? Ha, ha! *You* can do what you like, boy; Auntie won't shed a tear."

Silence fell as they began the long walk home. It seemed a long time since that first walk through the town on the day of his arrival with Patricia at his side. He wished that she was here now, not chuffering away in the direction of Truro. Then it had been high summer. Now winter was on hand and the sea in the harbour was grey and choppy. He glanced at the man walking beside him. Perhaps it was fancy, but Uncle Perry seemed recently to have lost something of his buccaneering look. Instead of being a hunter, you could fancy that he was now one of the hunted.

If Anthony had ever paused to look back over the weeks which followed Pat's departure he might have seen them as a bridge between two periods. The first was the period of decay, when the restaurant was shut and all life and vitality had gone out of the house and nothing at all seemed to happen; the second was the period of crisis when all that had been festering under the surface since Joe's death came to a head. But Anthony never did look back on this interim period. To him it was a time best forgotten.

To him it was a series of dull, grey, lonely days during which he slept and rose and washed and ate and pottered about the house, staring at the whip of the rain on the windows or going out for a brisk but dismal duty walk under heavy skies with a sharp wind cutting round the corners, or shopping for Aunt Madge with a huge wicker basket which now was never more than half filled while the shopkeepers rubbed their hands and treated him with respect though all the time out of the corners of their eyes they were watching him queerly. A period, he would have said, when nothing worth noting happened.

He would have been wrong. Had he been a little less unobservant, a little more aware of the undercurrents moving around him, he would have marked a number of minor events which showed which way the stream was running.

First there was the dismissal of Fanny. This happened so quickly that he could hardly believe his eyes. One day she was there, the next gone. Nor could he obtain from either of the adults an explanation for her going. When he put his questions Aunt Madge turned up her eyes and Uncle Perry grinned and shook his head behind his sister-in-law's back. Obviously she was not dispensed with for reasons of economy or because she was superfluous to the running of the household, as the two boy waiters had been when the restaurant closed. She had been very useful about the house, and the house was not the same for her absence. Only when he learned that she had been given a week's money in lieu of notice did he begin to suspect that she had been dismissed for some offence. Perhaps she had been caught stealing knives.

Anthony began to feel that the house had too much in common with the story of the Ten Little Nigger Boys. First Uncle Joe, and then there were seven. Second the two boy waiters, and then there were five. Next Patricia, and then there were four. After this, little Fanny, and now there were three. Anthony wondered when it would be his turn.

It could not come too soon. After Fanny's departure Aunt Madge took to staying in bed still longer in the mornings, and often the boy was the only one stirring before ten o'clock. Breakfast was not until eleven when Perry would join them, jovial but unshaven. Whereas in the old days Mrs. Veal was always cooking, the closing of the restaurant appeared to have robbed her of the incentive, and meals were now designed for the least possible trouble.

There did not seem much prospect at present of his becoming another little Nigger Boy, he thought. His aunt had never been one for going out much, but another phenomenon of these strange weeks was that if she did leave the house Anthony must go with her. Not Perry but Anthony. He spent many a dreary hour in the dusty anteroom of Mr. Cowdray's office while she conferred inside, later to walk back through the main street adjusting his pace to her slow, heaven-ordained progress. At first she wanted to take his arm, but he contrived to fall out of step so often that eventually she abandoned the idea.

Twice every Sunday he had to go to church with her. Again the slow parade through the narrow main street, dressed in their Sunday best, people nodding and wishing them good morning or good evening. She always insisted on sitting in one of the front pews and in staying behind to speak to the vicar after the service. Then came the slow walk back with more nodding and an occasional pause to pass a word, usually arriving home to find that Perry had burned the dinner or let the supper potatoes boil dry. Then Perry had to tell exactly what he had been doing while they were out and Aunt Madge would chudder away at her grievances all through dinner.

Anthony often thought of the remark made by Perry after they had seen Pat off, and he came to notice that if they were all three sitting in the parlour together in the evening and Perry rose or shifted his chair, Aunt Madge would at once look up from her knitting and adjust her eye-glasses and never take her gaze from him until he sat down again. Sometimes, too, she quietly watched him from a distance when he was washing up or sitting in his shirt sleeves in the kitchen smoking and reading his paper. Her face was like that of a plump Persian cat which reflected the temporary lights and shades of the outer world but gave away little of what was happening inside.

One evening they sent him out for beer. He ran across to The Ship and Sailor on the corner of the main street and found the bar crowded. Mr. Treharne was behind the bar and he took the boy's order while talking to another man. Only when he handed the jug back over the counter, did he turn upon Anthony an inquisitive, knowing look.

"Don't see much of your Uncle Perry these days, boy," he said. "He's well, I hope?"

Anthony was getting used to sly glances.

"Yes, thank you." Politely he passed over the money.

"Used to be one of our best customers," said Mr. Treharne. "Folks' habits change, I suppose."

"Can't come out for his own beer now," said one of the men at the bar. " 'As to send the nipper."

Another said: "Reckon he's found a pair of apron strings lyin' around."

There was a general laugh at this.

"*And* they ain't his mother's."

With cheeks burning Anthony waited patiently for his change.

"Ever 'eard o' the Table of Affinity, eh, boy?" said the first.

He pretended not to hear.

"Go an' ask your uncle. Maybe he do know . . ."

"Deceased wife's sister or deceased husband's brother, 'tes all the same. A pity for she. They can't call the banns."

"Reckon they've done all but."

Another roar of laughter greeted this.

"What's it like in thur, boy, eh?" said the wag. "Must be a cosy nest. Think there's room for me?"

"Let the boy alone," growled someone. "'Tesen't narthing to do with him."

"No," said the wag. "' 'Oo blames the gooseberry fur 'anging on the bush?'"

With the laughter following in gusts Anthony pushed his way out through the crowd. In the welcome darkness outside he stopped a moment and found that he was trembling all over.

CHAPTER TWENTY

Patricia settled into her new work very quickly. She found her occupation, though always making demands on her nervous energy, curiously restful from one point of view. It was impersonal in the sense of having no concern with her private affairs, and after the hurly burly of the two previous months she gladly sank her individuality into that of the tireless Miss Gawthorpe.

She did not go home each week-end. She made the excuse that she could not get away, but this was not the real reason. Having got this post under a mild form of false pretences, and finding the work not unpleasant, she lived in a daily but decreasing terror of being found out. There were, she knew, people in Falmouth who would "feel it their duty" to write to Miss Gawthorpe if they knew she was employing "that Patricia Veal." Her chief hope of escape was to keep out of their sight.

There occurred, however, a half term, and with it no reasonable way of avoiding a two-day holiday. She found the house dingier and more untidy and not so clean and her stepmother larger and more puffy, like a cake with too much yeast in it. Perry's chuckle was as frequent as ever, but was on a furtive note and there had been an increase in that curious nervous twitch about his mouth as if his upper lip were biting upon something which could not be properly secured. Anthony looked thin and self-contained and was less free in his manner, especially towards her. The candid gaze had gone from his blue eyes.

At the first opportunity she brought up the subject of his schooling with Madge.

Madge hedged. Or rather she created vacuums around isolated words, which was her way of being non-committal. Pat asked if she had heard from his father again and Madge said, no. Pat had the impression that she was still hedging. What did they propose to do with him after Christmas? Had they made any inquiries at Falmouth Grammar School? Madge turned up her eyes and said something about Perry having it in hand.

"Oh, Perry," said Patricia. "You can't really leave anything to him. Not, I mean, like fixing up a boy's schooling. Isn't there some law nowadays about children *having* to go to school? He's missed one term already."

Her stepmother said something indistinct about being very well aware of the law. She gave the impression that she would make a move almost any time now. There was clearly no point in spending a lot of money on the boy if he was likely to be moving again. Really just a question of finding a stop-gap.

This seemed the chance the girl had been waiting for. "If it's only that – and of course you're probably right – why not see about sending him to Miss Gawthorpe's? There are boys of twelve and thirteen there, and we do teach them manners, which is more than some schools do."

Madge fumbled with her cameo brooch. In the deep lace folds of her dress something rose and fell and a faint breath of a sigh escaped.

"Away from home ... Oh, no. My responsibility. No mother. I couldn't ..."

153

"I should be there to look after him."

"Oh, no . . . The travelling and . . ."

"I believe Miss Gawthorpe might put him up. There is a bedroom vacant there, and I think she might be glad of someone to help in small ways. I haven't actually asked her –"

"I should think not . . ."

"I haven't actually asked her, but in that case I think she might be content with the ordinary day fee."

Mrs. Veal shook her head. "Oh, no . . ."

Patricia could always understand and appreciate a reasoned argument, but she still had a small girl's dislike of an unreasoned refusal.

"Why not?"

"Useful . . . he's useful here. Fanny has gone. A great deal to do. Your uncle naturally isn't . . . And I . . . Hi am not too well. Severe headaches. Rheumatism. I sometimes wonder how I carry on. A great help . . . Anthony. Besides . . . my nephew. Responsibility . . . And he's happy here."

"Why not put the idea to him and see if he likes it?"

Madge's chins shook above her lace collar. "Children. No idea . . . what is best for them . . . adult matter."

"I suppose you think I'm still a child," said Patricia, feeling angry. It was not altogether being frustrated in this way that irritated her. But Aunt Madge seemed to have become so much more pontifical since she went away. This absurd dignity had been growing worse ever since she came in for the money."

"Not at all," said Madge. "But the matter. Hi must decide."

"Well, do for heaven's sake do something," the girl said, swallowing her annoyance. "If you won't send him to Miss Gawthorpe's send him somewhere so that he has an interest in life. I don't think he looks as well as he did, and it surely can't be good for him just to mope about the house all day."

"We will decide. I will decide . . . as I think best. I will think . . . Hasty decisions never . . . Plenty of time. Christmas is . . ."

So Patricia left on the Monday morning without being able to fulfil the promise she had made herself. She felt thwarted and unreasonable, and vowed that if it were not for Anthony, Falmouth and stepmother would see no sight of her during the Christmas holidays. Something of her disappointment showed in her parting with Anthony, and he for his part felt separated from her by far more than a few weeks of idleness and doubt. This time they did not kiss, but shook hands quietly, and very soon he was walking back through the town alone with his own thoughts.

Some time after Patricia went Aunt Madge finally agreed to allow Louisa's representatives – not Louisa – to make a search of the house for any later Will which Joe might have made. Mr. Cowdray put this to Madge as a reasonable way of settling the dispute, but perhaps what weighed most with her was his remark that rumours were going about the town that Miss Veal had been unfairly dispossessed, and this seemed the obvious way of quietening them. Madge for all her dignity was very sensitive to public opinion.

The first Anthony knew of it was a suggestion from Aunt Madge that he should go across the river to St. Mawes and take his lunch with him. The idea was such an odd one coming from her that he was too surprised to raise any objection, so the picnic was arranged. As an outing for a warm June day there was a good deal to commend it, but undertaken in November it was a fiasco. Having eaten his sandwiches much too early, he mooned about St. Mawes gazing in at the handsome houses and gardens of the retired people who lived there, then took an earlier ferry back than he was expected to take and arrived at his home to find some of the rooms practically dismantled and his uncle and aunt arguing among the debris.

She greeted him very sourly and Perry informed him that his aunt had decided on a day's spring cleaning and that he was lucky to have missed it. This did not look quite like spring cleaning as he understood it. There were no buckets of water or brushes or dusters about, and nothing looked any fresher, but he spent the rest of the afternoon and evening putting things back and was told just before bedtime that on the following day the house was to be gone through by Miss Veal's representatives in case Uncle Joe had made a later Will.

It seemed to him that this would result in all the things he had put back being pulled out again and that they might have saved themselves the trouble. But of course they were such a house-proud pair that they naturally wouldn't want the searchers to find any dust.

It was on the tip of his tongue to remind them to look behind the picture in the office where he had once seen his uncle put a document, but he supposed that would be one of the first places they would have looked as soon as Joe died. Probably Perry was looking there the morning when he had wakened him. By now he had become quite used to the smell of Uncle Joe's tobacco coming from Uncle Perry's pipe.

He still wondered sometimes who had made the hole in the floor and when. The hole had not just happened of its own accord, and the cork was a biggish one which had been cut to fit. He wondered if Perry had ever had the room. Several times he had intended to mention it to Tom Harris, but each time it slipped his memory. Last time he went to Penryn there had been another man there who seemed to know a good deal about his household, and he had not altogether liked that.

Then by chance he met little Fanny. The men had come to make the search: Mr. Cowdray, an auctioneer from Penryn and his assistant; and he had gone out for a walk, taking the road through the town and towards the sea front.

He had not seen Fanny since the day she left and, having always associated her with a cap and apron, he scarcely recognized the little figure in brown with the curly feathers round the collar and the prim little muff. She would have passed him by with her eyes down, but he stopped and said, "Hullo, Fanny," and asked her how she was getting on. She looked at him aslant, as so many people did nowadays and said, "Oh, all right."

"Sorry you left," he said awkwardly. "What did you go so quickly for?"

"Well, I ain't one to stay where I'm not wanted."

"I've got no one to sew my buttons on now," he said.

She looked less unfriendly.

"I'm home, helping mother. I ain't going out to service again, not just yet. You got anybody in my place?"

"No."

Anthony put his hands in his pockets and kicked at a

stone. "Often thought of asking you something," he said. "Who had my bedroom before I came?"

Fanny looked at him sharply. "Nobody. Why?"

"Oh, nothing."

Fanny fumbled with the parcels in her basket.

"Did Uncle Perry ever sleep there?" he asked.

"No, he didn't, and you don't need to mention yer Uncle Perry to me! Anyway, I was only there eleven month, and that was a month too long. After Mr. Veal died ..." Her eyes glinted a moment and she looked suddenly grown up. " 'Twas the cook's room. Afore my time. When I went there there wasn't no cook."

"Did Aunt Madge have it when she was cook, then?"

" 'Ow should I know? I suppose so. Yes, I should think. A sight better'n the poky little 'ole they gave me. *She'd* see to that. Don't *she* sew your buttons on for you?"

"Um? No. No, I manage myself."

"I suppose *she's* just the same, eh? Waggin' about like a queen."

He was surprised at the hostility which had come into the girl's voice.

"Oh, she's all right," he said defensively. "Why shouldn't she be?"

"Why shouldn't she be! 'Deed, yes! She's fell on 'er feet 'andsome, 'asn't she?"

"I don't see what you mean."

She tossed her head. "Well, you wouldn't, would you? You're 'er nephew. You'd stick up for 'er if she was 'anged for 'igh treason."

"No, I wouldn't," he said doggedly.

"You say you wouldn't, but you would. I know. Hoity-toity, off we go to church together!"

The boy felt himself going red. "It's nothing to do with you, anyway. What's wrong with us going to church? You've only got a grudge against her because she gave you the sack."

"No, I 'aven't. I wouldn't lower meself."

"If you haven't, what did she sack you for then?"

Fanny's eyes went smaller. Her thin face pinched itself up like the closing of a hand.

"She didn't 'appen to tell you that, I s'pose."

"No."

"Well, why don't you ask 'er instead of me? Try it on, Mr. Clever, an' see what she says."

"Afraid to tell me?" he challenged.

"I don't tell things like that to kids. You be careful of your aunt. She's got a dirty mind, she 'as."

"It must have been something awful you did."

" 'Twasn't nothing of the sort. 'Twas 'er dirty mind an' nothing more to it. 'Er and Mr. Perry between 'em. Wasn't my asking, I can tell you."

"Didn't you want to leave?"

"Oh, I should've lef' whether or no! Didn't like it well enough the way it was going."

"What happened?"

She hesitated and again arranged her parcels. "I'll be going now. I got to go. Ma's expecting me."

"Go on," he said persuasively. "Tell us. Be a sport. Wasn't it your fault at all?"

This cunning appeal was too much for Fanny.

"Course it wasn't! You know what your uncle is. 'E started tickling me. Same as 'e's done before; same as 'e's done to you; there weren't nothing to it. But she came round the door quiet like, and she was *mad*. Thought she was goin' to 'ave a fit. I'm well out of that 'ouse, I can tell you!" Her eyes, in which there was a trace of embarrassment, searched his thoughtful face for blushes or condemnation, but this time neither came. "You know now, Mr. Clever. But don't say it was my fault, because it weren't. And if Mr. Veal'd been alive nothing wouldn't've happened." She paused again, waiting for his response, seeking it because it did not come. "You're welcome to your nice big bedroom at that 'ouse. I wouldn't 'ave it as a gift, I can tell you. Never know what's goin' on in that 'ouse, do you?"

With this parting shot, and still unsatisfied, Fanny gave her basket a contemptuous jerk and went on her way.

When he returned home, studiously late this time, the searchers were gone, and he could tell from the faintly self-righteous expression showing over the top of Aunt Madge's boned collar that they had been unsuccessful.

At supper Perry laughed and joked like his old self, but Anthony's responses were slow. He was still thinking about what little Fanny had said. Sometimes he turned his thoughtful blue eyes on the jovial man at the table, and his mind conjured up the scene Fanny had described. That she might have been lying never occurred to him; the incident rang true. It had happened like that.

After a time he began to think of the spy-hole in his bedroom, and his eyes turned on his aunt, whose knife and fork were working up and down like pistons. Her table manners were studiously refined in company but not so select in the bosom of her family, and her plump little cheeks were puffed out with what she was chewing.

Somehow, almost in the last few hours, the matter of the envelope in the picture had become real to Anthony. For a long time he had forgotten the incident, even when there was the wrangle over the Will; or perhaps it would be more true to say that the memory had remained at the bottom of his mind as an unimportant one. Lately it had come to the surface, floating about without serious or connected thought. He had felt that someone besides Uncle Joe was bound to know of the existence of the cache and to have examined its contents. Now he began to think he had taken too much for granted.

He wondered what to do. He might just say at the end of the meal: "Oh, about this Will; I suppose you've looked behind the oil-painting in the office, haven't you?"

But that put the initiative in their hands. He didn't fancy that. He might leave the issue three weeks until Pat came again. Or he might ask Tom Harris's advice. But Tom, he knew, was away, staying with his sister at Maenporth. He wouldn't be back for a week.

There was of course one other way. He could look for himself.

CHAPTER TWENTY-ONE

Ever since he came to Falmouth there had been nights on which he had been sleepy and others when he could not settle off and tossed and turned for hours. This was one of the latter, so he had no difficulty in keeping awake until half-past eleven, which was about the customary time for the others to retire. From then on, however, began a struggle. The minutes were dragging at his eyelids, and although he felt a bit strung up, yet at the same time he was falling asleep. He had had to lie in the dark all the time, because from the bottom of the stairs you could see a light under his door.

Soon after twelve he found he couldn't wait any longer. He lit the candle and climbed out of bed, putting on his coat and trousers over his night shirt and taking care to avoid the loose boards as he moved about. Then, just to be on the safe side, he slid under the bed and pulled out the cork. There was no light below.

Opening his door was difficult, for if it was done slowly the creak was enough to wake the dead, and if it was done too quickly the sudden draught made the upper sash of the window rattle violently. But he had practised earlier that evening and he was successful in making no noise. He wedged it open with a spare sock and, shielding the flame of the candle with his hand, began to go down.

With no idea of ever having to make a secret descent he had often played at going up and down without treading on a creaky stair, and he knew by heart the numbers to avoid: one, three, nine and twelve going down; four, seven, thirteen and fifteen coming up.

On the landing below it was necessary to pass Aunt Madge's and Uncle Perry's doors, for these two doors faced each other and the office was between Aunt Madge's room and the drawing-room, from which a door led off into it. As he had only been in the office once there was no means of knowing whether this door creaked; there was no guarantee that it was not locked, but he had seen the adults go in and out freely during the daytime.

With his hand stretched out to grasp the knob he realized that the best means of entry for him was the parlour. This would mean passing two doors instead of one but would keep him further away from Aunt Madge, and he did know that the drawing-room door did not squeak.

He slipped into the sitting-room, and as he did so the French clock under its glass shade on the mantelshelf chimed the half-hour after midnight. The room still had an occupied smell, and some of the ash from Perry's pipe lay in a grey heap upon the top bar of the grate. The embroidered bag with Aunt Madge's sewing in it was slumped upon a chair with something of the shapelessness of its owner. When he put back the bound volume of *The Quiver* this evening he had not turned the key in the bookcase and the door gaped an inch open.

160

After a pause to gather his courage he turned the knob of the door leading to the office, and the door to his relief opened easily and silently. Feeling uncomfortable about his way of escape, he left this open behind him and set the candle down on the office desk. The picture of the old lady faced him on the opposite wall. It was the head and shoulders of a little grey-haired woman in a lace cap and her small black eyes seemed to be fixed upon something just over Anthony's shoulder, as if there were a person standing behind him. He saw that he would need a chair.

He carried one across. He felt very uncomfortable about the curtains not being drawn, but he could not move them without risking noise and the window looked out over the harbour. No man was tall enough to stand with his feet in the mud and stare in at a second-storey window; nevertheless one could not get over the feeling that someone might.

The chair creaked under his weight and the picture-hook nearly fell off the rail, but at last he was safely down with the old lady between his hands.

He carried her to the table which had once been littered with papers and set her face downwards. There was no obvious catch as he had expected or anything which suggested to the casual gaze that the back was detachable. He tried to remember what he had seen his uncle do. There was no glass in the frame. He unscrewed the two hook by which the picture was hung but this had no effect. Then he turned the old lady over to face him and the painting and the back fell out of its frame upon the table.

The noise made him sweat, and little pricklings of nervousness ran out to his finger-tips like pins and needles. After a moment he summoned up the courage to continue and as he lifted the picture away from its back he saw the envelope which his uncle had put there.

So his latest idea had been the best. He had been wrong not to think of it before, not to look before. Perhaps he was still going too fast. This was probably something to do with the shipping line; he had seen ...

He slid the document out of its long envelope and opened it with a crackle of parchment. He read hastily through about half and that was enough. He put his find on the table and picked up the frame to put it back, his mind already leaping ahead to what he should do next.

The point was, whom should he trust? His duty was to hand it to Aunt Madge, his inclination, to keep it until Pat came home. Or again he might take it tomorrow to Aunt Louisa. But he didn't like her well enough, for all that she seemed to be working with Pat's good at heart. And taking it to her was too much like rank treason. Aunt Madge and Uncle Perry looked after him and were not unkind. They might be as peculiar as some people thought, but they were honest in all their dealings and they had been kind to Pat and not wanted her to leave home. Since Pat left, Aunt Madge had made quite a fuss of him; the fact that he could not somehow take to her was surely his fault, not hers. To give this document to the opposite side was a rank betrayal he could not quite face.

He might let Tom see it, or first tell him about it, or better still go straight to Mr. Cowdray.

But that was obviously showing a distrust for Aunt Madge. She would see that he had gone behind her back, and it would be horribly uncomfortable facing her afterwards. He could hardly go on living here unless he took the Will to her first thing in the morning.

Anthony began to see that the possession of such a document as he had found was more of a responsibility than he had bargained for. All very well for grown-ups to make decisions, but he was so young and so alone in the world. He didn't know when his father would be able to send for him, whether he even wanted him or not. Tom did not want him; Patricia could not have him; where would he go if he left here? Why turn against the people who gave him shelter? He almost regretted having found the envelope. If he had looked and there had been nothing there, then his conscience would have been clear.

But first get the painting back. This was something over which he had not expected to have any difficulty, and not until he had tried three times to fit the back into the frame did he realize that the frame had "sprung". He broke out into a new perspiration as he failed at the fifth attempt. The only way seemed to be to take the picture and hide it and hope that no one would notice that it was missing from the wall.

"Stap me, boy; I thought you were asleep hours ago!" said a voice in his ear.

Anthony jerked his head up, and his heart and throat

congealed, so that he could not even cry out. He could only hold the table and stare at Perry and try not to fall. Perry, in a nightshirt and big coat and his black hair all towsled.

"What's the matter, boy; been sleep walking? Don't look so scary; I'm not going to eat you."

Then he saw or pretended to see for the first time the document Anthony had found in the picture. He picked it up and opened it.

"What's this, eh? Don't say it's what ... Hm. Where did you find it, in that picture? Glory be. What made you look behind old Granny. How's it work? Show me."

"I – I don't know. I – it just came to pieces. Er – Uncle Joe showed me once ... but I forgot how he did it. I –"

"What made you think there was something here? Rot me, what a place to look!"

"I ... saw Uncle Joe put something one day. It – never occurred to me it would be – anything important – till this search today. Then I thought I'd ... just look."

"Um," said Perry, staring at the paper and twitching his lips. "Can't say whether it's important or not, not just at a glance. Don't think it's much, you know. Fancy old Granny having a secret for us like that. But if you'd known the old Four-Master you'd know it was quite in keeping. Not that it's likely to be important. I'm pretty sure it's not much; but perhaps it will be as well to let old man Cowdray see it, eh, boy?" He pushed back his hair and met Anthony's gaze. "Did you read any of it?"

The boy said: "I only just glanced at the front and then I tried to put the picture back. I ... can't get it back." In order to hide his eyes he turned to the table and tried to force the picture into its frame.

"Easy does it." Perry slipped the document into his pocket and bent to help. But something had gone wrong with the frame when the back fell out. "Oh, blast that! We'll be waking the old lady. Leave it now, boy; it's time for our beauty sleep. Now if –"

"Did you see my light?" Anthony asked.

"No. You dropped something overboard, boy. Well, well, you never know what's going to turn up in this world, do you, now? Everybody searches the house and finds sweet Fanny Adams, and then you go adrift in your sleep and tickle up old Granny and out comes this. But I think it's a mare's nest, boy. I think it's nothing important. I think it's nothing much. Keep it to yourself for the time being, what?"

"Oh, yes," said Anthony.

They had come out of the office into the sitting-room. "Keep it from Aunt Madge, too, shall we?" he said in a conspiratorial whisper and dug Anthony in the ribs. "Just the two of us in the secret. Then tomorrow I'll lay off to board old Cowdray and we'll see what sort of a signal he runs up."

His manner was so friendly that Anthony felt ashamed of himself. Ashamed of himself for feeling frustrated in his purposes. He knew now that in his heart, for all his professed loyalty, he had never had the least intention of handing over to his uncle and aunt anything he found in the picture, certainly not if it was a Will. They might give him shelter and food and reasonable consideration but they did not give him confidence. He might defend them before any outsider who presumed to criticize, but he could not defend them to himself.

He did not sleep much that night, and more than once he wondered how Uncle Perry had come to hear the noise he had made with the picture frame, for Uncle Perry's bedroom was on the other side of the passage. He thought he could guess the answer to that.

The next morning *The Grey Cat* was in harbour. She had slipped in some time during the night and was a little nearer the quay than her usual anchorage.

Although he had been sorry to see her go, Anthony was far more pleased at her return. He was lonely, missed Patricia more than ever, and his meetings with Tom were too infrequent to be looked on as more than an isolated adventure. Now for a week or more there would be the gruff Ned Pawlyn to bring a breath of fresh air into the house. Never, he felt, had he so much needed it.

The captain and mate put in an appearance while he was at breakfast, and he at once dropped his knife and fork and rushed out to meet them. But it was not Aunt Madge's rebuke which made him stop and blink. Captain Stevens had as a companion a dark, thick-set man none of them had seen before.

"Morning, ma'am," said Captain Stevens, removing his cap. "This is Mr. O'Brien. Mr. Pawlyn went ashore at Hull,

He said he felt the need of a change. Morning, sir," he added, addressing Perry, who was just making a dishevelled appearance. But it was to Madge that the Captain gave his account of the voyage. Joe's widow not only held the money, she also held the reins of business, and although one or two of the older captains might feel a prejudice against dealing with a woman, there was no question of shifting any of the responsibility upon Perry. Aunt Madge was now the *J. Veal Blue Water Line*, and no one who wished to continue in her employment must make the mistake of thinking otherwise. And, however much she might neglect the re-opening of the restaurant – which entailed a resumption of the old routine of hard work – one had to admit that she seemed perfectly capable of continuing to conduct the *J. Veal Blue Water Line* on the basis that it was bequeathed to her. Captain Stevens had not been in the house ten minutes before she announced that a new cargo was waiting for him as soon as he had discharged his present one.

Four days went by after this disappointment and Perry said nothing to Anthony about the picture. Several times during the week the boy thought he saw his aunt regarding him curiously, and not once during the week did she ask him to go with her. But so far as Perry himself was concerned there was not the smallest indication that the incident had ever occurred. The boy began to wonder whether Perry intended to forget the whole occurrence and rely on his superior age and position to override any questions that were put him. If so, Anthony was determined that Uncle Perry should be mistaken.

But on the fifth day Perry came to him and waved the document in his face.

"Well, boy, we were blown off our course a bit that time. I could see it myself when I read it, but I thought 'twould be fairer not to tell you until old man Cowdray had cast his optics over it, see?"

"What is it?"

"I told your aunt. I thought it for the best after all. I thought it not important, but I thought it for the best. We took it to old Cowdray. It's what I guessed. It's a copy of the Will we already have. Just the same, word for word. See, look for yourself."

Anthony took the document and unfolded it quietly.

"Folk usually keep a copy for themselves. Solicitor makes it out same time as the original. It's for reference, d'you see?"

Anthony read through the first part of the Will. "Yes, but . . ." He broke off, keenly aware that his uncle was watching him while pretending not to. "But if it was just a copy like this, why should he put it behind the picture?" His intended question had been something quite different.

Perry chuckled and lit his pipe. "Come to that, why put anything there at all, where like as not it would never be found? You didn't know Joe as I did, boy. He'd got the mind of a squirrel. Liked hiding things. Some folks do. There was a man I knew in 'Frisco. When he died they found he'd papered his bedroom with dollar bills and stuck a wallpaper over them. Might never have been discovered but the man who took his room noticed a bit peeling. Friend found him two days later, room full of steam, three kettles going, still busy. When you've seen as much of the world as I have, boy, you'll know it takes all sorts."

"Yes," said Anthony.

"How was it you said you came to know of the hiding-place, did you say?"

Anthony tried quickly to remember what he had said. "Uncle Joe showed me. One day – I was in there, you see, and he showed me how it worked, just for fun."

"Was there anything in there then?"

"I'm – not sure. I think – He said he sometimes put things in there."

"Well, 'twas a good thought to try." Perry chuckled again, but his mouth twitched. "A bright idea, if you follow me. I wonder you didn't think of it before, though. I suppose you'd have given it to Aunt Madge if I hadn't come up and frightened the wits out of you?"

"Yes . . . I . . . I'd hardly thought. I didn't really expect to find anything, you see."

Perry seemed satisfied. "Well, pity it wasn't a deed of gift making over to us a thousand pounds, what?" He dug him in the ribs again where he knew him to be most ticklish. "A thousand pounds each. Then we'd have gone off on the spree, just the two of us together, boy. How would that suit?"

"Fine," said Anthony quietly.

"We'd go off to Marseilles and Alexandria; those are the places for a good time cheap. I knew a girl once ... And then we'd go across the Atlantic to Canada. We wouldn't wait for your old father to send for you; we'd go and find him. That would give him a shock, wouldn't it? We'd turn up at his camp one day, just when he came back from his diggings, and somebody'd say: 'Dick, here's a young man called to see you,' and he'd say: 'I wonder who in tarnation that can be?' And he'd go inside and you'd be standing there waiting for him. . . ."

There was a good deal more of this before the conversation ended. Perry was trying to divert the boy's mind and partly succeeding. While something in him rejected the vision as a spurious one, Anthony was yet beguiled by it because it approached so near to many he had had himself. The mood in which he fell in with Uncle Perry's clumsy romancing and laughed at his jokes was therefore only partly assumed; and Perry the deceiver was himself deceived.

Never in his life would Anthony quite regain the frankness and freedom of manner he had lost during his stay with the Veals, that fresh, clear-eyed candour which feared nothing and withheld nothing. Always there would remain as a mark of these days a hint of reserve which would make him a little difficult to know. People would say of him: "He's charming, but hard to understand;" and they would never know that they were reaching back into an untidy kitchen of Victorian days with Perry manoeuvring and bluffing and pushing back his hair and Aunt Madge's shadow in the doorway, and the water lapping against the old stone quay outside.

CHAPTER TWENTY-TWO

Further delay, the boy felt, would not help him or anyone else. Already he was greatly to blame for having waited so long. He must move at once.

He did not know where Maenporth was, but he slipped out just before supper and asked Jack Robbins, who told him that it was a few miles beyond Swanpool.

That evening there were visitors to supper: Captain Stevens of *The Grey Cat* and Captain Shaw of *Lavengro*, which had come in a couple of days after the other ship. They were both due to leave again soon, and Aunt Madge had shaken herself out of her sloth and cooked them a supper reminiscent of the restaurant in its best days. But this was even better because it was free and Joe had always charged them full price.

Captain Shaw, a fat man with a trace of Mongol blood in him, grew expansive with the wine and began to pay Aunt Madge extravagant compliments which she lapped up like a dignified tabby offered a bowl of cream. Then, having made himself popular, he began to undo the good work by referring to Joe and the way he had starved his beloved ship; if they ever revictualled in Falmouth they always ran short of provisions and supplies before the voyage was done, and if they victualled at any other port Joe always complained of extravagance and took a percentage off the captain's wages.

Aunt Madge was nothing if not jealous of her late husband's reputation, and she began to look as if the cream had turned sour. Perry grinned and twitched and rumbled in the background like an extinct volcano, content it seemed to let someone else have the limelight and divert Madge's attention from him.

Presently the party adjourned to the sitting-room upstairs, and Anthony went with them and sat and looked through another volume of *The Quiver* while they played whist. At nine-thirty he wished them all good night and went slowly up to bed.

He sat on his bed in the dark for fifteen minutes, and then picked up his shoes and came down again. Never since he had been here had anyone climbed the second flight of stairs to see if he was in bed – the fact that his light was out was deemed good enough – so he felt fairly safe in taking the chance. And if they had gone to bed before he returned, as seemed probable, he knew a way of prising open the scullery window and there shouldn't be much difficulty in wriggling his body through.

As he passed the parlour he heard Captain Shaw's thick voice: "Aye, aye, Mrs. Veal, I grant you that. But how was I to know ye had the ace?"

He slipped out through the back door and was rather upset to find a thin mist lying over the river. There would in any case be no moon tonight, and he had hoped the stars would be out. At present the mist lay on the water more than over the town, but as the night advanced it might spread, and he had never been to Maenporth in his life.

All his cautious, baby instincts told him to give up the project; the thought of creeping upstairs again and sliding between the sheets suddenly became infinitely desirable; he could put the visit off until tomorrow when the weather might be better – or even until Saturday when Tom would be home at Penryn. He might go all the way and be unable to find the house. If the fog came down he might even lose his way and wander through the secret little lanes all night. Then the fat would be in the fire; if Aunt Madge knew he had been out she would take care that he didn't go again. Better to return.

But there was growing up in Anthony already an obstinate dislike of being overborne by his weaker instincts. He quietly shut the door behind him and put on his mackintosh and cap and a scarf. In this life you had to do what you meant to do or else shrivel up in self-contempt.

He set off at a trot. The faster he moved the sooner he would be there, the sooner he was there the less chance there was of Tom's being in bed, the sooner he was back the better prospect he had of slipping in before the door was locked.

Up Killigrew Street and across Western Terrace and down the hill to Swanpool. There were still plenty of lights about and a number of pedestrians. The grey mist began to move around him in waves, increasing when he got near the sea, but it was not a cold mist and he was soon perspiring. By the time he had passed the cemetery and reached the bottom of the hill it was bellows-to-mend, and he fell into a walk. The swans were asleep hidden somewhere in the rushes, and ahead of him the waves cracked dismally and rattled on the pebbly beach. The sound was sad and old and impersonal, as if it spoke of creation and decay.

From the mouth of the little cove he mounted the next hill and thought he would never get to the top of it. Then by great good fortune he came upon a pony and trap turning out of a side lane.

"Please, sir, is this the way to Maenporth?" he called up into the darkness.

"Ais, sonny. Straight acrost the moor, then down-along the hill and turn ... Are 'ee going thur? Jump up, I'll give'ee a lift."

Anthony accepted the invitation, glad not only of the lift but of the company. The farmer was curious to know what a youngster like him was doing out past his bedtime, but he evaded a direct answer until they had gone down another steep hill and through a narrow thickly wooded lane which came out once again within sound of the sea.

"Now, son, this is whar'ee do want to go. Down this yur path: that 'ouse nigh buried 'midst the trees: that's Mrs. Lanyon's 'ouse. This old broom of a fog. See it now, do'ee? *Tha's* a boy. Now, Emmie, *ck, ck*, come on, my 'and-some ..."

Anthony walked down the dark, muddy lane towards where the gables of a sizeable house showed among the fir trees. The sigh of the sea was abruptly cut off by the dripping hedges as he walked up the short shingle drive and pulled the front-door bell.

There were lighted windows in the front of the house and a glimmer in the hall which increased as a uniformed maid turned up the lamp before opening the door.

"Yes?" she said.

"Is Mr. Tom Harris staying here, please?"

"Well ..."

"Could I see him, please? He ..."

"He's busy now. What do you want?"

"Tell him it's Anthony. He asked me to call."

The maid hesitated, then opened the door. "You'd best come in. You'll have to wait, I expect."

With a sense of timidity the boy entered the hall and the maid turned the lamp up. Hunting trophies and a few shields came to view and peered down at him suspiciously. Then the maid went into a room on the left and he caught sight of a well-lit drawing-room and people sitting round on chairs. At the end of the room was a piano and several people standing up with violins and things.

She reappeared. "He said for you to wait. He said he'd not be long."

"Thank you." When he was alone he stopped twirling his cap and dropped it on a chair and sat on it. Wisps of fog had followed him into the hall. Then someone began to play the piano in the room. It was a pleasant sort of piece to listen to, not with any detectable tune but a lot of nice ripples running up and down, up and down, like the sea coming in on a sunny day.

The music suddenly became louder and was damped again as Tom Harris slid out of the room through the smallest gap he could make in the door. He came towards the boy smiling and handsome and gentlemanly in a black evening dress suit.

"Hullo, Anthony; this is a surprise. Come in here. My sister's having a musical evening. You've some news?"

He led the way into a small library, taking with him the hall lamp. Usually Anthony had seen him in tweeds, and he was suddenly struck by the different worlds in which Tom and Patricia revolved. Patricia had hinted as much to him, but he had never personally realized what she meant until now. Tom was a gentleman. Pat, although he had never known her to be the least bit common or vulgar, was not quite what the world at present understood as a lady. Tom had been brought up to find his pleasures in this sort of an evening: people dressed for dinner and having musical evenings and card parties and the rest. Pat had spent her evenings in the atmosphere of the restaurant. Even though she no longer did so the deeper differences remained. This was another gap between them, perhaps wider and deeper than their lovers' quarrels.

Anthony did not reason all this out, for he hadn't the time or the experience; what he sensed was the outlines of the difference, and, aware of himself as a connection of Pat's, he felt the inferiority for her. Then he told his story, forgetting social complexes as he went on.

In silence Tom heard him out almost to the end.

"Do you think he was lying to you this afternoon? What makes you sure? Did you read the document you found?"

"Yes. It wasn't the same."

"In what way did it differ?"

"The Will I found seemed to leave the – the property nearly all to Pat. I think it just left the restaurant business to Aunt Madge, but I didn't get a chance of reading it all through."

"Any other divergence?"

"Di . . ."

"Difference between what you found and what he showed you."

171

"Yes. Well . . . what I saw Uncle Joe put behind the picture and what Uncle Perry showed me can't be the same thing. I saw Uncle Joe sign the other, and the captain and mate of the *Lady Tregeagle* witnessed it. The thing Uncle Perry showed me wasn't signed or witnessed."

"I wish you'd told me this before, Anthony, before investigating yourself."

"I know . . . I know. Sorry." He could not quite explain the complex pull of loyalties which had made him reluctant to inform against his aunt in such a way as to make it obvious that he did not trust her.

"You see we've nothing at all to go on. If the Will was as you say, they – well, they may have destroyed it. Then it's only your word against his."

"But there's the captain and mate of the *Lady Tregeagle*. I don't know –"

"When *Lady Tregeagle* left she was going to Alexandria. She may pick up another cargo there and be months returning. And, of course, their testimony proves very little without a document to back it up."

"But if they said –"

"Yes, I know." Tom began to walk up and down the room. "If the mate and captain of the *Lady Tregeagle* were prepared to swear that they had witnessed on such and such a date a Will made by Joe Veal, and you swore that you had found such a Will, your aunt would be in a very difficult position morally. But legally, without the document we could save our breath. Besides, Joe being so secretive as he was, it's unlikely he told the captain and the mate what it was they were signing. I'm afraid, old boy, that there's nothing to be done."

Anthony stared up at the young solicitor as he turned from the window. All that day and for three days before, a conviction had burned in him that his actions of the other night had irrevocably destroyed his hopes of helping Pat. Tom's attitude confirmed this. But the odd thing was that he felt Tom did not care. He remembered Tom's attitude once before when he had seemed relieved that Pat had been cut out of her father's Will. If Tom really loved Patricia he should be more concerned for her future than his own gain . . . even supposing that there would be any gain to him in Pat's loss, which at present seemed unlikely. He personally might have made a complete failure of his

172

attempt to help, but it was wrong to treat the news with indifference. After the excitement of stealing out of the house and the long run and the drive through the mist Anthony felt suddenly let down. He had brought news of vital importance; possibly he was too late with it, but the only chance of not being too late was to take some action at once. He had not stopped to reason what action *could* be taken: Tom would know that; the main thing was to get the information to him. Let Tom turn on him furiously now for his mistakes if he chose, but not treat the information as if it did not matter.

Harris stopped and looked at the boy with his intent brown eyes. "Does anyone else know of this?"

Anthony shook his head.

"Do you think Perry knows you suspect him of lying?"

"No. I don't think so."

"Has he any idea that you've come here?"

"Oh, no."

"Well, then, he mustn't have. You realize that, Anthony. He mustn't have any idea. We must keep this a dead secret between ourselves."

"What are you going to do?"

Tom shrugged. "What is there to do? I'll make further inquiries, but it's most essential that Perry shouldn't know we're suspicious. Do understand that. Because – because, you see, if he so much as suspects a thing, the new Will, if it still exists, is likely to be burnt. Give him time, Anthony. There's nothing to hurt for a day or two. Give him time."

Faintly to their ears came the sound of applause as the pianist finished her second piece.

"I'd better be going," said Anthony.

"Has Patricia been over since I saw you last?"

"No."

Tom said: "You can't walk straight back. I'll get you some sandwiches and something to drink."

He protested that he didn't want anything, but Tom left the room and presently returned with a dish of tongue sandwiches and a cup of steaming coffee.

"If you wait an hour," he said, "Mr. and Mrs. Vellenoweth will be driving back to Falmouth and can give you a lift."

"I'd rather go, Tom. You see, they might miss me. It's not very far, and . . ."

173

"Perhaps you're right. It was sporting of you to come here like this. Will you have tea with me at Mount House next Sunday?"

He met Tom's eyes for a moment. "Oh, I don't suppose there'll be anything fresh by then."

"Come, anyhow."

"I'll try. Sometimes Aunt Madge wants me to go out with her."

As Tom saw him to the door, string instruments could be heard tuning up in the drawing-room. Tom put a hand on his shoulder.

"Don't think I'm unmindful of your help, Anthony. It has been worth a good deal to me, and we shall get over this disappointment. To have known that another Will has existed is a big step forward. Even that much will mean a great deal to Pat, to feel that her father fully forgave her. I'll warrant she'd as soon know that as know that the money was actually hers."

"Ye-es."

"One thing I want you to promise me."

Anthony twirled his cap and peered out into the misty darkness which was soon to receive him.

"If Patricia should by any chance come home this week-end, I want you to promise not to breathe a word of this to her."

"But —"

"I want you to *promise*."

Anthony twirled his cap. "It's her money. I couldn't . . ."

"Nevertheless I want you to."

In the distance could be heard the faint hush-hush of the sea. Near at hand water was dripping into water.

"We agreed to trust each other, didn't we?" said Tom.

"Ye-es."

"Well, I want you to trust me on this point. I want you to promise not to tell her anything about this new Will until after you've seen me again."

"But why?"

"Why? Well, it's for her good that she shouldn't know, I assure you."

Anthony eventually promised. Unless he wished to quarrel with Tom and accuse him of not playing fair he could hardly do otherwise, and he hadn't the courage to do that to his face. Besides, he had no real facts to go on, only a sense of general disappointment.

But when he promised he did so with his fingers crossed, like they did at school when the speaker was supposed to be absolved from doing what he said. He knew in his heart that this was only a moral quibble which really evaded nothing; he had never used it before in any serious matter. But his new-growing duplicity was finding many outlets.

If the opportunity came he knew he would tell Pat everything.

The night received him like an over-attentive and slightly sinister friend; its damp embrace cloyed, and he pulled off his muffler as soon as he was in the lane. There was no air, only a drifting mist which had to be breathed in wet and breathed out in a finer form as if the moisture had been refined into steam.

The fog was thicker than when he had gone in. Branches dripped high overhead and somewhere near water was running in a ditch. After the lights of the house he was quite blind, and he had to grope his way foot by foot in the direction of the main road. But he was used to darkness from his Exmoor days and as his pupils expanded he began to move more freely. Once the road to Falmouth was reached there were few chances of going wrong; only one sharp-right turn to take at the top of the hill.

For a long time he was too preoccupied with his thoughts to feel any sense of his own isolation. Tom wasn't playing fair. This was not a solemn compact to help Patricia as first planned, but a one-sided flow of confidences with nothing in return. Tom, he felt, was using him to obtain this information, and the information was not being turned to Pat's benefit, but to Tom's own. There had been the incident of his last visit to Mount House when the tall grey-haired man was present, a stranger to whom he was apparently expected to speak as freely as to Tom. Now there was tonight with its impression of divided loyalties, its sense of confidences withheld. However it had begun, he was being treated as a child again, as a pawn in a game considered outside his comprehension.

Midnight was past before he reached Swanpool, and until now perplexity and disappointment had been stronger than any childish fear. Only when he began to walk down the long snaky hill which led to the pool did he realize that in a few minutes he would have to pass the cemetery. Only then did he realize with an extraordinary shock of conviction that this was the occasion he had dreamed about; when he would meet Uncle Joe at the gates and walk home with him, and when they reached the restaurant they would find it in ruins and the ball of moss would be in his hand and something unnameable stirring in the shop.

CHAPTER TWENTY-THREE

For perhaps half a minute he stopped in his stride and considered turning back. Then common-sense reasserted itself, reason gently unclasped those alien fingers; he smiled unconvincingly and went on his way.

Strange that a simple, tree-rimmed reedy pool which one has seen so many times by day can by night become lonely and fogbound and sinister. All the way round its edge he was pursued by the sound of the waves breaking on the steep, pebbly shore. It was like the tipping of bags of small coal: the first heavy fall when the wave broke, then the rattle of the small coal as the bag was pulled away. It was like the loneliness of life, the loneliness of himself.

He began to climb the hill towards the cemetery, thinking hard of his grievances and mistakes, striving hard to regain that armour of preoccupation which had protected him so far; no doubt his own mistakes far outweighed his grievances; Tom was right to look on the matter of the Will as a cause already lost; his own proper course should have been to have waited until Pat returned for Christmas; and – and then . . .

And then there was a light in the cemetery. A white glow like the rising moon below the horizon.

He stopped and told himself that the light came from one of the houses behind. He went on a few paces and stopped again. The light was in the cemetery and near the gate. It was not the light of a lantern or of a torch or of a candle, but just a white glow showing through the fog. An indistinct glow in the swirling mists.

He couldn't understand it. He went on a bit farther, stopped again, biting his finger-nail. Nothing to do with him; run past and don't bother to look. Something perhaps which had no right to be there, but it was not at all his business to inquire what.

On a clear night he would have been able to trust his eyes. The fog had spread its web over the land and even normal things were imbued with enormity and suspicion.

By now he was close beside the cemetery wall. He edged along it until he came near the top corner where Uncle Joe and Aunt Christine were buried side by side. The fog was thicker than it had yet been anywhere. But he was now so near that nothing could hide the exact location of the light. It was beside the gate, about twelve paces inside, and came from behind a wooden or canvas screen which apparently had been erected across the path just there.

A possible explanation suddenly came to him, and his slow breath of relief mingled with the fog. Someone no doubt had died and the sexton, being pressed for time, was working on after dark to prepare the grave. To confirm this view his nearer approach brought the sound of a scraping spade and the thud of heavy earth.

Then he heard the murmur of voices.

There was still no reason why he should have inquired further. He could have walked on up the hill and kept his eyes and his thoughts averted. But a force stronger than fear made him stop at the gate of the cemetery. He felt himself to be in the grip of some compelling attraction. And there was an inevitability about the location of the diggers.

As he went in a figure loomed up, and he ducked down against the first grave-stone with a thumping heart. Tall and dark the figure, with an oddly shaped hat. It was a canvas screen, he saw; there were several figures behind it, and he thought at least six lanterns. The figure which had passed him had taken up its stand by the gate, thus cutting off his retreat. Recklessly he climbed across the stones, striking his boot on one, but there was noise behind the screen and he reached it unheard.

Nightmare-like now, he was gripped with an urgent necessity to know the worst; so inimical did delay seem that he might have taken out his knife and slashed at the canvas to see what was happening within. But there was already an inch-long tear through which he could peer.

There were five lanterns and seven men and a number

of gravestones. So bright were the lanterns that he could see the lettering on two of the grave-stones, words which he had come to know by heart. One of them had only just been put up. Two men in shirt sleeves were in one grave almost up to their shoulders and partly screened from view by the pile of mineral-yellow soil which they had dug up. Another grave was also open, and beside it and beside an even larger mound of rubble was something Anthony had seen before. Two men with masks and aprons were bending over it. A third, in a silk hat, was standing well back from them. Two policemen made up the party.

Anthony turned and ran, ran careless of noise and stumblings towards the outer gate. He ran as if the Devil and all Hell were after him. He ran on wings of fear, while ice-cold sweat stood out on his face and hands. He reached the gate and was through it while a figure turned and grasped at him. He ran along beside the cemetery blindly and wildly, turned away from the other gate and up the hill. No dreams troubled him now, no fear of dreams. He would gladly have gone back to all the bad dreams in the world. What he was running away from was reality. All his life as a result of this experience he would do the same.

He ran up the hill and across the main road and down the hill, with the thick mist closing in behind him and the hand of Fate heavy on his shoulder. Twice he almost fell, and in the wider spaces of the Moor where the landmarks were less easily seen he strayed across and lost his sense of direction.

Had he come to a stop there his instincts and fears might have been brought to a stop as well. Even a short pause might have set him thinking. But he found the next narrow street just in time and fled on towards his home. In no time, though his breath was coming in great gasps, he was before the back-door of the shop. Panting, he stood on the mat and tried the handle. It opened and he saw that the kitchen was lighted. Before he could withdraw Aunt Madge caught sight of him. But he was not sure that he wanted to withdraw. He was too far gone for man-oeuvre or temporizing.

They were clearing away the remnants of the evening's feast.

"Anthony!" said Aunt Madge. "I ... Bed, I thought you. How have you ...?"

He sat on the nearest chair and panted for breath; in this warmth there was less air. The perspiration under his cap was still cold, as if it were a part of the mist and not of his own body. He put his head down.

"Disobedience." Aunt Madge's voice came through walls of fear and nausea. She began to talk, to scold, to chew the cud of her grievance. For a time her words glanced off unheeded, only one or two coming through like solitary survivors of an attacking army. They kept him in touch with his surroundings, they and the grip of his chair. His normal boyish mind kept struggling to revert to its own preoccupations; solid, decent, homely things; the smell of new bread and kicking a ball in a narrow street, the feel of the ball in his fingers; lemon pudding and sleep; rowing across the harbour, Pat's laughter, his mother's voice: thoughts that were his brain's warmth and refuge. But not yet, not yet could he escape. This other thing was too near, it blocked everything else from view. Life it seemed never would be the same again, for how could the ugliness and horror ever grow smaller? His dreary existence of these last weeks seemed golden with health by comparison with what the future must be.

He heard his aunt call something and Perry emerged from the scullery, an apron still about his waist.

A hand touched his cap, lifted it off, and his head was turned up towards the light.

"Hell's hounds! Where've you been, boy? Been swimming? Your hair's as wet –"

Anthony looked up and his voice came back.

"They're taking them away! I saw them. The police it is! I don't understand!"

"Who are? Taking who away?" said the voice on a different note.

"Uncle Joe. Aunt ... Christine. I came past. They were digging. They'd put a screen round. The ... *It* ... was on top. They'd ... the lid ... they'd ..."

Tears choked further words. Tears streamed down his cheeks for about a minute. The hand had left his head. Uncle Perry went away and sat on a chair.

The tears were a safety valve letting out dangerous accumulations of terror. He constantly smeared his face with

179

his sleeve and the back of his hands. When the tears began to stop he groped for his handkerchief and wiped the last of them away. He saw a drop or two fall beside Perry's chair and thought that perhaps he too was crying. Then he saw liquid trickling down the side of his chin and Aunt Madge withdrawing a glass which she had been trying to put between Perry's teeth.

"Your uncle," said Mrs. Veal. "Been took queer. Been — been drinking too much. This excitement. I never. What have you been doing, Anthony? Hi wish to know the truth."

Even in this crisis he knew that the whole truth would not do.

"I — I sneaked out, Aunt Madge. I wanted — wanted to see where the swans slept at night. Jack told me — Jack told me they didn't nest like other birds —"

"Yes, yes."

He realized she was not interested in this part of his story. Her eye-glasses were not quite still; there was a tremor moving through them, as a newspaper will quiver when there is machinery beating somewhere below. Her small eyes seemed to have disappeared behind them, as if they were hiding themselves in the folds of her puffy face. Anthony went on to tell what he had seen. While he was doing so Uncle Perry belched and a thin trickle of saliva joined the driblet of whisky on his chin.

Abruptly Aunt Madge set down the tumbler and took out her own handkerchief.

"Envy, malice, hatred, all uncharitableness," she said in a high-pitched voice as if it were being squeezed out of her. "My life ... All my life. Pursued. Saul, Saul, why persecutest thou me? All my life. People. Evil tongues. My dear mother. My dear sister. Always the same." She put an uncertain handkerchief waveringly up to her small snub nose. "People, evil people, whispering. The way they insinuate. All the wickedness of this world. My mother, one of the noblest of women. Never loved any one more, unless it was my dear husband. Persecuted by evil tongues. Always the same. I have been. Bearing my cross of loneliness. And now. Desecration of the hallowed dead. Wicked evil tongues. They know I'm all alone. Poor widow. They think they can do anything. But they can't. I'll see

180

them prosecuted. I'll see them ... utmost letter of the law. My poor husband. Insinuation ..."

Perry lifted his head from the side of the chair. His face was the colour of Aunt Madge's pastry before it went in the oven. His skin was the same texture too, thick and soft and slightly pitted; his face was twitching persistently.

"Deliver my soul, O Lord, from lying lips," said Aunt Madge, hoarsely and rapidly, "and from a deceitful tongue. Sharp arrows of the mighty, with coals of juniper. Woe is me, that I sojourn in Mesech, that I dwell in the tents of Kedar. Remember, Anthony, when you are grown up. A lesson in the wickedness of the world. Remember your aunt." She waved her hand. "Calumny is her lot. She has bore herself with Christian fortitude. When thy enemy smitest thee upon the one cheek ... Remember a delicate woman broken upon the wheel. Never have pity, Anthony, for Philistines shall put out your eyes. They will stop at nothing, dragging even the bones mouldering to dust." Her voice quivered higher. "*Dragging* them, I say, out of the ... The Serpent has them in his power. Wicked evil that they are! Won't even let the dead, the blessed dead, rest in peace. Interfering, *dragging* them out of their sleep. Vile, vile in your sight! The light of the wicked shall be put out!"

Perry's hand closed round the glass and slowly transferred it to his mouth. It clicked against his teeth and the liquid disappeared as down a drain. He tried to get up from his chair, but failed.

"Why should they do it, Aunt Madge?" Anthony asked. "Why should they do it? And who is it, anyway?"

Perry's next attempt put him upon his feet, and he reached the cupboard in the corner where the whisky bottle was kept. Aunt Madge lowered herself into a chair and took off her pince-nez and wiped them. When next she spoke her voice was lower. Her eyes had reappeared.

"Being unwell does not entitle you ... Perry, not neat alcohol. We must act. We must take steps ... restitution of our rights. We must see Mr. Cowdray. We must—"

"I said this'd happen!" Perry drained his glass and glanced sidelong at the boy. "God! I said this'd happen. All along."

"You should be in bed, Anthony," said Aunt Madge.

"You must have been ... Yes, upset, I'm sure. Go to bed. Better in the morning."

"But what are they doing?" he demanded.

Aunt Madge put on her pince-nez. "A dispute. Over the ... your dear uncle. The Veals have a vault in the old church-yard ... the parish church. That woman, your Aunt Louisa, wished him to be buried there. We did not. They have made a lawsuit of hit. They have acted while we ... We must do something. Something must be done in the morning."

"There's nothing we can do now," said Perry.

Aunt Madge's pince-nez continued to wobble but she did not assent to this view.

Anthony woke very late the following morning. He had gone to bed with little more said, but he had turned and tossed for endless hours in the darkness, sleepless and alone. He knew himself lost and without guidance.

Instinctively he felt himself to be in a position which would have puzzled many a grown-up. He was helpless before the drift of events. Could he have become a fatalist to order he might have saved at least some of the anxiety of the night; but no fatalism and no resignation could prevent the fevered living-over-again of what had happened.

Once, after hours of tossing and turning, he crept out of the room to go downstairs to see what the time was; but a light under the door of the drawing-room and another light reflecting up from the ground floor showed that nobody was in bed but himself.

Dawn was late on that misty December morning, and he just remembered hearing the seagulls crying and seeing a greyness encroach upon the bar of night between the curtains; he was about to get up and pull the curtains when he fell asleep.

Perry woke him.

"Show a leg, boy. It'll soon be seven bells in the forenoon watch. Show a leg; we've good news for you."

He had pulled back the curtains and the window let in a shaft of wintry sun. It also showed up Perry's recently shaven face trying its best to look swashbuckling and doggish. The attempt was not a success. Red-eyed and collarless, he smiled unconvincingly at the boy. The mouth was trying to turn up but the lines turned down.

182

Anthony slid quickly out of bed.

"News? *Good* news? What about?"

"Never mind; boy. Wait till you get below; your aunt'll tell you." Perry went unsteadily out, leaving a strong smell of rum behind him.

Anthony followed with the least possible delay. He found them both in the kitchen. Aunt Madge was reading Malachi. Her little lips were forming the words as she went from line to line. She was wearing the same dress as last night and he suspected it had not been off; it's stiff lace collar and heavily brocaded front with flaps and frills over it looked out of place this morning. She had not even taken off her earrings or the four strings of pearls.

"And the day that cometh shall burn them up," she said. "News. Your father. A letter this morning."

Daylight had undermined some of the terrors of the night. This announcement abruptly drove away the rest to a distance at which they could be tolerated.

"What does he say? Does he –?"

"You're to go out. Early boat. He's sent money. Passage paid. And ye shall go forth and grow up as calves of the stall."

Anthony let out a whoop of delight.

"Did it come this morning? When have I to start?"

Aunt Madge turned over a page. "That is left ... Hi thought. Fare is booked from Bristol. No regular service from here. *The Grey Cat*. Leaving on tonight's tide. Calling at Bristol. And he shall turn the heart of the fathers to the children. We thought ... Your uncle and I. Save the train fare. Bristol the day after tomorrow. Captain Stevens knows you. He would look after you."

"Yes," said Anthony. "Go to Bristol by sea, you mean. I'd like that. That'd be fine. By sailing ship. Yes, thanks, Aunt Madge. Would that be tonight?"

"Tonight."

"I must pack. I can hardly believe ... It's nearly twelve now. What time do they leave? Does Captain Stevens know?"

He hurried upstairs again, bursting with excitement. But behind the excitement, like the structure behind an ornamental façade, was relief. Relief to be leaving this house and its shabbiness and hysteria. Relief at the thought of leaving the horrible scene of last night three thousand miles behind. It wasn't explained. Nothing was explained; some instinct told him that there might come a time when these perplexities and unsolved relationships would irk him, when he would blame himself for leaving them without a backward glance, the weakness of this escape might leave a hard core of self-despisal, overgrown but not overthrown, which some day would serve him ill. But at this instant he had no second thought, only a surging happiness at the idea of casting everything away. Somebody else could worry about the policemen in the cemetery. Someone else could argue out the problem of the Will. Somebody else could carry tales to Tom Harris. Not he. Not he.

Only one thing he would have liked to do, and that was to say good-bye to Patricia. That being impossible, he would drop her a short note; he had her address and could get a stamp from the near-by post office.

The day was a bright one and mild, a fresh southerly wind having puffed away the remnants of fog. It seemed in keeping with his mood of relief that the sun should shine and the harbour look as bright and gay as in summer. There was little time to lose, since *The Grey Cat* would be weighing anchor at seven. Even in a few months he had collected all manner of souvenirs which he was anxious to take with him, and these had to be fitted somehow into his one wicker travelling bag.

All the afternoon both Aunt Madge and Uncle Perry were very quiet. No doubt they were worrying about the news he had brought last night. But neither of them seemed anxious to go out and consult Mr. Cowdray, unless they had already been out before he woke. They had an odd air of waiting, of sitting still and having nothing to do. Aunt Madge took down a number of flypapers in the kitchen and put them into the stove. Perry had reverted to his rum again. His face had that heavy, studious look which told its own tale. He always looked as if he was going to produce some great thought and never did.

The sun went down that night behind the town glowing red among the clustered black clouds. For half an hour after it had gone all the old town of Falmouth stood out clear-etched in the twilight glow as if impressing itself indelibly upon the boy's brain; the church steeples and the grey houses and the narrow quays and the climbing cottages looking down over the pink flush of the harbour.

He finished such preparations as there were to make and knelt for a moment at the window of his bedroom. Not many minutes' rowing away were the tree masts of the barquentine which was to take him on the first part of his long journey. He felt no apprehensions that the journey might be tedious or difficult: his only wish was to be gone.

Perhaps it was only in these last few hours that he had begun to realize how much the happenings in this house had weighed on him. Like a man who had been carrying a burden, he had not felt how much his shoulders were cramped, his breathing restricted, until the weight was eased and he was standing there waiting for it to be finally lifted off. Most burdensome of all perhaps had been the necessity for making judgments of his own; not decisions, but judgments of people. He had been pitchforked from a world of friends and acquaintances, in which he had instinctively drawn his opinions from his mother, into a new circle in which he had to form every judgment upon complete strangers for himself. He had at first seen many things through Pat's eyes, but for the last two months he had found himself forced more and more back upon the bedrock of his own immature sense of values, and these were blown like a leaf in the wind turning one side and then the other up. To be released from all his contacts here, to wipe out all the past mistakes and begin anew, this was almost the greatest relief.

As the brightness faded from the sky there crept over him, without any sort of prompting, the conviction that even now he was not leaving all the problems behind as he had supposed. Somehow, in some manner, they were now a part of him and had to be resolved. Most gladly he would have forgotten the horrible scene of last night. But it would not be forgotten. It was only over-laid for the moment by the happy and exciting news of today. Some time it would return. He had seen something which no manner of excuses from Aunt Madge and Uncle Perry would explain away. Something which was not a final event in itself but which had to be searched and sounded to the depths. He was young but he was not a fool. His judgment of events was often faulty but not always. Aunt Madge's lame explanation did not convince him. The police were in it. That was what frightened him. The police were in it.

As the light of the thin crescent moon began to show up

he saw a small dinghy cutting a dark rippling arrow through the silver water. Captain Stevens coming to fetch him.

Not before time. Five o'clock was past and he would be happier away from the house. Once in the ship he would recover his confidence and his good spirits of this afternoon. Once in the ship he would really begin to believe the journey begun. Not until then.

Now there were good-byes to be said. Must not forget to thank them for their kindness. His father would be sure to ask. (Or at least his mother would have been sure to do so. He suddenly realized that he hardly knew his father.) Anyway, he owed them thanks, Aunt Madge and Uncle Perry: they had given him food and a home; he had barely given them loyalty in return.

He picked up his bag, his cap, his coat, two parcels, looked round the now familiar room, at the sloping raftered ceiling and the pieces of cheap furniture, which had the friendly pull of five months' intimate association Then he went down the two flights of stairs into the kitchen. He found Aunt Madge and Uncle Perry with hats and coats on and valises packed, waiting to accompany him.

CHAPTER TWENTY-FOUR

By the frail light of the sickle moon following the sun towards the south-west, *The Grey Cat* slid quietly out of the harbour under a strip or two of canvas. Once past Pendennis Point she shook out the rest of her sails and bent and quivered under the touch of the wind like a horse feeling its master after a long rest. Then she moved off slowly with the wind on her starboard bow, dipping lightly in the choppy sea, her lights winking their farewell to the shore bound castle and the line of darkening cliff.

The barquentine had never been designed to carry passengers, and accommodation was uncomfortably cramped. Captain Stevens had given up his own cabin to Mrs. Veal, and Anthony and Perry were to share the store-room which led off from the main saloon on the opposite side and which had been hastily made habitable by the provision of two floor bunks fitted up unpleasantly like two premature coffins by the ship's carpenter.

As Aunt Madge said, addressing nobody, the inconvenience was only for a couple of days. They had important business in Bristol and at the last moment had decided to take this opportunity of settling it. Together with this business matter they could discharge their duty to Anthony's father by accompanying the boy and seeing him safely aboard his ship for Canada. Uncle Perry said it did his old guts good to feel the deck under his feet again, and Aunt Madge said it would be a nice change and a rest for her; she had been feeling thoroughly run down and she wished she had thought of the idea before.

Anthony did not believe a word of it. He didn't know quite what was happening, but he was beginning to have a fair idea. Uncle Perry didn't in the least look as if he was deriving any pleasure from being at sea again, and unless he was very much mistaken Aunt Madge was the last person in the world to accept this sort of discomfort out of a sense of duty to *him* or even in the interests of her own health. She would, one guessed, almost prefer to die in comfort rather than live without it.

But there was very little he could say or do. If he had been powerless to influence events before, he was certainly no less helpless now. He comforted himself with the thought that so long as he was going to meet his father it was not really his business to inquire into the motives of the people who went as far as Bristol with him. So long as he was moving, and moving in the right direction, the entanglements would slip off one by one.

Captain Stevens, although he put a good face on it, did not look pleased at having the owners aboard and had insisted in putting himself right with the Board of Trade signing them all on as part of his crew at a shilling a day. Anthony wished that Ned Pawlyn had still been a member of the ship's company.

That night he spent in uneasy, sickly slumber, listening to Perry snoring and muttering to himself in the opposite bunk, and when he did close his eyes it was usually to start into wakefulness as last night's detestable scene flashed suddenly before his eyes, or at some unfamiliar sound, the tramp of feet above his head or the clink, clink of glass as Perry poured himself another tot of rum. Perhaps there were others who could not forget what had happened yesterday.

All the night the barquentine was beating into a tenacious headwind, which increased sharply during the dark hour before dawn. Presently he heard Perry being sick, and shortly afterwards he began himself.

After that he lost count of time and sequence, except that at some period of his illness a member of the crew came in and turned out the smoky, swinging oil lamp and let in grey fitful daylight through the port-hole.

Then later, after discovering within himself that he had no further incentive to live, he was sick for the last time and fell asleep.

When he awoke the colour of the daylight had not changed, but he felt that a considerable time had passed. Uncle Perry was no longer in the bunk opposite. Light-headed and painfully weak, he pulled himself gingerly out of his bunk and was at once flung on the floor beside Perry's. He clawed himself slowly upright and looked out of the port-hole.

The first impression was that all was lost. There was no horizon that he could see and nothing that he had ever visualized as a seascape. The port-hole was crushed down among walls and valleys of racing grey water towering at all angles above his vision and from time to time burying the window in total darkness. There was no such thing as a level, no datum line of balance or equilibrium. It was impossible to tell how far the sea engulfed the port-hole, how far the port-hole buried itself deep in the sea. There was no means of knowing the difference between the two or even of knowing that there was a difference. The sky when it was visible was a low, tattered shawl of brown. All the noises of ship and sea were dominated by a high-pitched variable whine like the heart-beat of an infernal dynamo.

Giddy and in danger of more sickness, he felt he could exist no longer without some water to moisten his parched throat; so he pulled himself to the other side of the cabin and opened the door.

Voices greeted him. Perry and Aunt Madge and Captain Stevens were in the dining saloon, which was in a state of chaos and semi-darkness. No one noticed him enter; there was far too much noise to take heed of a little more: rattling doors, straining woodwork, creaking chairs, loose things carrying on a scattered conversation of taps and rattles; above all, the roar of the sea and the scream of the wind.

"Persistent neglect of running gear, ma'am," the captain was saying. "We've got to take that into account. I wouldn't mention it only ... mind you, it's not a question of danger yet – and these 'ere sharp sou'westers often blow themselves out as quick as they get up. But I'd not fancy tackling the Bay in this weather. Not as things are aboard. Mebbe you remember I asked –?"

"Turning back," said Aunt Madge hoarsely to the table. "Absurd. Hear no more. Wind'll go down. Face it out in due time. My dear husband always said, *The Grey Cat*, utmost confidence, captain and ship."

"Thank you, ma'am. It's my wish to please you. But I've got my crew to consider. I put the facts before you just in case. We can ride this out till nightfall. If it don't abate we'll have to turn and run into the nearest port."

"Think you could make the Scillies?" Perry asked, pushing his hair back.

Captain Stevens tapped the water out of his sou'wester. "I don't. And shouldn't want to."

"I don't fancy the Bay meself in this weather," said Perry. "Stap me, I've seen the seas flying as high as the royals. It makes a man cautious. But maybe it'll abate before morning."

"Of course it will." Mrs. Veal put a handkerchief to her mouth and wiped away a hiccup. Apart from the fact that her cheeks seemed looser than ever and to shake with the pitching of the ship, the monument was not yet overthrown. A night of nausea had not prevented her putting on her pearls and her ear-rings.

"Well, there it is," said Stevens. "I trust you're right. The cook'll prepare you some hot cocoa if you've a mind for it. That's the best we shall be able to do just at present."

By means of various fixtures he pulled himself round to the saloon door and went out. About half a gallon of water came down the companion and slipped about on the floor of the saloon as if seeking a way of returning to its own element.

Anthony let himself go and brought up with a rush against the table. "I want a drink. Is there any water?"

Both stared at him suspiciously as if they suspected him

189

of eavesdropping. Perry's face was yellow with sea-sickness and rum. "In there," he said, jerking his thumb.

The boy entered a little wash-up, and found some water in a carafe fixed to the wall. He drank it too greedily and was sick again. He stayed in the wash-up about half an hour, feeling too ill to move, but at last plucked up the strength to crawl up a hill back into the saloon.

Neither his aunt nor Perry was there; presumably they had gone into her cabin, for the space of movement was very limited. In the din he found a chair and sat on it and leaned his head back and watched the whole saloon at its dizzy acrobatics. After a time he found his eyes accustoming themselves to the changes of position; he was moving in exactly the same relationship and that helped. He began to feel better. The time by the clock above the door was nearly two, so they had been at sea nineteen hours.

There was a clatter of boots and Mr. O'Brien, the mate, came into the room. He took no notice of Anthony but, maintaining his balance in a remarkable way, went over to a cupboard, knelt before it and began rummaging inside.

Anthony said: "This is a bad storm, Mr. O'Brien."

The mate gave him a half glance but did not reply.

"Are we in danger?" the boy asked.

Mr. O'Brien thumped something back into the cupboard. "Not if it was a ship ye was in, me little fellow," he snapped. "I wisht I'd never signed on but stayed in Hull with me two feet on dry land. Well, well."

There was a crack above them and a thud, and water suddenly came down the companion ladder to join up the pools which already existed.

"Are we far from Bristol yet?"

O'Brien rose to his feet. His fat red face under the sou' wester gleamed with water. Salt had whitened the stubble of his beard.

"I wish we was nearer. But, Holy Mary, why Bristol? If I could see the colour of Mount's Bay I should be satisfied."

"Well, we're going to Bristol, aren't we?"

O'Brien buttoned up his oiler. "Not this trip, young feller. Oporto we was making for. But where we shall make landfall if this breeze don't drop, God only knows."

Anthony ran after him as he went to the door.

"I know the ship's going to Portugal. But we're calling at
190

– at Bristol first to pick up more cargo. That's – that's where I'm getting off."

O'Brien pushed away his detaining arm.

"Och, I've no time to stand here arguing the toss. Ask your mother, or whatever she is. She'll set you right."

Nightfall brought no abatement of the wind but only a slight shifting of direction.

At 8 p.m. Captain Stevens came down and with a steady hand entered the following particulars in the log:

8/12/98. Days on passage, 2. Course SSW. Wind and weather: SW 7–9. Rain squalls; steep seas. Ship taking seas solid over fo'c'sle head, pitching and labouring.

Later came three other entries.

9/12/98. Midnight. Wind and weather: SW 9–10. Running before full gale under foresail and tops'l only. Course now approx. NNE by ½ E. Heavy squalls. Two helmsmen. Heavy damage on deck.

2 a.m. Wind and weather: W by S 9. Fore topm'st carried away. Seas breaking over all the time. Ship labouring heavily.

4 a.m. Wind and weather: W by N 9–8. Bare poles. Trying to set up jury rig for'ard. Water gaining on the pumps. In much danger of being pooped.

A superstitious person might have imagined that Joe Veal was taking some part in the situation and exacting his revenge. If nothing more, his parsimony was coming into its own.

But Madge Veal was not a superstitious woman. She was far too self-centred to believe in omens. She was not interested in retribution, divine or astral-human, nor if she had been would she have thought herself a subject likely to incur it. Anything she had done she had done with the best of intentions; indeed, she had never acted but on the highest principles and from the highest possible motive, that of her own welfare.

But Perry . . . Perry, like all sailors, had a strong thread of superstition in his character. Not that he had been a

191

sailor any length of time. Three years of hardship before the mast when a young man had given him a working knowledge of the argot but no further desire to employ it in its proper element. After that when he travelled he travelled as much as possible on dry land. Cab-driver in Cape Town, waiter in Buenos Aires, casual cow-hand in Texas, hobo, soft-drink attendant at a drug-store in San Francisco; these were casual points in the career of a rolling stone who had attracted a record low level in moss. Then a lucky ticket in a sweepstake had put him on top of the world and given him the money to travel home to England first class. It had been the beginning of a run of luck which had brought him a comfortable corner by his brother Joe's fireside and the favour and side glances of his brother's statuesque wife. It wasn't that he'd ever been really attracted by Madge, it was only that he never could resist an implicit challenge of that sort: there was the mischievous temptation to know what the statue was like when it was tipped off its pedestal.

Well, he knew now.

He had thought then that it never would end, that run of luck; there seemed no reason why it should. But imperceptibly the change had come. Not at any single point could he say the vein had given out; nor was he the sort of man who would ordinarily concern himself with regrets that it had done so. Not ordinarily.

But these last few weeks he had begun to wish he had never left San Francisco.

He knew now, although his mind was working in a haze of rum and sea-sickness, that there was only one serious concern in his head: to cut the painter and slip away. To do that he would take any reasonable risk. His was not a conscience which had been unduly exercised in the past; it had accepted shady little episodes and adventures without protest. But the essence of them was that they were *little*. He knew his limitations. And for the last few months he had been playing right out of his class. For the last few weeks he hadn't been able to call his soul his own.

The knowledge was on his lungs. Not so much his conscience as his lungs. The knowledge was a weight; it was a tangible thing. Sometimes he found he could hardly breathe for it. The only palliative was rum.

As the storm grew worse he left Madge and went to lie

down in his bunk, aware of the quiet figure of the boy in the other bunk. If he had any beads to tell he would have "told" them. He could not escape a superstitious twinge at the fury with which the gale had broken upon them, but he still had the gambler's belief that his sudden bad luck was about to change and that the gale might yet turn to his own benefit. Now that they were being forced to run for one of the Bristol Channel ports he might get a chance to slip ashore unobserved.

What disconcerted him in this hope was the manner in which Madge was bearing up. By all the laws this storm should have shaken her nerve. The only sign she gave was that of going into her most withdrawn mood. But she was far from any mood in which she could be easily given the slip.

The boy stirred and sneezed but didn't speak, although he was certainly awake and had seen his uncle come in. Perry had never wanted to bring the boy at all. To him he represented an encumbrance and an added risk. But Madge, with an inside knowledge of the facts, had said that he could not be left behind to bear tales and tell everyone where they had gone, or at least *how* they had gone. During his five months' stay he had seen too much. Little boys had big eyes. Besides, he had done all her shopping for her. If examined by some imprudent prying busybody he would give too much away. And, though she did not put it into so many words, Anthony still fulfilled a purpose he had fulfilled for some time: he lent respectability to a *ménage* which without him would be morally suspect. When they reached Portugal, Aunt Madge said, they could put him on a boat to Canada from there; it would be a nice surprise for his father who, even if he hadn't sent for him, would certainly be glad to see him. But Perry was not quite sure if she meant this; he would never be sure of anything Madge said again. He was coming to appreciate Madge's conscience which, if always active, was always malleable; he had known it to make the most acrobatic *volte-faces*. He was not exactly comfortable about the future of the boy.

Anthony would have been much better left behind.

But as the night advanced Perry's fuddled humanitarian promptings were lost in fear for his own safety. In his few years at sea he had known enough of storms to recognize the dangerous quality of this one, and his experience of ships was at least sufficient to tell him that the barquentine was fighting for her life, and fighting with declining heart.

At five o'clock Captain Stevens was brought down into the water-logged saloon amid the wreckage of the furniture. A wave had brought a broken spar round and knocked him down with it. He was conscious but in considerable pain. Nobody but himself had the least knowledge of medicine, but he said he thought he had broken some ribs. At this stage Perry realized that their chances of survival were becoming slight. In the Atlantic they might have drifted before the storm until it abated. In these narrow seas they were likely to pile up on the rocks which could not be far away.

They took Stevens into his own cabin where Mrs. Veal sat stubbornly in a corner and would speak to no one but herself. Perry made an effort to get him comfortable in his bunk and then put on the captain's oilskins and went on deck. At least he succeeded in opening the companion doors and putting out his head as one will put one's head out of a train when it is rushing through a tunnel. (There is only the noise and the pitch blackness and the flying wind.) The doors banged to after him as he retreated into the cabin and more water followed him down.

He wiped water from his face and poured himself out a tot of rum.

He sat there all alone, feeling desolate and trapped and frightened. He would have given a good deal merely for a confidential friend to talk to. But in one cabin there was a sick boy distant and reserved; in the other was an injured man watched over though not tended by a woman who frightened him more than anything else in the world except the things she had done.

So there was nothing for it except to get drunk, and that was something beyond his powers; all he could do was take enough to solace his loneliness and deaden the worst of his fear.

A member of the crew sighted land at 6.35 when dawn had begun to thin the blackness of the flying night. For twelve minutes with O'Brien and another man at the wheel, barely able to cling to it and constantly washed by half seas, they kept their distance from the high desolate coast. More desperate attempts were made to increase the jury rig, not without success, and O'Brien brought her up a little to the north. But then as they plunged on he saw through the slow, fitful daylight that the coast ran out ahead of him across the path of the wind.

He knew then that *The Grey Cat* was on her last voyage.

A wave came over and swept the length of the deck, licking like a hungry animal over a bone which has already been picked clean.

"May!" he shouted at the top of his voice to the carpenter. "Below! Get 'em up."

May the carpenter did not hear what was said, but he understood the gesture that went with it. He glanced backwards at the hurrying mountainous seas, then quickly unlooped the rope about his waist and dived towards the hatchway.

Perry was still alone in the saloon, leaning heavily on the table with a glass before him and water swilling about his knees. He had been singing glassily to himself, having almost achieved the end he had not thought possible.

" 'Elp me to get the cap'n up," said May. "We're drivin' in 'pon the land. Stand a chance."

Perry followed him into the cabin. May had already explained the position to Mrs. Veal. She was standing up, steadying herself by holding to a bookshelf which had long since emptied its books into the water at her feet. She had put on her hat and coat, and her pince-nez was awry. She looked highly indignant that this was happening to her and peered at May with hostility for disturbing her.

"On deck," Perry said thickly. "All hands. Safest place now. There's rocks ahead. Get the boy. Bring him up. Safest on deck."

Captain Stevens said: "Leave me here. Look to yourselves."

"Come along now," said May.

Between them the two men lifted the captain from his bunk and staggered with him out of the cabin. For the moment the onset of immediate danger had cleared Perry's brain; he was not so much afraid of the sea. The companion was not sufficiently wide to allow of three abreast, but he brought up the rear without stumbling.

Left behind, Madge took off her pince-nez and carefully stowed them away in an inner pocket of her dress. Without them her face looked curiously bare, bare and plain and commonplace; passing in the street you would not have given it another glance. She drew on her kid gloves, fastened the two buttons of her black astrakhan cloak, took out her hatpin and thrust it back in a different position, picked up her bag. Her mind could not visualize what the scene was likely to be on deck. She could not dissociate herself from the conviction that she would step into a dinghy and be rowed ashore. That was the only fitting way out. Her sense of dignity would not allow it to be otherwise.

She splashed her way across the saloon to the stairs but turned back towards the spare cabin. There was the boy in there. She reached the door of the spare cabin and then saw that there was a key in the lock and that the door was of good teak. She turned her head without haste in the direction of the companion way. The others were already on deck. She put out a gloved hand and turned the key. Then she took out the key and dropped it in the water.

She turned away and crossed the saloon and began to climb the slippery companion ladder towards the deck.

EPILOGUE

By noon of that day the worst of the gale had spent itself, though the seas were mountainous and puffs of foam still eddied about the streets of Sawle. Before dark the sky cleared and the sun came out.

All day the village had been in a hubbub. Most of the survivors were housed in the Tavern Inn, but one or two had overflowed into the cottages of hospitable neighbours. Altogether it had been a busy time, and when evening came the bar of the Tavern Inn was crowded with men in need of something to wet their parched throats and congenial company with whom to share the experiences of the day. Wrecks were not so frequent as they had once been, and this one had yielded interesting dividends in crew and cargo.

All the members of the life-saving rocket crew were there, except Tom Mitchell, who was a little boy and had been put to bed, and Abraham Jarvis who was a teetotaller, and Mike Smith who had begun celebrating too early and had gone to sleep outside his own front door. There had been one or two reporters down during the day asking questions and taking photographs and generally getting in the way, and tonight two had arrived from Plymouth and had attached themselves to Benjamin Blatchford, the captain of the crew.

Now that all that could be done while daylight lasted had been done, he was not averse from giving them an account of the wreck in return for a measure of free beer. Ben Blatchford had a wholesome dislike for charity; he would not have accepted a free drink from a foreigner in ordinary circumstances; but in this case he was giving the two reporters something in exchange, so that set things to rights in his mind.

The bar was full of smoke and noise and good-humoured banter.

"Mind you," he said reasonably, " 'twas Abe Jarvis's idea to pull the old gun round upon that point. I think 'twould have come to one or another of us soon enough, but he thought on it first. 'Try 'er over to Sawle Point,' he said. 'Run her down right b'low Hoskin's field.' And sure

197

'nough, though 'twas plaguey work gettin' 'er thur, once she was thur, first rocket fell plumb acrost the barque. Handsome bit o' shooting, 'twas, though I say it myself. We'd the wind almost abeam, see? A nice judgment was all that was re-quired."

"About how long did it take to get them all off, Mr. Blatchford?" asked one reporter with gold-rimmed spectacles.

". . . Once the line was took fast, you mean? I couldn't say that fur certain; we wasn't looking at no clocks. A 'our, p'raps. Thur was no time to waaste, mark you, not a minute to waaste. We was all sweatin' bad when 'twas over, though the wind was as cold as charity. That's what I said at the time. 'Thur's no time to waaste, lads,' I said. 'We must get the line acrost now,' I said, 'or else . . .' "

The reporter nodded sympathetically. "Yes, I suppose it was touch and go. Who did you rescue first; the lady passenger, I suppose?"

Ben Blatchford wiped his beard. "No. They sent the ship's boy over first to test the line. Then the captain –"

"The captain? I thought usually –"

"He was 'urt about the ribs. He was in a bad way when he come over. We thought he was dead, but 'e was only knocked out. They do say he's been took to Truro Infirmary. The lady came third. Then seven of the crew, mate last. That made the lot."

"Was she the captain's wife?"

"No."

"Ah," said the other reporter, scenting romance.

"They do say as she owned the ship."

"Is she still in Sawle, do you know?"

"In the Tavern Inn when last I heard. They give her the best room over the parlour. So Mrs. Nichols says, and I've no cause to think 'er a liar."

"Another pint, Mr. Blatchford? Certainly. Three pints, *if* you please, miss. I wonder if we could see her, George? Might add a feminine interest."

"I'll have a shot later. Carry on, Mr. Blatchford, what were you saying?"

" 'Lo, Tom," said Ben Blatchford, putting down his mug. "Got away from the missus at last? Rare good job she made of getting that barrel ashore this morning. What was in it?"

"Well, I s'pose you 'ad your eye on it yourself, Ben Blatchford?"

A good-tempered wrangle sprang up amid the smoke, and other voices joined in. Mr. Nichols, the landlord, leaned his elbows on the bar and argued with a fat man in a tight red jersey. In the corner a blind man nodded his head and grinned and chewed his toothless jaws. Presently Blatchford gave his attention to the reporters.

"Do we understand that a man was drowned, Mr. Blatchford? A member of the crew?"

"No, 'twas a passenger. Tried to swim ashore wi' a line when they thought we was not going to get a line aboard. Foolish that, but they say there was no 'olding him. Said 'e'd been a champion swimmer and wouldn't listen. Many a man's done it before. 'Tis a question of keeping your nerve, see? Before now, I've seen 'em try to launch a boat. A pity, for 'tis just throwing away good lives. We always try to signal to 'em to stay where they are, but they won't see."

"This passenger; was he any relative to the lady, do you know?"

"Brother, I bla'. But you'd best ask her, didn't you?" Ben Blatchford's small grey eyes brooded on nothing as he re-lit his pipe. "He'd be sucked out, ye see. They always are. They say when he went under they pulled in the line, but it had broke. What else did they expect? 'Twas a pity, too." Blatchford's eyes transferred themselves to the spectacled reporter. They seemed to mourn the loss of a man.

"Those two were the only passengers, I suppose? Sad, as you say, that one of them should have been lost. All the crew were saved, I take it?"

The Cornishman's eyebrows came together in a slow frown.

"Thur was one other passenger."

"A man? He was saved, I presume?"

"No-o.... A boy. A lad of eleven or twelve, I s'pose. No.... He got lef' be'ind."

The noise in the bar had increased during the last few minutes, and the two reporters pressed forward so as not to miss any word which came from the bearded lips of the man who was speaking to them. But for a moment he did not go on.

"Left on the wreck?" prompted the spectacled reporter. "Then there were two lives lost. How did that happen?"

199

"Gracious knows. There was some confusion betwixt the first boy that come over and this one, they do say. An' then wi' the captain being knocked out ... Mebbe you can imagine what 'tis like on the deck of a ship which is being washed b' the sea. 'Tisn't a time when you always remember to count 'eads. I reckon 'twas the leddy's fault; he was with she, and she ought to have seen he was took off wi' the rest." Blatchford stroked his beard. "One thing did seem a straange thing to 'appen. He'd somehow got himself locked up in a cabin in the captain's quarters. Whether he'd locked himself in thur fur safety, or ..."

The reporter motioned for another refill. "Has the boy's body been recovered, do you know?"

Blatchford's eyes travelled to the approaching mug. "Oh, the boy was all right. 'E were as safe as any of 'em. We found him thur still in the cabin when the tide went out. Scared, you know, as any young tacker would be. Scared, but keepin' his end up like a good 'un. Just broke down a bit when we busted the door in. Boys o' that age have plenty o' give an' take, as you might say. Like a sapling, bend but won't break, see? I well remember when I was ten ... Yes, 'e's upstairs too. They put 'im to bed, and I bla' Landlord Nichols gave 'im a tot o' brandy to keep the chill out ... But I can't understand 'ow that thur door came to be locked."

In a cottage on the opposite side of the square from the Tavern Inn two of the crew, Anderson and Mallett, had met again after having been separated by minor injuries and lack of dry clothes. They were both men who had been with Stevens in *The Grey Cat* for some years.

They sat for a time before the fire, glad of safety and a pipe of tobacco and not anxious for speech. The two old people who owned the cottage had left them alone.

"Funny thing," Anderson said at last. "Funny thing about old Veal's brother, Perry Veal, or whatever 'e was called. Funny thing about 'im. You was near 'im when 'e says 'e'll swim. I'd got me finger broke an' I'd not much mind for anythink else, like. But I sees 'im wavin' 'is 'ands like a preacher. What was 'e wantin'?"

"A line," said Mallett.

"Well, wasn't you wantin' to give 'im one?"

"O'Brien wasn't. O'Brien didn't want to. O'Brien

thought as they might still get a rocket over. 'E didn't see as Veal'd do it, champion swimmer or no. With the Old Man bein' knocked out ... Well, it was like this. You mind when we struck? D'you see 'em come up on deck about five minutes before?"

"Yes."

"Well, it was like this. May come up first, more or less carryin' the Ole Man. Then come Perry Veal staggerin' as if 'e was in two ships and near gettin' washed overboard first wave. You seen that. Then Mrs. V. clawin' 'er way up, 'at goin' one way an' bag the other. Well, two minutes later they was flattened up agin' the after bulwarks along of me and Peter."

"That was when we struck."

"Aye. Aye, we struck just then. An' over we went in a 'eap, clingin' for dear life as if we was all goin' over the side. Then the mizzen topm'st cracked right over our 'eads, an' she come up again, drainin' all the sea off of her deck like Niagara Falls. I was next to Perry Veal and the old lady was the other side of 'im. 'E was brimmin' over wi' drink, I could see that. I don't know 'ow you was fixed, but where we was, tilted the way we was, we was sheltered from the worst of the wind. And we looks up and tries to see what the coast looks like before the next wave smacks over the top and washes the guts out of us. An' then, mark you, I 'ears Perry Veal say to Mrs. V., Where's the Somethin'-or-other?"

"Where's the what?"

"I don't know what. I don't catch what. And she says: 'Follerin' me up. Just be'ind me.' Then they lies quiet for a few minutes while O'Brien tries to get the distress flares goin'."

"They was a wash-out."

"Like everythin' else. Then, when we was splutterin' and breathin' in a bit of air after a back-wash, I 'ears Perry Veal say again, Where's the Somethin'? Bag, I thought, but 'e talked so thick."

"Boy, mebbe."

"Well, I might've guessed that if I'd knowed there was a boy except for Mike aboard. An' she says, high-pitched an' hoarse, ' 'E was follerin' me up, I tell you!' Then Peter sighted the rocket crew on the cliffs, and for the next ten minutes I was watchin' them too close for to have time to spare for Perry Veal. But when I looks next 'e was still clingin' there, lookin' at 'er like as if 'e'd never moved in ten minutes. Just starin' at 'er till I thought 'e'd got a fit. Not lookin' at the rockets fallin' in the sea. Lookin' at 'er. Then O'Brien crawls over and says: 'It's a poor chanct we've got, bhoys. Every man for hisself if she breaks up.' Then Perry looks at 'im like 'e was dreamin', an' his face twitches, and then he looks at Mrs. V. again, and when O'Brien 'as crawled away he shouts the same question at 'er as before, though she's 'alf drowned with water suckin' about 'er waist. An' when the water goes back she doesn't answer 'im nothin' this time, but just looks at 'im one of 'er hoity-toity looks. Then —"

"I know them. She give me one when she come aboard a couple of months ago."

"Then that's when 'e breaks out. 'God almighty!' he shouts at me, with the sea sprayin' over us like bits of stones. 'I ain't in wi' this bitch. See? I ain't God almighty! I'm gettin' out o' this. God almighty, I ain't in wi' this bitch!' Just like the sort of face Tim Chudleigh got when 'e took the D.T.'s. Then 'e lets go 'is 'old, even though we're just waitin' for another wave, and crawls after O'Brien back to the poop. An' some'ow 'e ain't washed off like a whitebait, and gets to the poop, and that's when you sees 'im arguin' with O'Brien."

There was silence after Mallett had finished speaking. They both drew meditatively and appreciatively at their borrowed pipes. Anderson had always been a slow thinker. But he usually got somewhere in the end.

"Reckon there was somethin' betwixt those two," he said at length. "I shouldn't think 'twas all D.T.'s with Perry Veal."

Above the bar of the Tavern Inn was a long dusty passage with an elbow bend in the middle; this fed the bedrooms of the inn; and at about the time that the bespectacled reporter was thinking of slipping away from the bar and interviewing Mrs. Veal, a tall, slender young woman came out of one of the rooms, closing the door softly as if not to disturb a sleeper. She was dressed in a long grey frock and still wore a grey hat with a veil, but no outdoor coat. She walked along the passage and, lifting up a corner of her skirt, ran quickly down the dark stairs, slipped past the bar and turned into the kitchen.

Mrs. Nichols looked up from her crochet-work and was inquiring:

" 'As 'e woke up yet, miss?"

"About five minutes ago. I thought he might like something to eat. I wondered if I might make some gruel. That was what the doctor said, wasn't it?"

" 'S, I think. But sit you down, dearie; I'll make it for 'ee. No, no, no trouble 'tall. You must be wearied out coming all that way in Jess Parson's wagon. I don't knaw 'ow 'ee kept saw clean. No, no, I'll make it. Sakes, I don't, in ole Jess Parson's wagon all cagged up in mud."

"I was lucky to have the lift," said Patricia.

"Well, yes . . . I s'pose 'ee was frightened out of your life when you 'eard 'bout this 'ere shipwreck. But there wasn't no need to worry, you see. They'll be right as ninepence in the morning. Least . . . 'Twas a mortal shame that Mr. Watsit was drowned. Relation of yours, wasn't 'e?"

"My uncle."

"Dear life, now isn't that sad? Well, well, that's a poor job. Well, well, dear soul."

Conversation continued while the gruel was made. Dazed and uncertain herself, Patricia could only parry the polite little questions put by the polite little woman stirring the pan. She had only been here an hour and most of that time she had spent beside Anthony's bed while he slept. There she was away from prying eyes, which she most wished to avoid. They had told her her stepmother was sleeping too, so she had not seen her yet. In any case she had a strange reluctance to see Madge until she had first talked with Anthony and learned more of this unexpected trip. Queer, her dependence in this crisis on Anthony. She felt that from Anthony she would get the truth as far as he knew it without subtlety and without evasions. That, she felt, she needed more than anything else.

Also they had told her the facts concerned with Anthony's survival, and although a doctor had examined him she wanted to reassure herself that he had come to no serious harm.

The gruel was ready and she took it from the hands of Mrs. Nichols and went out into the narrow passage leading to the stairs. As she reached the bend to go up the stairs, two men came in at the private door of the inn talking to Nichols the landlord, who had been called out of the bar. Pat shrank against the banister and started up the stairs. But to one of the men that figure was beyond mistake even in the gloom of the hall. She heard him mutter an excuse and spring up the stairs after her. He caught her at the turn of the landing.

"Pat . . ."

"Well, Tom . . ." She turned half defiantly, half defensively, to face him.

"What are you doing here, Pat; surely you were not on the ship? I . . ."

"I heard of it this afternoon. Anthony had written me a letter. I came over as quickly as I could. They're – my relatives, aren't they?" She spoke quietly, unprovocatively.

"Have you seen Anthony?"

"I'm taking him this gruel." She took a step to move on.

"Pat, I'd like a word with you. Is there anywhere we can go?"

"I can't stop now. I must take this in."

"Take it in and come out again, can you? I must have a word with you." He spoke as quietly and gravely as she. They were not talking like strangers, but like people who had known each other years ago. He had taken off his hat, and his hair gleamed in the dim light.

"I ought to stay with him. Besides . . ." She did not finish the sentence but he understood it.

"You may not have anything to say to me, but . . ."

She hesitated. "Oh, it isn't that . . ."

"I'll wait for you."

She entered the bedroom and found that in the interval Anthony had gone to sleep again. She waited five minutes in the hope that he might wake and give her the excuse not to return at once to the passage. When he showed no signs of doing this she put a plate over the gruel and left the room.

She found Tom where she had left him.

"There's a sort of parlour in here," he said. "There's nobody else about."

She followed him into a small room at the end of the passage. In one corner of it a table-lamp showed an ancient yellow light like something which had been burning for centuries. The room smelt of mildew and stale lavender.

She went over to the window and stared nervously down into the square, where various horses were tethered and people moved about and talked in groups in the starlit, windy darkness. He stared at her and tried to think how best he might put what had to be said.

But the sight of her had pushed the carefully formal speeches out of his head. When he had not seen her for some weeks he fancied that the old lure was fading, but as soon as he set eyes on her nothing else mattered.

"It's weeks now," he said, his thoughts coming to his lips. "It's weeks now ... How have you been getting on?"

"Very well," she said almost inaudibly. "Thanks to you."

"To me. . . ."

"Yes. Miss Gawthorpe didn't tell me she was your cousin."

"Oh . . ." He hesitated, not quite sure of the tone of her voice. "So you know that?"

"I found it out this week. It was kind of you to arrange for my future."

Now he knew that his "kindness" was not appreciated.

"How did you know I was looking for a job?" she asked.

"I just heard." He was not going to let Anthony down.

"I gave in my notice yesterday."

"You ... but why? Miss Gawthorpe finds you very satisfactory."

"I might have known," she said bitterly, "that I shouldn't have been engaged without references. Thank you for standing sponsor for me."

"Oh, nonsense. Miss Gawthorpe wanted someone reliable. It happened that I knew of someone. She wouldn't have taken you or kept you if you had not been suitable. There's no reason at all to give notice. That's absurd."

"I frequently am absurd."

He said: "Seeing you now after so long revives ... all the old hopes and dreams. For me, Pat, there'll never be anyone like you. I've tried – to take a different view, but it's no use."

"I'm sorry . . ."

He took a step nearer and then stopped. "This wasn't what I had to talk to you about, but seeing you again ... Before we drop it, Pat, tell me once more if it has to be all over between us. For my part –"

She said: "After everything, how can there be anything

more? No, Tom, how can there be? We've never – deceived ourselves. Tell me what it is you have to say."

Silence fell between them, and much more besides, the shadows of old memories. The memories, bitter and sweet, were like puppets, jerked into motion with a pseudo-life of their own but deriving from impulses outside themselves. There was no chance at all of ignoring them; they were a part of their relationship.

She turned and walked towards the door with an instinct for escape. Her movement was hasty and impulsive, thrust on her by inadmissible emotions.

"Where are you going?"

"If you've nothing else to say ... I must see Madge. I haven't even spoken to her yet."

He barred her way. He was torn between impulses. The issue was so vital to him that he wanted desperately to pursue it. But he knew that if he did so she would leave him, and it was impossible that he could let her go to see Madge.

"Let me pass," she said.

"I've got to tell you, Pat. I've got to tell you. Somebody has to. Your – your father's body was exhumed the night before last. His and ..." He could not get beyond that.

She put a hand on a chair and stood and stared at him as if suspecting some trick to detain her. Then she saw that he was completely in earnest. All the other feelings which had so engaged her a moment ago drained away, were engulfed in a great chasm of surprise and horror.

"Dad? ... What for?"

"There was a suspicion about the cause of his death. You see ... I began, the police began to make inquiries. I began ... and that started ..."

"What suspicion?"

"Something that wasn't without cause. They've found more than four grains of arsenic in your father's body."

Madge Veal had been sitting before the fire without stirring for nearly an hour when the knock came on her bedroom door. She had a faculty for remaining perfectly still like a brocaded effigy in a waxworks; at such times her personality was purely negative, it seemed scarcely to exist; her body was like an empty house in which a single nightlight burned to show that the owner would be back.

She had asked for the fire as a special favour, saying that

she was cold in bed and felt she had caught a chill. But in fact it was not so much the warmth she needed as the encouragement of the brightly flickering flames. All her life she had found comfort in gazing into the fire; it stimulated her thoughts, and this evening her brain was rusty and tired and disjointed like an old railway line which has been long in disuse.

For years her thoughts had known the comfortable tracks to follow; one ran along them for months almost without consideration; strict guidance was unnecessary, conscience and instinct doing all the necessary work. To be jolted on to unfamiliar lines was, she felt, grossly unfair, and subconsciously she was trying to think herself into a state of mind in which she could abjure the necessity of following them to disaggreable conclusions.

When the knock came it was not unwelcome as a diversion; the effigy slowly came to life and put on an extra dressing-gown before calling, "Come in."

A thin man with gold-rimmed spectacles gingerly entered, and she at once regretted not having added her pearls. She pulled a scarf up under her varous chins and looked down at him from above them.

"Yes?"

"Mrs. Veal?"

"That is so."

"You'll pardon my intruding, ma'am. I could find no one to bring me. I represent the *Western Daily Post*."

"Yes?" She had become very jealous of her dignity.

"I'm taking down a few personal notes about the shipwreck. I was told the position of your bedroom. I hope I don't intrude."

"You may come in," she said coldly. While he moved further into the bedroom she eyed him up and down and the thought came to her that she would have been glad of someone to talk to, if only it could have been someone intelligent and understanding like Perry. Had reporters any intelligence?

He began to make the conventional inquiries about her health and safety, and while she answered him the need to unburden her grievances became steadily more important.

"You were the owner of the ship, ma'am, weren't you? Very sad indeed. Did you often travel in her?"

"Oh ..." Mrs. Veal waved her hand. "From time to
207

time. Since my dear husband's death, of course, not the inducement."

"No, no."

"Bristol," said Mrs. Veal. "Business there. My poor brother-in-law. A wicked, wicked shame. The captain had no right ... expose to danger. Should have made for port earlier. My poor brother-in-law ..."

"Mr. Perry Veal. A great pity. I understand he was lost trying to swim ashore with a line."

The reporter discreetly waited as Madge Veal began to fumble among the many folds of three dressing-gowns and presently produced a handkerchief.

"I look upon it – shall always look upon it, gave his life for me. Great gentleman. Said to me: 'I must go, Madge. I'll bring you help. Never fear.' 'Never fear,' was what he said."

The reporter made a note of the words. "What were your feelings when the ship struck, Mrs. Veal?"

"Only man ever understood me. My dear husband, deeply sympathetic, but his brother Perry, finer mind. Great loss. I mourn, Mr. – er ... Many ways, wish I had been taken. I look to the afterlife and reunion." She dabbed at her nose. "Many fine spirits. Passed on. One wishes that one were in closer contact. I often think. Very sensitive to such things. Deeply sensitive. Coarse-fibred people."

The man glanced up. In an appropriately sympathetic voice he said: "How long had you been at sea when –?"

"Suffered," said Aunt Madge, turning up her eyes. "All my life suffered. Persecution, grievous thing, Mr. – er ... When my dear sister died. Eve of her thirtieth birthday. Acute gastritis. With her to the end. People said. But what did I gain who lost a sister. Were devoted. Devoted. My mother and I were all in all to each other after that, but were we not indeed before?"

"Your nephew, I believe, was very fortunately rescued later? If –"

"Been determined," said Mrs. Veal, "all my life to go on, follow the straight path. The straight and narrow. It invites the scoffer, philistine, scurrilous tongues. Sustained by conscience. An unhappy woman, Mr. – er ... You see before you one. Stung by scorpions." She waved a hand at him, forgetting for the moment that she despised him, remembering only that he was the audience she must have.

The experiences of the last three days had upset her more than she thought. Her cheeks trembled with indignation. "Your paper. Put that in. Stung by scorpions. We all have our crosses. Hi try ... Consolation in conviction. The lonely people of the world."

Through a mist of preoccupation she was aware that he was addressing her.

"Mrs. Veal."

"Yes?" She paused and her small mouth hung open like a little bag which someone had forgotten to fasten. "Yes?"

The reporter said in a depressed voice: "Could you tell me your emotions, just simply and – and simply, when your ship came ashore. It is unusual to have a – a lady aboard and I'm most anxious to get a woman's point of view."

She looked at him with contempt. "All my life, fate has deprived me ... loved ones have fallen by the way. By the way, Mr. – er ... It has been my misfortune. *NOT* my fault. I do not complain. My dear, dear sister in the flower of her youth. My dear mother when her advice, most needed. My good, kind husband. I am. Lonely woman. Stricken with sorrow. My husband's first wife, she often said to me, 'Madge, you look bowed with secret grief.' It was the truth. Only Perry felt and understood. He only knew what it was."

The reporter fidgeted and glanced towards the door. He had not been taking notes.

"That's very, very sad, madam. Naturally we always regret intruding upon –"

"Unusual," said Mrs. Veal doggedly. "The one who stands out. Always picked at by the herd. An unusual woman. Hi often think. Destined. One does not know. The end is yet to be."

"Yes, yes," he said.

"The end is yet to be! Mr. – er ... Put that in your paper. Joan of Arc did not know. Jeanne d'Arc. Envious men may deny me ... Right of speech is mine. Always remember that, right of speech. Don't go," she said as he made a movement to rise; and so sharply did she speak that for the moment he accepted her veto. "Don't go. I have much to tell you. Afterwards. You'll be glad."

Pat found herself back on the sofa in that musty old parlour of the Tavern Inn. She didn't know how she had got there, and Tom was trying to persuade her to drink something from a glass.

She sat up. "I'm all right. I'm all right. It – just made me sick."

He sat back upon his heels and waited quietly for her to recover. A sudden gust of wind boomed down the chimney and shook the old building in its depths. He saw now that her colour was returning.

He felt it particularly unfitting that he should have had to strike this final blow. Patricia, for all her slenderness and youth, had always been so inwardly strong and self-sufficient; while he, outwardly confident enough, had never been really confident in her presence. (Or only once, and that had been when his desire for her had outweighed his deference.)

That had been one of the stumbling blocks in their relationship, but the fact that she was down at last brought him no comfort or satisfaction. He raged against the circumstances which had weighted the dice against her. In the space of two years she had lost both her parents; her marriage had come to grief; the standard of life she had grown used to had been overthrown, the money rightly hers had been given to someone else. She had gone out to earn her living among strangers. But now something was upon her less bearable than any of the foregoing. Something crooked and unclean and not to be thought of. But something which would have to be thought of. In the next few days and weeks it would take a larger and larger place in her life until there would be room for nothing else. Then, perhaps it would be in three months, perhaps six, the bubble of talk and trial and publicity would be pricked and she would be left to herself again, empty and neglected and alone. Alone but with a stigma of talk and rumour still clinging to her like cobwebs from a sewer. Wherever she went they would go, casting an unrelenting stain over her cleanness and her youth. "Oh, do you know who that is staying with you, Mrs. So-and-So? Patricia Veal: *you* remember, the Falmouth poisoning case. No, she was only a step-daughter, but of course they were a peculiar family. I've heard it said – mm-mm-mm-mm ..."

That was her future unless ... He realized that this was the very first time since she left him that they were alone together and she not trying to get away. He wished he could somehow heal the wound his words had inflicted, a wound which was going deeper with every minute that her brain worked, here alone with him in the lamplight. They were alone together but that counted for nothing.

He said: "When this is over ... It'll take time, Pat, obviously it will take time. When it is over ... Oh, I know this isn't the time; there couldn't be a worse. But I may not get another opportunity." He still sat on his heels beside her. She made no response. "This ... all this trouble that's coming. We could help each other. It's bound to be hard to get through alone. Life's pretty rotten for you since your father died; it will stay rotten for a time. Afterwards ... I've had an offer of a partnership in Cape Town. All South Africa's unsettled. Two things it needs are honest politics and honest law. I'm going to take the chance. There we could really start afresh, really afresh. The past could be more easily forgotten. We're both young. We can wipe things out and begin again."

His voice, which had become eager and moving, tailed off. He looked at her.

"Perry," she said. "Was he in it? His own brother. That's the hardest of all ... to understand."

He got up, sat on the edge of the couch, leaned his head on his hand. The moment was gone.

Neither of them knew how long passed before she said: "What made ... *you* suspect?"

"Oh ..." He tried to bring back his thoughts to the subject which, until he had seen her, had prominently occupied them. "Something about your father. His appearance wasn't quite natural. The clumsy way he handled things as if there wasn't much feeling in his fingertips; the look of his skin. Then I'd been reading for an examination in criminal law. Not that I suspected anyone in particular at first. Thought perhaps he took some sort of drug. I ... didn't see enough of him and there was nobody I could inquire from."

"When was this?"

"I noticed it particularly the first time I saw him after you had gone back."

Two men were mounting their farm horses outside in the square. You could hear them talking to the horses, shouting to each other, then the lumbering clop-clop of iron hooves on cobbles.

"Go on."

"I might have done more. I wish now I had, but I was very unsure then. And I'd quarrelled with him and wasn't on speaking terms with you. I dropped one or two hints to you, but you naturally thought I was only trying to scare you into coming back. It was dangerous to start talking outside. I made one or two inquiries about your mother . . ."

"Oh, dear God!" she said. It was a cry of pure distress. He took her hand and held it.

"Oh, Tom!" she said. "Oh, Tom!"

They sat there for a long time in silence. Presently tears began to run down her cheeks. "Don't cry, Pat," he kept whispering. "Don't cry, Pat."

He forced himself to go on, trying to pick his way.

"After – after your father's death I began to feel there must be something, some cause. I went to see the doctor concerned, but of course he would tell me nothing. What sealed everything was the Will. I felt there was no doubt then. When your father made that Will he signed his own death warrant – forgive me for being blunt. But I was very relieved when you didn't come in for the money. I had been afraid that you might be next. That's why I hoped no later Will would be found. That's why I plotted and schemed to get you away from the house, out of danger."

"Thank God I haven't been to see her," she said through her tears.

"At last I got the police interested. Inquiries were made at likely shops. Nothing led anywhere. Anthony gave us the clue. He said one day that he did a lot of shopping for her. When he went through the list we at last came to – to fly-papers. He'd bought them at various shops in the district twice at Penryn, once even at St. Mawes, though none had been bought since last August. Inquiries were made about the type bought and an analysis made of them. Each one contains enough poison to kill a man. That gave the police evidence to take action."

He still held her hand and she made no attempt to release it. She needed companionship in the dark.

"What are they going to do now?"

"The police? Nothing until tomorrow. They haven't quite finished all ... all the reports haven't come through yet."

She said half passionately, half fearfully: "I wish it was tomorrow. I wish it was tomorrow."

In the bar Ben Blatchford and the younger reporter were still standing side by side at the counter, although there had not been much conversation between them since the other man left. Two miners had walked in from a neighbouring village and were being regaled not only with beer, but with a lively account of the day's pickings in flotsam. The captain of the rocket crew, while not taking a prominent part in the discussion, was listening with an attentive smile. The reporter was reading through the notes he had made.

He felt a touch behind him and found his colleague had come back.

"Any luck?" he asked.

The other man shook his head and began to polish his glasses. "Hopeless. Couldn't make head nor tail of her."

"You got to see her, then?"

"She wouldn't talk sense. You know the sort: you ask a straightforward question and they go off into the story of their lives. Death beds of all her nearest relatives, *with* details of what they died of. She kept on burbling about being misunderstood and nobody loving her. I think she's got a mash on this fellow who was drowned. But as soon as I turned the conversation on that she was up and away about something else. Couldn't pin her down. We'll rig up some sort of a story, but I made my excuses as quick as I could."

"What now, then?"

"We ought to catch the midnight train from Truro. Look, I'm going to have a shot at interviewing the mate, who's been put up at a cottage across the way. You got all you can out of this man?"

"Ye-es. I think so. But there was one thing. These notes—"

"Get a photo of him if you can. It'll fill up. I'll be back in twenty minutes."

Left to himself again, the younger reporter read his notes again. This was his first assignment and he didn't want to fall down on it. He looked at his watch. Then he touched Blatchford on the sleeve.

The old man turned and regarded him with eyes which

213

had grown more friendly and benevolent as the night advanced.

"Yes, boy?"

"Many thanks, Mr. Blatchford, you've been very helpful. Do you happen to have a photograph of yourself, free of copyright, that you could let us have?"

"Well, boy, I've a snap that was took last August month of the whole rocket crew, and I'm thur wi' the rest. 'Ow would that do, eh? I don't know whether 'tis free of what you say, but I'll not charge ye fur it."

"Thanks. That would do very well. We're leaving soon, so perhaps you could get it for us? The – er – I . . . in looking through these notes it's occurred to me there seems a slight contradiction, so to say, between – er . . ." Under the keen eye which was now turned on him he stammered and hesitated; then he gathered courage and plunged on. "Look, Mr. Blatchford, earlier when we began to talk, I have it down here that you said there wasn't a moment to lose in saving these people from the wreck."

"Nor was there. Nor was there."

"No, certainly; very good. But you said – mind you I'm only trying to clear the matter up – in speaking of the boy you say that he was saved later, much later, by a rescue party which boarded the ship, and you spoke as if it was only natural that he should be. I suppose that's all right; but if as you said every minute was precious –"

"So 'twas. So 'twas." The tough weather-beaten face twisted slightly and the eyes glinted. "Precious to we. We always get a pound for every life we saave bi' the rocket. They was safe enough where they were if the ship didn't break up. Naturally the ship *might*'ve broke up, but we was anxious to get 'em off whether or no. Tide was goin' out fast. In another hour they'd 'ave been able to walk ashore." Blatchford exchanged a few words of farewell to a friend leaving the bar. Then he turned back to the reporter. "Now 'tis real nice to've seen you gentlemen, but you'll be careful not to put that in your papers, won't you. Folks might think it read straange. But I'm an honest man and you ast me an honest question. Sometimes things do work out straange round these shores, and it's no fault of we as've lived 'ereabouts all our lives."

After the reporter had gone Aunt Madge went back to her

seat by the fire, aware that she had been casting pearls before swine. She was sorry she'd wasted her breath in trying to explain as much as she had; the man had no soul above the common herd. You could not expect such a man to be sensitive and understanding when so few people had the quality of brain to appreciate her confidences. Only Perry had fully shared her way of thought. Perry and she had been soul mates. In the maelstrom of the Cornish sea he had been lost, and she would never see him more. The thought was a deep grief to her.

True, there was still a faint, uneasy memory that all had not been quite well between them at the end, that in his courageous effort to save her he had appeared distraught; but her brain was rapidly disposing of this remembrance. Each time she thought of it the lines were less distinct, the occurrence lit by a softer light.

Soon she would forget it altogether, having convinced herself that it was unimportant and did not affect the deep, rich stream of their love and understanding. Only Perry had known all. Or not quite all, but she thought he understood all. One day soon she had been going to tell him everything in a burst of confidence. Now it would never be.

In the cottage opposite the bespectacled reporter was busy taking notes and wondering how to describe Mr. O'Brien's accent. Just once or twice while he listened to the mate's ready flow and contrasted its factual pungency with Mrs. Veal's windy hesitations there came to him a twinge of uneasiness, such as he sometimes had when he went to a racing meeting and on impulse put his money on another horse from the one he had all along intended backing: a sort of mental dyspepsia of second thoughts.

Not that he was aware of having missed something which would illuminate his story of the wreck, but he felt once or twice that a cleverer man might have been able to turn her peculiar personality to some account. She was a bore, but an unusual bore. He had watched her closely at first, and listened closely, keen to catch the thread of sense which must lie behind it all. Then he had failed and lost interest and become impatient.

So Madge Veal sat by the fire with her secrets still safe and the reporter made up his story with the larger part of the story left out. Later he would bite his nails in fury and regret.

He might have comforted himself when the time came by reflecting that he failed to understand her where cleverer men had failed. Where all men would fail who tried to assess her behaviour by their own.

For her brain was like a dusty room which had had its doors all locked and barred, a room in which the air had grown stale and noxious for lack of contact with the outer air. Her egoism provided the bolts and keys, sealing up the smallest crack whereby there could be any contact between other people's ethics and her own. Within this room her commonplace, rodent, dangerous personality had had its living and being, like a prisoner free within limits, building up its self-deceptions, concocting its own excuses, imagining its own triumphs, plotting its own satisfactions, growing large and fat and white like a slug under a stone.

Only during the last few days – for the first time for years – events, especially the news Anthony brought, had burst open some of the doors and left them wantonly swinging. She had hastened to press them to again, her etiolated mind recoiling at the touch of the cold air. She had fought then like a querulous invalid from whom the bedclothes had been pulled away, fought tooth and nail to cover and protect herself again. She had succeeded, but only by admitting the existence of disturbing facts inside the protective screen. Even now they were still here, and Perry had been insistent that they were of a nature which would not remain sterile but would grow and develop and have a fruition of their own.

It had needed hard thinking to put them in their place. That was why she had felt lonely and off her balance to-night. That was why she had said so much to the stupid staring reporter, talking in spite of herself, ventilating the stored complaints of a lifetime, justifying herself, pitying herself, inviting his commendation of her behaviour, using him in some degree as her confidant. It didn't matter. No harm was done. He had taken nothing in. The mere fact of having been able to talk to a man and of feeling herself so greatly his mental superior had had a reassuring effect; that and the relief of having talked it all out had brought reassurance. Before the comforting warmth of the fire and the self-supporting glow of these reflections she began to doze.

She was very tired. As she dozed she thought of her sister, a tall, comely girl who had had all the good looks of the family. Half dreaming and half waking, she thought of the strange way in which her sister had lost her good looks before she died; her cheeks had sunk and so much of her beautiful fair hair had come out; the family were renowned for their fair hair; her mother had retained it to the end. She thought of her mother, and how one year she had been essential to her well-being, the next superfluous, the next obnoxious, and the fourth she had not been at all; her death had been quite sudden. One, two, three, four, the years had peeled off like ripe plums falling from a tree; like flies falling from a flypaper.

She began to think of flypapers and of flies dying and dropping off them like the years. And in her sleepy mind she began to confuse people and flies, flies and people, so that each had the same relative importance to herself. Sometimes before she had done this; it was a convenient way out of many a moral impasse; her thoughts often repeated themselves in this way, working their way into grooves and sophistries of their own. The older she grew the more unreal became the affairs of other people, the easier it was to reduce the concerns of all living things outside herself to a common level of triviality and unimportance.

As she dozed her over-clothed, flaccid body drooped into new and more indolent shapes, as if the cold Cornish sea had washed away some of its familiar contours, as if someone had shaken the yeast cake when it was rising. Her pince-nez sat slightly awry, the lines of her mouth drew themselves out like slackening purse strings. When she awoke the facts would have adjusted themselves more closely to her liking. Until then she would sleep.

In the last few days the rude world had broken into her privacy, upon her complacent day-dream. Doors had been shattered, but her patient, persistent, third-rate mind was already building them up again. They should be built stronger than ever before.

At this moment she lacked Perry, who had never imprisoned himself within such lofty seclusion and had therefore a more ready appreciation of the dangers of the outside world; she lacked Perry to insist that no repairs her egoism could effect were strong enough to stand before the impact of what was to come.

The machinery of the law, however trumpery it may be to anyone concerned, as Madge was concerned, with the higher values of her own life, has an unwelcome appearance of reality while it is in motion – as Perry had never failed to appreciate – and deeper resources even than egoism are needed to reject the impression made by steel about a wrist or rope upon a throat.

Pat woke. She had been sleeping for some time, her head in the crook of his arm. She was not cold for the room was not cold, and he had drawn his overcoat across her. The lamp had almost gone out. A small, dying yellow bead of light barely lifted the heavy darkness away from them.

She was not aware of having accepted this position but had not been forced into taking it. Somehow they both felt the need of companionship, and for tonight at least she could not bear to be left alone. She didn't want to go to bed or in fact to move until daylight came. Daylight would bring its own tests and problems but would, by driving away the darkness, help her to meet them. She felt lonely and sick and afraid and yet temporarily at rest, as if in this one corner of an alien and ugly world lay safety and peace. She was afraid to move lest she should break the thin shell of their isolation. Above all else she felt sick as if everything she had eaten in her life, everything and everyone she had known, had suddenly become unclean.

She raised her eyelids to get a glimpse of him without moving her head. He was dozing, his head inclining to one shoulder. Whatever else, he represented stability and cleanness in a tainted world.

He had said more, avowed more tonight than he had ever done before – except perhaps in his letter. She liked him in this eager mood when he carried conviction without eloquence. That was how they had married. Their marriage had been a mistake, but it did not appear so big a mistake tonight as it had recently done. She wished he was never dry and reserved and hesitant and inclined to look on the legal title to a thing as the be-all and end-all of possession, upon flesh and blood as inferior to pen and ink and a revenue stamp.

Perhaps he had never thought that. But a habit of shyness and reserve had been imposed on him all his life. She had to admit that he had shown very little signs of this side in his recent meetings with her.

It occurred to her for the first time that perhaps her judgment had been coloured by her father's prejudice against all lawyers, by his insistence that the one she had married ran true to his general estimate of them. The influence had been there without her realizing it.

Tom stirred and woke, and she found herself looking into his eyes. She was suddenly in contact again with the personality she had been dispassionately considering. The change was drastic. Of all the prospects now open to her the one thing she could no longer do was consider him dispassionately. His eyes, his looks, brought back all the liking and disliking to its original personal equation. There was no avoiding it.

He said: "I've been dreaming I was on trial again for assault and battery. You came and testified for me."

She lowered her eyes. "What time is it?"

"Not late. There are still voices in the bar. Do you want to move?"

It was a question she would have preferred not to answer. Presently she said, "No." Bluntly and honestly.

The monosyllable sent the blood coursing through his veins. In self-defence he took the admission at its lowest value to himself. During the last hour all his hopes had been given up.

"What'll happen to her, Tom?" she asked.

"Who?"

". . . Madge."

"A clever Q.C. may get her off, but I don't think so. If the – the second analysis confirms the first then there won't be any escape."

"Perry didn't come back to England until after mother had died," she said almost inaudibly.

"No. Whatever his part, he came late to the scene. I don't think he was more than an accessory to her."

"I wish these next weeks were over. I wish . . ."

"They'll pass, my dear. It's a question of keeping up until then."

Silence fell.

"Dear God," she said suddenly, a twitch of horror going through her. "My mother ... It – it doesn't bear thinking of."

"It's a nightmare," he said. "Look on it as that. There'll be an awakening."

"Yes, but always, always it will have happened."

He did not reply to that, for he did not know what to say.

Time had passed in the old inn. Almost everyone had retired for the night. The bar at last was empty, except for the smell of stale beer and the tobacco fumes curling like fog about the low ceiling. Mrs. Nichols, dozing off to sleep beside Mr. Nichols, was aware that she had intended going up to see if the young lady wanted anything, but she had been busy at the last preparing the other two attic rooms for the two men who had come in very late and who her husband said must be accommodated. When she finished that it was so late that she had hesitated to go up and disturb her. Perhaps she was still with the boy. A pity there had not been anything better than an attic room to offer her. It was seven years since they had had such a full house in December, when the *Madrid* ran aground by High Cliff.

In his attic bedroom the detective who had travelled with Tom Harris lit his pipe and wondered what had become of the young solicitor. He had already been to his bedroom, but there was no response. Presently, when he was sure that the house was quiet, he would take a stroll round. It was not his business to sleep tonight.

In the parlour little had changed. The lamp had gone out and the lace curtains let in a glimmer of starlight.

She slept again, fitfully, uneasily, but he was awake. He didn't want to sleep during this time. Her piled fair hair had come loose and was straying across his coat. Her breathing was quiet but not quite regular.

His mind wandered lightly, irrelevantly, over his past life, coming back to its present surroundings with a twinge of pleasure and sorrow. He knew that over Falmouth estuary the water would be whitening under the stars. The trees about Penryn, quieter now after all the wind and rain, would stand in groups upon their lonely hills and whisper of man's mortality. Human life was a stirring, a thin fermenting between the breasts of the world, a reaching for the light and a gathering of the dusk. A shifting and temporary interlocking of relationships between light and dark. The worst heartache and the brightest happiness would soon be still. They loomed large as mountains, like clouds they were as large as mountains but dispersed like smoke.

He thought of his schooldays and his mother, and Anthony lying sleeping in another room, and Patricia marrying him, proud and defiant, yet warm and lovable; sweet and kind and forgiving but hasty-tempered and undisciplined and rashly impulsive. Cold and warmth; they were here in his arms now. Anger and love. Waywardness and obedience. Incalculable but loyal. Would he have her any different? Not if he could have her at all. Birth and death, daylight and sunset: they were the impersonal things. Now, now was reality, the few hours in between of youth and understanding.

He thought of his profession and his future. South Africa drew him, accompanied or alone. There, among the great mountains and river and forests, small humans were quarrelling as if the world were theirs and theirs not the most temporary lease. He thought of the shipwreck and the baleful wind still moaning from time to time round the inn. He thought of Anthony and *his* future. They owed him much more than a casual thought ... Affection and a return of loyalty for loyalty.

"Tom," she said.

He hadn't realized she was awake again. He stared at her in the darkness, knowing his expression couldn't be seen.

She said: "Why do you want me to come back to you?"

Trying to keep the feeling out of his voice he said: "I've already told you why."

"For you it means giving up so much," she said indistinctly. "Your place is here, in Penryn, working in your own firm, doing the work you were meant to do. Why give all that up? You're known in Cornwall, known and respected. It means starting somewhere quite new —"

"I'm going to Cape Town in any case," he said.

"There's your mother. Why spoil her life? Why should I come between you?"

"You haven't. We're on perfectly good terms and I think you could be. She's become reconciled to the idea of my going abroad in any event."

She stirred restlessly, but didn't try to move away.

"I'm – I'm not your type, Tom. Honestly. I don't fit in. I felt that always before. Why should it –?"

"One doesn't have to fit in in a new society."

"I don't even fit in with you. I'm – not worth your career. I'm restless, capricious, changeable . . ."

"I want you as you are. Life can be too safe, too easy. You've made me see that. We're different, but we can each help the other. It's just a question of taking the chance." He said no more, hardly able to believe that so much progress had been made, afraid to spoil it by a wrong emphasis, the ill-chosen word.

Silence fell in the room. In South Africa the strange stars had moved on two hours ahead in their flight towards a new dawn.

Then he said: "There's bitter feeling between the British and the Boers. No one can tell how it will turn. That's another chance."

She did not reply.

"All this unpleasantness that's coming," he said, "will pass quickly enough. It's the further future that counts. If we back it for all we're worth it won't let us down."

"Give me two or three days more," she said. "Will you? Then I'll decide."

He said quickly: "As long as you like."

"No. Not as long as I like. Two days more. You see – you see, Tom, I'd like to put a term on it. We got married in such a hurry, on the impulse of the moment almost. Then I left you in the same way. When I married you I thought it was for good. I truly meant it to be. Then when I left you I meant that to be for good as well. Now if I come back to you I want that to be all quite changed. I don't want to come back on impulse like a – a beastly shuttlecock. I want it to be entirely deliberate. And if I *do* come back – it's really going to be for good this time."

He put his hand on her hair for a moment and thought she did not notice.

"For better or worse," he said.

"For richer, for poorer, in sickness and in health. Easy to promise and hard to fulfil. I – I've always felt ashamed

222

of leaving the way I did, for the reasons I did. They seemed good enough at the time, Tom. But sometimes I was desperately ashamed. Somehow, it was because I hated myself so much that I tried to hate you. But – I didn't seem to be able to help it. All sorts of things came up, confused the issue. I – I've tried so hard to hate you. Remember that."

"So long as you failed."

"I failed."

There was silence in the room.

"Nothing else matters," he said. "Nothing. Nothing. Sleep now."

Her head settled more comfortably upon him. Her breath for a time continued to have a catch in it that would not quite settle down.

He listened to it and wondered if she could hear the beating of his heart.

In another room Anthony slept. About him the human comedy had played itself out, swinging him with it from time to time as it gyrated. For the most part he had been uncomprehending, either as a spectator or participant. The larger issues had passed him by, happening just beyond his purview, casting shadows upon his life but leaving him out of sight of the main procession.

Lonely and forlorn, he had come to the house of Joe Veal at the crucial moment of its decay. Like a sick plant the outer petals of the family had one by one peeled off, at length revealing the worm in its heart. Now the ruin and disintegration was complete. Torn between conflicting loyalties, having no mature standards by which to judge, he had contrived to steer a middle course of which no adult need have been ashamed. Much that was unpleasant had happened to him and more was yet to follow.

But at present, worn out by sea-sickness and nervous strain, he had forgotten what had happened and was ignorant of what was to come.

He did not know how Pat had contrived to be here so soon. He did not know how the cabin door had come to be locked, nor exactly how, when he should have been drowned, he had yet come to be saved. He did not know that the polite gentleman who had questioned him at Tom Harris's would come to see him again in the morning and take down a statement which he would later be required to confirm before a stern old judge in a court of law. He did not know that his young personality and companionship were yet to prove the final cement which would bind together during the next two difficult years the young couple who, after an initial breakdown, had just resolved to begin again.

Nor did he know that his father was married again, to a widow with two young children, and that they could see no place for him in their household. Nor did he know that he would never see Canada, but would travel to South Africa instead.

Being a normal boy and not a seer, he knew none of these things, and for the present did not care. He had been cold and frightened and sick, and now was warm and safe and comfortable.

Anthony slept.

THE END